Praise for **BAD THINGS HAPPEN** *HERE*

'Fuses elements of mystery and romance as Luca's _____ ly told coming-of-age story unfolds against a _____ th. There is not a word wasted in th_____ tale.'
– *Kirk*_____

'An atmospheric and multi-_____ mystery that surprises until the haunting end.' – Klara Thomas, author of The *Cheerleaders* and *The Weekend*

'A heart-racing stay on Parris Island! Couldn't put down *Bad Things Happen Here* as, along with Luca, I had to know who did it. I loved all the twists and turns as Luca gets closer to the truth.' Tracy Darnton, author of *The Truth About Lies*

'Deliciously dark and haunting, *Bad Things Happen Here* is an expertly woven knot of mystery, romance, betrayal and death. Barrow's storytelling will have you untangling theories until the very end. Pack your bags, prepare to enjoy your trip – but stay ready.' – Ciannon Smart, author of *Witches Steeped in Gold*

'A beautiful, racy, and haunting story of standing out and following your gut when the world around you is falling apart.' – Ashley Woodfolk, author of *Nothing Burns As Bright As You*

'Compelling and compulsive. Barrow expertly crafts a dark tale of sun-drenched dread that lays bare both the long-reaching impact of trauma and loss as well as the ways in which tragedy can so easily be disguised as destiny.' – Stephanie Kuchn, author of *Charm and Strange*

BAD THINGS HAPPEN HERE

REBECCA BARROW

HOT
KEY
BOOKS

This work contains themes of self-harm, suicidal ideation, and physical and sexual violence.

First published in Great Britain in 2022 by
HOT KEY BOOKS
4th Floor, Victoria House, Bloomsbury Square
London WC1B 4DA
Owned by Bonnier Books,
Sveavägen 56, Stockholm, Sweden
www.hotkeybooks.com

A CIP catalogue record for this book is available from the British Library.

ISBN: 978-1-4714-1124-3
Also available as an ebook and in audio

1

Typeset by Envy Design Ltd
Printed and bound in Great Britain by Clays Ltd, Elcograf S.p.A.

Hot Key Books is an imprint of Bonnier Books UK
www.bonnierbooks.co.uk

For me

Beautiful how
it all pours out,
after dark,
after light.

—Maggie Rogers, "The Knife"

1

Parris, the island where it seems girls go to die.

And like always, Luca is the only one to remember Polly on her birthday.

Luca drives with the windows down, air twisting her curls around her face. Maybe that isn't true. Maybe people do go to Polly's grave, put down flowers that will sit and rot among the headstones. Perhaps they stop to clean off the photograph Polly's mom chose, the one with her hair slicked back in a bullet bun and red-painted lips hiding her braces.

Luca wouldn't know, because she never goes there. That's not where Polly is, to her. It's just a box in the ground and a stone in a place far too somber for a girl like the one Polly was.

It's still early enough that the island is quiet as she drives across it. Not that it's ever busy, really, but the roads are almost completely empty, every light green as she heads toward the bridge.

It rises up into the blue sky, the only way out of this place. Luca doesn't drive across, though, but pulls to the side and turns the engine off. She gets out of the car, the stems of the orange carnations she brought with her pressed between her palms. Then Luca steps down, beside the bridge, onto the uneven rocky ground where nobody's really supposed to go.

But we did, she thinks.

Her and Polly, climbing down these rocks, so they could reach the water below. That's why she comes here. Or that's mostly why.

Below her the ocean swirls, a calmness to the waves that's unusual for this spot, and Luca throws out the carnations one by one, the bright blooms drifting down and down and down until they meet the water. "There you go, P," she says. "Happy birthday."

Three years she's done this. She brings the flowers, she sits for a while; she starts to tell Polly something that's happening and then stops, because what could she ever say that would mean anything now? *School is shitty. Our favorite breakfast place closed. I realized I was in love with Jada right after you died and I told her about the curse and then she stopped speaking to me.* What does any of that matter to Polly now? What does any of it matter when Luca is alive and she's dead?

She was scared, the first time, to come back. To return to this place where the curse had surfaced. But then she had realized that really, this might be the safest place for her to go. After all, the curse never strikes the same place twice.

So she came, the first year, and the next, and now. And Luca will come back in a year and do it all again, like the ritual can change anything. But it means something to her, to do it. It means something that there's somebody to remember

Polly who really *knew* her. After all, Polly's parents left the island soon after she died. Jada hasn't talked to Luca in almost three years, acts like she and Luca and Polly were never even friends. And everybody else, well, they didn't *know* her, and they don't talk about her. She's sure they have their reasons. Thinking about her is unnerving; they don't like to look death in the face so close. Something like that.

Luca closes her eyes and remembers that last year, that last birthday. Fourteen years old. Polly is fourteen and Luca is seventeen now, will be eighteen in two short months. There was always that distance between them, Luca being born in the long days of summer and Polly coming so much later, arriving in the world during the spring bloom.

She waits there for as long as she can bear. Maybe it's an hour, maybe it's a minute. But when she's done, Luca opens her eyes and looks down at the water again. She kisses her fingers and then holds them out to the air, her only goodbye to the girl she's let down the most.

"I love you," she says, words she never said when Polly was alive. "I'll see you next year."

And she leaves. She's always leaving Polly behind, further and further with each day.

2

When Luca wakes on Friday and pushes back the covers, there is a line across her legs, turning her light brown skin golden. A beam of sun pushing through the crack in the curtains.

She closes her eyes against it. Sometimes she is so sick of the sun that she could climb up into the sky and rip it down with her bare hands.

She gets out of bed and goes to the balcony, stepping out into the early morning quiet. Down below, the backyard is a carefully controlled explosion of flowers, surrounding the wide deck and curling past the pool, edging their way along the green, green lawn. At the end of the garden is the beach, and then the ocean, glittering bright under the sun, as it always does.

Luca turns her gaze left, to the edge of the property next door. The house where Polly used to live. The house that has been sitting empty since her parents left, as if people thought it was haunted.

But then this spring it sold, sign outside, and now new people will live there, new people will sleep in Polly's bedroom and walk her steps down to the beach and it's really over, Luca thinks. It's done: no more Polly. This is the last place that felt like she was still alive, the house suspended in time, a living, breathing space seeming to say, *I will stay for as long as it takes. I will be here until the truth is known.*

But no more.

Luca sighs and steps back into her room. She gets dressed, sort of: high-waisted vintage-style bikini (she does not subscribe to such outdated rules like "fat girls should wear one-pieces," fuck that) and a sheer black robe, and twists her long curls into a knot on top of her head.

Sometimes she is tired of the sun, but all of the time, she needs it to live.

She makes her way through the house: past the framed photos along the upper walkway, down the soft-carpeted stairs, cutting through the open living room where her sister's diploma hangs above the piano. *Only temporarily,* Whitney says every few weeks. *Once this internship is over, I'm thinking about going to New York.* Or Chicago, or Austin—the place changes, but the fact that Whitney is not leaving doesn't. No one really leaves Parris. Whitney had gone to college, but she came back, just like everybody else did, like Luca is destined to do someday.

Outside she takes off her robe and slips into the pool and stays there, suspended in the water as the sun moves through the sky and time seems so still.

So she doesn't know what time it is when a shadow falls on her as she floats on her back.

"Do you ever get out?" the shadow says.

Luca turns over and swims to the edge, holding on to the side and looking up at her sister. "You look like shit," she says, but she doesn't mean it. She never means it, even when Whitney looks like she does today: clearly hungover, in last night's dress, lipstick still stained on her mouth, her long dark hair pulled up in a sloppy ponytail. Whitney is her big sister and always beautiful because of that.

"Ha." Whitney kicks off her heels so she can sit and slide her feet into the water. "Did Mom ask where I was?"

"I haven't seen her," Luca says. "I can't believe you were out all night. I thought it was a work thing. You hate them."

"It was," Whitney says. A small smile is on her face. "And then it wasn't."

"You could have called me." Luca flicks water up at Whitney. "I would have come out."

"You would have hated it," Whitney says, and tips her head back, squinting at the sun. "The new people are here."

Luca sinks a little, letting the water cover her chin. "What?"

"Saw them as I came in," Whitney says. "So. That's it, I guess."

That's it.

Although it won't be it, Luca knows. Her mom will invite the new people over for drinks, maybe dinner, and she'll make Luca and Whitney be there, because it's *polite* and *nice*, and Luca will have to put on a smile and pretend that she hasn't hated them since she first heard they existed.

"What are they like?"

Whitney shrugs. "I think it's just two of them," she says. "A woman and her daughter, I guess. I saw their stuff, mostly. Nice art." Then she pulls her feet out of the pool. "I'm starving. Are you hungry? Let's go get something to eat. And coffee. I need coffee, desperately."

Luca tries her hardest not to look over at the wall that separates their property from the Sterns'.

Not the Sterns' anymore. Whoever these new people are.

"Yeah," she says, nodding at her sister. "Give me a minute to change. I'll meet you out front."

3

A drop of water trickles down Luca's neck as they wait in line at Darkroom, Whitney's preferred caffeine dealer. It's the usual afternoon crowd: moms with babies in thousand-dollar strollers, kids like her on summer break, a few basic white guys stabbing at laptop keyboards.

The line's going slow. Whitney's talking to her about what she's going to wear when they go out tonight, but Luca's looking up ahead to see who the holdup is, and she rolls her eyes when she sees Isaac Charles at the register, in that beat-up leather jacket he's always wearing no matter the heat and the scuffed boots with undone laces. Likes to lean into the wrong-side-of-the-tracks stereotype, except in Parris, there is no wrong side. Just the wrong kind.

He's getting his card out as slowly as he can and talking intensely at the barista—not *to* her, but *at* her. "Well, maybe you could swing by after you close up," he's saying, running a hand through his short but artfully messy hair. "You know Beth Palermo? Her parties always go all night. You'll have time."

The barista is clearly avoiding his gaze, busying herself

tapping things into the register. "Oh, I don't know," she says. "I have to open tomorrow, too. Super early, you know?"

"So come for an hour." Isaac leans over the counter. "Come on, Grace. Have some fun."

"Hey."

The sharp word comes right next to Luca's ear, and she lets herself smile as Whitney snatches Isaac's attention. *"Super* not it to hit on someone whose job depends on her being nice to you, asshole."

Isaac flushes, narrowing angry eyes. "I wasn't—"

"Yes, you were, Isaac," Whitney says. "And she's clearly not interested, so now that's done, you can fuck off and let her do her job and the rest of us get on with our day. Yes?"

He lingers a moment, as if torn between staying and fighting for the barista's yes, or doing what Whitney says, and then he pushes past them so fast that Luca almost doesn't hear the "Bitch" he throws over his shoulder.

Almost.

The barista visibly relaxes and Luca watches out the door, watches him striding down the street. "He is such a dick."

"That he is," Whitney says, and then it's their turn to order and the barista is saying thank you to Whitney, and Luca turns, gaze moving along the line behind them. And that's when Luca notices her.

The new girl.

Has to be, because Luca knows everybody on this island, if not by name then at least by face, and she would remember a face like this girl's. Would certainly remember an Asian girl, because Parris is exceedingly white and Luca is a mixed-race Black girl and those are the things you keep track of in a place like this.

She's tall, dark hair cut blunt at her shoulders. Wide eyes and a mouth to match, and as Luca watches, the girl sinks her teeth into her lower lip, staring up at the board.

Some small part of Luca that has lain dormant for years sets alight.

Look away, she thinks. *Look away look away look away—*

"Luca." Whitney's looking at her, eyebrows raised. "What do you want?"

"Oh. Sorry," Luca says, and then she gives the barista her order and Whitney pays and then says, "I have to pee," and disappears.

Luca moves down to wait at the end of the counter and pulls out her phone so that she has something to look at other than this girl.

She's staring at it when someone says, "I love your nails."

"What?" Luca looks up and the girl is next to her now. Up close Luca can see the deep brown of her eyes and a tiny scar below that bottom lip.

Do not look at that scar. Do not look at this girl like that. She took Polly's house and you are supposed to hate her, right, that's what you decided, isn't it?

"Your nails," the girl says. "I always rip mine off. But yours are perfect."

"Oh," Luca says, and she looks at her fingers, tipped with almond-shaped acrylics, bright red for now. "Thanks."

"I'm Naomi," the girl says. "Fontaine."

Do not play nice with her. What would Polly say?

Luca pushes her hair over her shoulder and gives the girl—Naomi—a tight smile. "Luca Laine Thomas," she says, the way she always does when she says her name, partly because it is her name and partly because she's always loved the way it sounds out loud. And then, because it feels like Naomi has the upper hand and she does not like it, Luca says, "You moved into the Stern house. Right? On the north shore."

Naomi looks surprised. "Yes," she says. "How did you know that?"

"Not many secrets in Parris," Luca says, and then Whitney is back.

"Hey," she says, and notices Naomi. "Hi. Oh! New girl. Right?"

Luca gestures between the two of them. "Whit, this is Naomi. Naomi, my sister, Whitney."

"Naomi," Whitney says, drawing it out in that way she likes to do. "I wondered when we'd meet you. We're neighbors, you know."

"Oh," Naomi says, glancing at Luca. "No. I didn't know."

A different barista sets their drinks down in front of them, and Whitney looks at Luca with a shine in her eyes that Luca knows all too well.

Naomi's phone chimes, and Whitney takes full advantage of the second Naomi takes to look at it, away from them.

She's cute, Whitney mouths.

Don't, Luca mouths back.

But of course she does. "You should come out with us tonight," Whitney says. "Meet everyone. I mean, you're gonna meet them all eventually, but it's better if you're with us."

"Tonight?" Naomi looks up and bites her lip again.

Luca looks away.

"Sure," Naomi says after a moment. "It's not like I'm doing anything else, so—"

"Perfect." Whitney grabs their drinks and heads to a table. "Luca, give her your number, okay?"

She's subtle as a brick through a window, but Naomi is looking at Luca and does not seem horrified. "You sure you want to come?" Luca says, a weak attempt at loyalty, still. "These things can be kind of . . . intense."

Naomi does not back down. "I like intense," she says.

Luca sighs. "Okay," she says. "Give me your phone."

After she's tapped her number in, she hands the phone back. "Thanks," Naomi says.

And Luca gives her another smile, sharper this time. "Don't thank me yet."

4

They eat dinner with their parents, a once-a-week event put in place shortly after Polly's death. A coincidence, Luca knows she's supposed to believe, as if her parents haven't always been completely transparent, as if she didn't see it for the *how to deal with your mentally unstable child in the wake of a tragedy* suggestion it really was. But it's okay, doesn't bother her. She knows—has known since she went to her first therapist at eleven—that her parents don't really know how to treat her, because neither of them knows what it's like to have a brain like Luca's. But they try, and isn't that what counts? They pay for good therapy and her medication; they do things like the family dinner and vacations when they would rather be working, because it's the best they can manage. And if her other options are the kind of parents who don't believe in mental illness, or the kind who would cling and monitor her every move, then Luca is glad she has the clueless-but-well-intentioned kind. It gives her a freedom, a space, where she doesn't have to pretend to be the good, sweet girl who just gets a little sad every once in a while.

Luca spins her fork through her pasta as her mother grills Whitney about her internship at the law firm. Besides, these dinners may have started as a response to what happened to Polly, but now they are more just regular dinners, the specter of Polly fading away, like she has from most people's minds.

The thing about Polly's death, her disappearance and reappearance in the shallows, is that it was not unusual. Maybe for another idyllic place it would be, but Parris is not like that. And the strange thing about growing up on this island, having it be part of you and you part of it, is that you forget these events don't happen everywhere, not in the way they happen here. You forget that not everywhere has the stories Parris does—Polly, lungs filled with salt water.

The daughter burned to ash.

The pageant queen left for dead in an alley and the girl on the yacht—all of them, these violent bursts that rip through Parris, leaving razor-edged holes behind.

You forget that not everywhere is cursed.

"We met the new people," Whitney is saying now, bringing Luca back to the moment. "Well. We met the daughter."

"Oh, you did? We should have them over," her mom says, and the lights of the dining room chandelier catch the gold in her blond hair as she turns to Luca's dad. "What do you think, Nick? Drinks? Next week, maybe?"

"Tuesday could be good." Her dad takes out his phone, even though the rule is no phones at the dinner table. "I have a dinner on Monday and the investors' meeting will run late on Wednesday, so yeah, Tuesday or Thursday should work."

"I heard the daughter is about your age, Luca." Her mom takes a piece of bread and rips it in two. "Is she nice?"

God, I hope not, Luca thinks. But she smiles at her mom and says, "I guess."

"We're taking her out tonight." Whitney reaches for the bottle of wine and tops up her glass, the liquid spilling out sunset pink. "Being good neighbors, you know."

Luca raises an eyebrow. "You just want to make sure she knows who's in charge around here," she says, and laughs when Whitney gives her the finger.

"Be civil," her dad says with an exasperated laugh. "Can we not just have one nice dinner?"

"Nicholas," Whitney says, even though she and Luca both know how much it irritates their father when they call him by his first name, like it annoys their mother when they call her Emilia, too. "All we *do* is have nice dinners. There were three different charity auctions last week alone. If I have another server shove another truffled Camembert tartlet in my face, I'm absolutely going to lose it."

Their mom stands, reaching for the bottle. "Just, please," she says, "behave yourself tonight. Okay?"

Under the table Whitney kicks Luca, and Luca puts on a pretty smile for their parents, the reassurance that their girls are the good ones, of course they are. "Don't we always?"

When dinner is done, her parents leave for whatever they're doing tonight, and Luca and Whitney go get ready.

Luca can hear Whitney singing in her shower even from

down the hall, and she loves her sister but she is a truly terrible singer, so she closes the door and turns up her music to drown Whitney out.

She changes her clothes—a black top that slips off each shoulder, a pair of tight black jeans, a gold chain at her throat—and then sits at her dressing table to begin the slow process of painting on a face. Not slow because she wears so much makeup, or is a perfectionist, but because she likes to take her time. It's calming, the routine of it. Filling in her brows, a high arch like Hedy Lamarr, slicking on shiny lacquer for a Josephine Baker mouth.

It's the routine and the memory of being five years old, playing with her mom's powder brush, Emilia applying her own lipstick to Luca's lips so they could match, for the five minutes before she wipes it off again.

The eyeliner takes the longest, the nerve necessary to carve out the clean-cut flick on her eyelids, but Luca is practiced in this and sits back, satisfied, to admire her work when she is done.

When her phone buzzes, she checks it: one new message from Naomi. is it okay if i get a ride with you? i don't drive and also i don't know where the fuck i'm going

Luca laughs and types fast. duh, of course, did u think we were gonna let u go by yourself anyway?

Naomi's response is almost instant. idk maybe ur into new girl hazing. should i come over when i'm ready?

sure. ring the bell, i'll listen for you

Luca sets her phone down, and there is something in the

top corner of her phone that she has looked at a hundred times today but has not registered before now, right now, this very moment.

Today is the nineteenth.

Today is the nineteenth and somehow Luca missed it, even though Polly's birthday falls four days before, even though she always remembers.

Except for this year, when she has forgotten that today marks the day that Polly disappeared.

"Shit," she says, her panic making the word an even uglier sound. "Shit, shit."

She has always thought it cruel, this chain of days. First Polly's birthday, then her vanishing, then her death. A neat row beginning with the best and ending with the worst.

But even so, she has not forgotten before, and this is how it starts, isn't it?

This is how I begin to forget her.

Luca sits forward, her chest tight and her breath coming shallow. *Not now, not now,* she thinks, because this feeling she is all too familiar with. The anxiety that plucks at her nerves and twists deep into her brain and makes her think things she would rather not, the obsession that makes her focus in on those thoughts, again and again and again and again and—

Her eyes fix on the tweezers lying on the dressing table, their sharp little ends, and here it goes, here it starts, *pick them up push them into your palm drive them hard until they pierce the skin until there's blood,* and *think about it, picture it, keep picturing it, keep picturing it—*

Her bedroom door opens. "You ready?" Whitney says. "Madison called and said—Luca. What's wrong?"

Luca holds out her hand but she cannot speak yet, and Whitney, because she knows Luca and she knows this, comes into the room and closes the door and kneels on the floor as she takes Luca's hand.

"Okay," Whitney says, half a whisper. "Okay, we're just going to sit here. And it'll be okay in a minute."

Luca breathes in cycles: in *two three four*, hold *two three four*, out *two three four five six seven eight*.

She breathes, and counts, and holds her sister's hand until her heart rate slows and the thought about the tweezers does not scare her. "All right," she says eventually, finally. "I'm all right."

When Whitney sees she is really okay, she stands and takes Luca's chin in her hand. "What happened?"

"It's May nineteenth," Luca says. "And I forgot. We all forgot."

She watches Whitney's expression shift a hundred times in a split second and then Whitney leans down, puts her forehead against Luca's. "Shit," she says.

"Yeah," Luca says. "Same."

"This doesn't mean anything." Whitney pulls back and looks at her. She has their mother's eyes, soft hazel, where Luca has the same almost-black ones as their father. "You know it doesn't mean that you don't love her, or miss her. It's only this one day. You remember her all year round. This doesn't mean anything."

Luca rubs her thumb over her bottom lip. "I'm going out

tonight," she says, "with the girl who lives in Polly's house now. A girl I promised myself I would hate."

"Why? Because her mom bought their house?" Whitney shakes her head. "You think Polly would care about any of that?"

Luca stays quiet.

Whitney tugs on one of Luca's curls. "She grew up here," she says. "Polly was one of us. She knew us, she knew *you*, and she knew exactly how much you loved her. If you think she would be pissed because you didn't remember that today was *the* day, you're *wrong*. Okay? So we're gonna go out now, we're gonna take that new girl out and show her who we are and know that she is not some kind of replacement, okay? No one could ever replace Polly."

"I know," Luca says quietly.

"I know you do." Whitney pulls Luca to her feet. "So come on. We have places to be."

And Luca lets Whitney lead, and she thinks, *I am sorry, Polly, I'm sorry,* and then she shuts the door on the moment.

5

It's a party like any other, because this is how it always is, and Luca lets Whitney lead the way, like she always does. She is always following in the wake of her sister.

Tonight there is this new person between them, Naomi following Whitney into Beth's, and Luca thinks that if things were reversed, if she were the new girl walking into the party, then she'd be majorly anxious, but Naomi doesn't seem nervous at all.

She'd been walking up to the house when Luca and Whitney opened the door to leave, and Luca had still been a little shaky, but Naomi had flashed this bright gleaming smile and maybe Luca is easy but she felt better after that.

"Come on," Whitney says over the music as they walk through the open-plan house, a constant flow of people around them. Beth's parties are always packed, the place everyone wants to be, when she lets them. "I'll introduce you to everyone."

"Everyone?" Naomi looks over her shoulder at Luca.

Luca shrugs. "You'll see."

Outside is where the crowd is, and over by the pool there's a fire pit currently surrounded by Everyone: Madison Rivers and Carter Muszynski and Beth Palermo, the kind of names other kids on the island just know, the same way they know Whitney and Luca Laine Thomas. They're Whitney's friends, really, but Luca has known them all her life too, from junior sailing to ballroom classes to getting quietly drunk at fundraisers, and Madison has been best friends with Whit for so long that Luca almost thinks of her as another sister. As the three of them approach Everyone, Luca gets this feeling like she doesn't want to do this, doesn't want to introduce Naomi to them, because they'll love Naomi and then they'll take her in, subsume her, and Luca wants this girl all to herself.

She doesn't stop, though, only keeps following her sister over there. Watches as a pair of skinny white boys in too-carefully shredded jeans approach the fire pit, lean in toward Carter, and say something that makes Beth, sitting in Carter's lap, wrinkle her nose. Carter waves them off, and the boys hang there for a moment, as Beth turns and stares them down. It's not until she bares her teeth that they scatter, slinking off like wounded puppies.

Every party, same thing. People who still think of Carter as the island's best and brightest dealer, a reputation he's never going to shake.

But then they are there at the fire themselves, and Everyone looks up and lights up when they see the sisters there. "Finally!" Beth says. "What took you so long?"

"What up, losers." Whitney falls into her natural place next to Madison. "This is Naomi. She just moved in next door to us. Naomi, this is"—she points—"Madison, Beth, and Carter."

Luca sits on the only empty couch and gives Naomi a nod, so she sits next to Luca. "Be nice to her," Luca says. "By which I mean absolutely do not be yourselves."

Madison laughs, and in the firelight she glows: her perfectly white teeth, her golden hair, the diamond on her left ring finger. "Aren't we always nice?" she says, an amused lilt to her words that says she knows exactly how not-nice they can be, when they choose to. "Anyway—hi, Naomi! Please ignore these two wicked witches!"

Naomi pushes her dark hair behind one ear, a small smile on her face. "I'll try," she says.

Luca notices the semi-lost look on Naomi's face and leans over to speak into her ear. "Okay," she says, "so, we've known Madison forever, and she's engaged to a guy she met in college, but he's not here, he's never here. I mean, she says he likes us but I don't buy it. And then we have Carter, kind of an asshole but mostly not, and mostly not to us. Likes to think he's a *reformed* asshole anyway, especially now he's not dealing anymore. Beth's the best, an angel—except for when she and Carter are in an off phase, which is almost every other week. I think they might be on right now, but who can even keep up?" She pulls back and arches one eyebrow. "Does that help? Or did I make it worse?"

Naomi lets out a small laugh. "I got it," she says. "I think, at least."

"Speaking of witches," Carter's saying loudly, drawing

Luca's attention back to him, "better be careful tonight. It's a full moon."

"Oh, please," Beth says. "Can you not?"

"Not what?" Carter says. "I'm just saying we all need to watch out. The curse hasn't struck in a while, and we all know what the full moon means."

Luca feels her cheeks warming, and the way Whitney glances over at her. The curse, right. Always a funny topic to bring up on nights like this, around the fire, sloppy-drunk storytelling, like it's nothing more than that.

They all believe it's nothing more than that, Luca thinks.

"Come on," Whitney says loudly. "We're not telling stupid stories tonight."

"I'm just *saying*," Carter repeats. "Witches burn, right? Just like that girl Isla Hollinghurst burned up in that house fire."

"Stop," Whitney snaps. "We are *not* talking about the curse."

Carter's eyes narrow. "Fine. Fuck a curse," he says. "Why don't we talk about the real reason she didn't make it out?" He grins, and there's a cruelty to it. "Why don't we talk about how it was her brother who set the fire and left her in there to die?"

There's a second of silence, like they all can't believe Carter actually said it—Luca can't *believe* Carter said it, that quiet, ugly rumor about Justin Hollinghurst, how he'd hated his younger half sister and her claim to his inheritance enough that he locked her bedroom door from the outside before setting the house on fire

But that was all it was, an ugly rumor. An explanation the

people of Parris whispered to each other, Luca knew, because the very idea of the curse made them so uncomfortable.

Still, Beth makes a noise of disgust at her boyfriend's words. "Let go," she says, jerking out of Carter's grasp, and he does, so quickly that Beth slips all the way from his lap to the ground, slamming into the tile.

"Jesus!" Madison says at the same time Beth says, "Fuck, that *hurt!*"

Carter puts his hand out to help Beth up, but he's laughing at the same time and Beth ignores him, stands up all by herself. "You are such an asshole," she says, shoving him. "You know what? Find somewhere else to sleep tonight."

Beth stalks away and Madison sighs. "Do you have to be this way, Carter? Do you try, or does being a dick come naturally?"

Now Carter makes a face. "It was a joke! Come on, no one really believes—"

"Oh, it comes naturally," Whitney says without looking in Carter's direction, and she gets to her feet. "I guess I'll go after her then, shall I?"

She doesn't wait for an answer, just walks off after Beth.

Luca looks at Naomi. "And that's our cue."

Luca gets up and grabs Naomi's arm, pulling her away from the fire pit and through the expansive yard toward the bar area. When they're halfway there, she realizes what she's done and burns a little, self-conscious, and drops Naomi's arm. "You want a drink?" she says over her shoulder, hoping Naomi can't see the flush in her cheeks.

"Jack and Coke," Naomi says. "So. That's everyone, then."

Luca winces as they join the line. "Sorry," she says.

"It's fine, they're your friends. No judgment."

Luca considers this. *Are* they her friends? Madison is the one she's closest to, by virtue of her being Whitney's forever best friend, Luca always trailing them around the Riverses' estate when they were kids. Beth is cool, but the kind of *cool* that means she lets Luca borrow her shoes more than that they keep each other's secrets. And Carter? He's always been there, the one who rolled them their first joints, the one they taught the reality of periods and bras and feminism to. She does love them, but truly, they are Whitney's friends first. Luca had always had Polly, and Jada.

Then Polly died, taking all her understanding of Luca with her, and Jada turned her back when Luca became too much for her. So now her sister is the only one she really has left, the one person who knows the unvarnished, unsweetened version of her.

But that feels like a lot to say to Naomi, something she doesn't need to hear, so instead Luca nods. "This is Parris," she says, like that's an explanation. "You get twisted up with people before you can even talk and then it's sixteen years later and you realize you can't imagine a world without their annoying asses in it."

Naomi looks somewhere past Luca. "I had a friend like that," she says, and then her mouth drops open, like she's surprised she said it.

"You're not friends anymore?" Luca grabs two cups: one

for Naomi's Jack and Coke, and one for her own vodka and lime—she doesn't drink much usually. Too much booze is not a good mix with her antidepressants, but one or two is enough to get her nicely tipsy.

"What?"

"You said you had a friend like that," Luca says. "Had."

Naomi is silent for a minute, and Luca can feel the space between them filling and then cracking. "Anya," Naomi says finally. "She died."

Luca's hand jerks and the whiskey she's pouring spills over her hand. "Shit," she says, shaking it off and then wiping her hands on her jeans.

Did she hear that, or is she fantasizing these things now? Because she remembers, a second ago, Naomi saying her friend died. And perhaps it's some broken wishful thinking on her part, that this new girl, this beautiful girl, this girl who lives next door, is also in the Dead Best Friend club, but maybe—

"Sorry," Luca says, shaking her head like it'll make things clearer. "Did you say she died?"

And Naomi nods, once. "It was a long time ago," she says.

And Luca wants to say, *No, I get it, I understand because that happened to me too, and I don't know anyone else who knows what this feels like—except for the other girl who was our best friend too, and she won't look at me anymore.*

Luca wants to drop the drinks and pull Naomi into whatever quiet space she can find and talk only about their girls, Polly and Anya.

But then a hand is snatching the cup of whiskey out of Luca's grasp and it's her sister, and she's downing it and throwing her arm around Naomi's neck. "Are you having a good time?" she says, not waiting for Naomi to answer. "Come, dance with me and Beth. Luca's a good dancer. Show her what a good dancer you are, baby sister."

Naomi is dragged away and Luca watches them go and the moment fractures and dissipates. *No, stop, go back*, she wants to say now. *Tell me everything.*

But she can't make time spin backward, and now Naomi is dancing with Whitney, an unselfconscious winding of her hips to the dancehall playlist.

Luca knows what Whitney's doing, but what she said is true—Luca is a good dancer. And she's always wanted to dance with a girl like Naomi.

So she goes.

They dance and drink and play quarters on Beth's parents' antique coffee table, and Luca loses track of Whitney somewhere around eleven, but she finds Madison instead, almost as good, and they smoke French cigarettes watching some girl show-off diving into the pool, and then she loses track of Madison, too, and Luca's only had a couple drinks—okay, maybe three—okay, maybe four—but Naomi is keeping up with her and for once Luca is not left on her own the way she usually is once Whitney disappears.

When they both have to pee, they go upstairs, because Luca knows every bathroom in Beth's house and Beth doesn't mind if she creeps around where no one is supposed to go, except when they are up there it seems like no one is following the rules tonight, because there are people making out up against the wall and one girl sitting on the floor smoking a joint.

But Luca tries the bathroom door and it's open, and she points at Naomi. "You first."

She leans by the door, waiting, and she's about to pull out her phone to text Whitney, tell her to meet by the pool in five minutes, when the girl with the joint speaks.

"Hey," she says. "Luca?"

Luca focuses on her and it's Tiff Lancaster, who drives a '66 Mustang that Luca covets, and Luca likes her fine, so she says, "Yeah, Tiff?"

Tiff climbs to her feet—Luca always forgets how tall she is, staring down at Luca from a great height—and leans opposite Luca. "May nineteenth," she says.

Luca shifts. "What?"

"It's May nineteenth," Tiff says, and offers Luca the joint. "The anniversary, right? Polly Stern. That girl who drowned. She was your friend, right?"

Luca blinks and she's in the police station three years ago, sitting on a cold metal chair and staring at the picture of a smiling Polly on the table and trying not to flinch at every word Detective Charles says. She blinks again and she's down in the depths of the station, a place where she is not supposed to be, but the officer who she convinced to lead her down there doesn't seem to know that. She's looking through the glass at Polly's body, Polly's dead body on a slab, the skin on her face gray and bloated, her eyes milky and ripe to burst, and she can only imagine what the part of her covered by a sheet looks like, can only imagine the rotting smell of her.

Then she's back in this moment, the one where it's as if Tiff knew she forgot, because in all the banal conversations she and this girl have had at parties and benefits and school events, Tiff has never uttered Polly's name. Not once.

But tonight.

The bathroom door opens and Naomi comes out and her face seems brighter than before. Luca can't figure it out, but then she understands it's just Naomi's lipstick, the fresh slick of red she must have applied while she was in there. "Hey," she says, looking between Luca and Tiff and then at the joint in Tiff's hand, still hovering there. "Okay?"

Luca pushes off the wall. "Wait for me," she says, her words too fast so they become almost nothing, *wayferme*, and she turns her back on Tiff-fucking-Lancaster and locks herself in the bathroom.

She snaps the light off, darkness covering all.

The buzz from the vodka is gone, and now that she feels entirely sober again she cannot stop thinking about Polly, Polly, Polly and she is taken over, consumed suddenly by the notion that something terrible is about to happen to her.

The curse, the curse. A thing that nobody else believes in, at least not past sixth grade, when the stories stop being scary and start being the shit that Carter pulled tonight. Stupid games, a way to give your girlfriend a good scare while you sit safe in the confines of your happy world.

But Luca believes it. She believes it, she can feel it, so much that it almost shocks her that she is the only one. That no one else feels the creeping grasp of something bigger than them, hears the hum running deep beneath the island. What else could explain everything that has happened here, that will continue to happen? It is just like every horror movie she has seen, every fairy tale told to her before bed as a small girl: there's a balance, an equilibrium that must be maintained. You can't outrun it, can't outsmart it. It takes what it requires, desires.

In the moonlight coming through the two tall windows, Luca moves close to the countertop. Without thinking too much about it, she presses her wrists against the sharp edge, watching herself in the mirror as she leans her weight forward and feels the pressure building against the skin and ligaments and veins there. She releases a long, slow breath between barely parted lips and then lifts her hands away, eyeing the indentations in her skin.

No permanent damage.

She raises her eyes and looks back at her mirror self. "Nothing bad is going to happen tonight," she says, her breath clouding the glass. "Stop it."

When she comes out of the bathroom, Tiff is gone but Naomi's there, waiting, like Luca asked her to.

"Okay?" Naomi says again, and she's looking at Luca like she knows the answer is no, and it's unnerving.

All Luca wants to do is slip into one of the several bedrooms farther down the hall and sleep.

But Naomi.

"Come on," she says. "We should get out of here before it becomes a total mess."

She leads, and Naomi follows.

6

They walk home slow, mostly because Naomi can't seem to manage a straight line, and Luca tries to keep thoughts of Polly out of her head by maintaining a nonstop stream of words in Naomi's direction, *Madison's wedding is soon and I don't know why she has to get married right now but I guess they're in love or whatever, and her boyfriend, wait sorry her fiancé, Peter, he's kind of boring but whatever, I still think she should get a prenup even though he's a Van Wyle and she says they don't need one, they don't care about each other's money, but better she's marrying him than someone from Parris, like remember that guy at the coffee shop today who was being an ass, Isaac Charles, yeah she dated him in high school, well she says a few hookups does not count as a relationship but he was totally obsessed with her, and if she was marrying him she'd need a prenup for sure, but enough about them, I guess Carter and Beth just broke up again tonight, for the billionth time, I mean Carter can be such an ass sometimes I don't know why he can't just be normal—*

When she finally takes a breath they're home, and Luca

feels her headache beginning. This is why she doesn't drink too much, she reminds herself. Stupid.

"Is this what it's always like?"

Luca looks at Naomi as they stop, standing in the middle of the wide street somewhere between each of their homes. "Yes," she says. This is Parris: late nights and the ocean during the sunlit days and walking home, two girls on their own, as if nothing bad could ever happen to them, even though at any second the curse could find and take them.

But Naomi doesn't know about the curse and Luca is not about to tell her. Telling her means talking about Polly, who used to live where Naomi sleeps now, and she can't, she can't, not tonight.

Naomi's watching her in that unnerving way again. It makes Luca's skin itch, pins and needles pushing up from her veins to the surface.

"Okay," Naomi says, and then she is hugging Luca.

It takes Luca a moment to register Naomi's arms around her, Naomi's body pressed against hers, and her breath stops.

Naomi is warm, her skin against Luca's clammy, and it has been obvious all night—all day, since Luca first saw Naomi in the coffee shop—but now Luca feels it must be noticeable on her own skin. Naomi must feel it where their bodies touch, how Luca's dormant desire has woken up and named Naomi as its target.

I want you I want you I want you, her blood pulses.

Then Naomi releases her and gives this small smile. "See

you later," she says, and then, when she is halfway to her house, she spins and calls out, "Oh. Thanks for tonight."

Luca says nothing, only raises her hand, and then she turns before Naomi can see it in her eyes.

As if she doesn't already know.

She takes quiet, careful steps through the house, because even though it seems impossible in a place this big, her parents always seem to hear her returning.

In the kitchen she gets a glass of water, and drinks the entire thing standing in front of the sink in long, thirsty gulps. She is about to fill the glass again when she hears the unmistakable sound of the front door closing, and noise in the hall.

So she sets the glass down and steps out into the darkened hall. "Isn't it past your curfew?"

Her dad looks up from where he's trying to unlace his shiny oxfords, brown eyes crinkling as he laughs quietly. "Shit. You caught me."

"I thought you and Mom were being boring grown-ups tonight," Luca says, hoping she sounds as sober as she now feels.

"It was a last-minute work thing," he says. "I had to play poker with the CFO of the company we're about to buy."

"Poker? On a *Friday*?" Luca widens her eyes. "Are me and Whit gonna have to talk to you both about your partying? It's really getting out of hand."

Nick finally gets his shoes off and comes over to Luca,

giving her shoulder a playful push. "Careful," he says. "I still hold the key to your credit cards."

Luca smiles. "I'm kidding," she says. "God, you really are boring."

Nick shakes his head. "Call me boring one more time, and I might decide *not* to ignore that you smell like you've smoked an entire pack."

Luca's cheeks warm. Her parents don't really care that she drinks, because everybody on the island does, and half the time it's happening at an event and they're the ones handing her the glass. But smoking is another story. "On that note," she says, "I'm going to bed."

"Don't wake your mother," Nick says, and Luca holds a finger to her lips before she turns and climbs the stairs.

She pushes Whitney's door open as she passes, but the bed is empty and the bathroom dark.

In her own room Luca wipes off her makeup in her bathroom and changes, crawls into bed, and then calls her sister. It goes to voice mail, and even though she knows Whitney never listens to them—because neither does she, nobody listens to voice mail anymore—she speaks when the robot voice tells her to. "As always, you vanished off the face of the earth," Luca says, rolling onto her side. "You are the worst sister. But it's fine, whatever. Naomi's cool. I think maybe she could be my friend. I don't know." She can still feel the warmth of Naomi on her. "But please don't do what you did tonight and try to, like, flirt on my behalf, okay? I mean it, Whit. Do it again and I'll kill you, I promise."

She laughs a little. "Find me when you get home tomorrow. Let's go buy shoes and get ice cream and I'll let you tell me about whoever it is that you ended up kissing tonight. Bye, Whit," she says, and she hangs up and falls asleep not a minute later.

7

It's late when Luca gets up the next morning, and so she's surprised to find her mother in the kitchen all dressed up like she's going to work. "Is it not Saturday?" she says, opening the cabinet to find some Tylenol for her headache (fine, hangover). "What are you doing?"

"I have a client coming in from out of town," her mom says from her place at the kitchen island, like they don't think of anywhere that isn't Parris as out-of-town. "This is the only day they could meet. What time did you and your sister get home?"

Luca goes to the refrigerator next, takes out the orange juice, and pours a glass. "Late," she says. "Well, I did. We got separated."

"Luca," her mom says, and it's that exasperated tone she loves to use on her younger daughter.

"What?" Luca says. "You know she's at Madison's, like always."

Her phone vibrates on the counter and Luca expects it to be Whitney—she seems to know when Luca's talking about her, always—but the screen says *Beth*.

never drinking again

breakfast tacos on me?

bring Whit and also a list of new boyfriend options bc
i think i dumped mine last night

Luca smiles as she types: come on, u and carter didn't
make up already?

he wishes. god knows whose bed he slept in last night
but it sure as shit wasn't mine. and it can stay that way

...... at least until next week

Luca's laughing when her phone buzzes again, but this
time the name on the screen isn't Beth, but Naomi.

Naomi.

Last night flickers back at her: the drinking, the dancing,
Naomi's soft arms around her. Her mom's talking at her, but
Luca is reading Naomi's message: sooo this is awkward bc i
don't like know how to make friends?? but did you maybe
wanna hang out today or something?

Emilia is still talking, but Luca cuts her off. "Yeah, great,
sure," she says, landing a kiss on her mom's cheek on her way
out of the kitchen. "See you later, Mom."

*Sorry, Beth, but there are more important things than break-
fast tacos.* She replies to Naomi: be ready in twenty.

8

Luca takes Naomi from one end of the island to the other, in and out of the lanes she's known all her life, past the gallery housing abstract art, around the redbrick building that is their high school.

It's not until they are watching the boats rock in the harbor that Luca realizes she has taken Naomi to only places where bad things have happened. Here, where the yacht carrying the remains of a girl named Laney Hart came in, twelve years ago. The alley behind the school, where Evelyn Mortimer, Miss Parris 1973, was found assaulted and abandoned with the crown still on her head. And the gallery, a sleek, mostly glass building that sits on the site of the former Hollinghurst mansion, the house that burned to the ground, taking Isla Hollinghurst with it, when Luca was only eight years old.

There are more, of course, going back farther and farther, but those are the ones that Luca thinks about most. Those are the ones she has brought Naomi to. *A curse tour,* she thinks. See, this is what happens: it guiding her, pulling her where it wants her to be.

Or maybe it was just me, she thinks again, because there is a lot humming inside her that she isn't sure how to approach.

So later still she drives them back to the northernmost point of the island, where there are no homes, only a winding road that climbs up and up and deposits you in a stretch of pale gravel. Luca parks and leads Naomi through long grass and tall trees until the trees fall back and everything falls back and they are on top of the island. Look to the right, and the ocean is its usual serene self under the setting sun. Look to the left, and there's Parris proper, laid out beneath them and covered in lights.

"Wow," Naomi says, taking a step to the edge where one side of the ground beneath them drops off, and then dancing back. "Whoa."

"Are you scared of heights?"

"No. When you've spent your entire life as a gymnast, you stop being afraid of most things, but especially heights."

"A *gymnast*? Wow, bury the lede much?" Luca says. "Are you good?"

"I was." Naomi glances back at her, like *move on.* "What about you? Afraid of heights?"

Luca moves closer to Naomi, nearer to the edge, and sits among the delicate wildflowers. "No," she says. "I'm more afraid of the things my brain says when it wants to *make* me afraid."

Naomi sits next to her. "What do you mean?"

Her question is more curious than needling, and Luca smiles into the dusk. "I have this thing," she says. "I don't know, I just think things without meaning to. They come and they won't leave even though I want them to. Sometimes they're the most pointless things, a song on a loop no matter how much I want it to stop. And then sometimes it's like—" She pauses. Does she want Naomi to know that sometimes when she's driving, she becomes fixated on the idea of ramming her car into the driver next to her? Or that she has constant waking nightmares of killing her mother, terrible accidents that she is responsible for? "Sometimes it's 'look at this look at how high up you are if you jumped from here you'd most definitely die how would that look,' and then I keep thinking about that until the next thing comes along."

The air is quiet around them and Luca thinks, *You've done it now, you told her all about your crazy too soon and now she hates you.* Exactly what happened with Jada, when Luca told her just how real the curse was. She remembers, often, how Jada looked at her like she was disgusted, how she walked away without a backward glance.

But when she looks up and their eyes meet, Naomi gives her a slow smile. "It's okay," she says. "I get it."

She says it like it's nothing, which means everything. Something inside Luca unfurls. "Queen of intrusive thoughts," Luca says. "That's me." She tips her head to the side. "So tell me the rest."

"Rest of what?"

"You know, your 'life story' or whatever. I need to know the dirt, so I can let everyone know all about you," Luca says, and for a second Naomi looks worried, like she thinks Luca's serious, but when Luca laughs, Naomi relaxes and laughs too. "Let's see, what do I have already . . . gymnast. Not afraid of heights. Can't keep a manicure in good condition . . ."

"What else do you wanna know?" Naomi shrugs. "My parents are divorced. My dad is in Chicago now. He has a new wife. I guess he'll have new kids soon."

Luca raises an eyebrow, watching Naomi's tone. "Stepmom? We don't like her?"

"Stepmom is fine," Naomi says. "Daddy's the problem."

"And where you moved from?"

"Oh, very repressed, very rich, very white," Naomi says with a smile. "So you know, this place feels just like home."

Luca rolls her eyes. "Oh yes, Parris, so wonderfully diverse and welcoming," she says. "What about your mom?"

"She's the good one," Naomi says. "Collects art. Does charity shit. Doesn't hold me to impossible standards I'll never get close to meeting, so. There's that."

They sit in silence for a while then, a silence that is both comfortable and not, the only kind Luca knows how to sit in. She is thinking of what to ask Naomi next when Naomi says, "This might be weird, but I heard something last night. About a girl. Who went missing or . . . something." She looks at Luca. "You know about that?"

Well, here we go.

Luca buys a little time getting a thin gray sweater out of her bag and pulling it on, wrapping her hands up in the ends of the sleeves. She can feel Naomi waiting and really, Luca has just been waiting, too, for this inevitable moment.

"Yeah," she says on an exhale, and she stares out at the lights of Parris. "Polly. She disappeared, while she was waiting."

"Waiting for what?"

Luca looks over at Naomi. "Me."

9

Three years ago, and she and Polly and Jada were friends.

But sometimes, Luca and Polly liked it to be just the two of them, so they could talk about things without worrying how shitty it made Jada feel, all the stupid charity events she wasn't invited to and the circles she didn't run in. They would ride around the island on their pastel bikes, short shorts and ribbons in their hair—Luca was real into channeling Rita Hayworth and Natalie Wood—and wander the edges of the woods and hide out, sometimes, at this small slice of beach beneath the bridge where nobody else went. Because it was difficult to get to, climbing over rocks to find the way down, and because it wasn't so much *beach* as *shore*, a bed of sand and small, sharp stones that the ocean rushed up to meet, crashing past the signs warning **UNPREDICTABLE CONDITIONS** and **TRAFFIC OVERHEAD**.

Sometimes Luca would wade in as far as she dared, which was never really that far; she was never able to ignore the warning signs *that* much, but it was farther than Polly could go. She would stand knee-deep and laugh at Polly on the sand, always watching and never venturing in. Because Polly was one of the worst things a girl born on an island could be: afraid of the ocean.

"Your house," Luca says, because she doesn't know the best way to start but this is one way, at least. "Your house—it was empty, before your mom bought it. But before it was empty, my best friend lived there. Polly."

Naomi pulls her knees up to her chest in a way that Luca has never been able to, not with her stomach and her tits. "She's the one who went missing?"

Luca nods slowly. "But she wasn't missing for long," she says. "Only three days, before they found her."

"Her . . . body?" Naomi says.

"Yeah." Luca jabs her thumbnail through a hole in her sweater sleeve, the thin fabric laddering. "Pulled her right out of the ocean."

The day Polly went missing had been one of those days for just her and Polly, except that the night before, Luca had texted to say, can we meet in town? I'm staying at Madison's tonight, because Whitney had just gotten home from college after her sophomore year. She'd come back a full week earlier than planned, and Luca was so thrilled to have her sister back for the summer and then Madison said, come over, let's slumber party, which they'd been doing since Luca was small, a cute little doll for Whitney and Madison to play with. They would put makeup on her and tell her ghost stories that she wouldn't learn were real until later, and it was tradition, the three of them.

So Luca had gone with Whitney and they'd spent the night at Madison's, drinking Campari sodas and eating the housekeeper's chocolate chip cookies and sleeping all three in the same bed, even though the Riverses' house had about a hundred guest bedrooms.

In the morning Luca woke up hungover, late to meet Polly like they'd agreed. She texted to beg forgiveness, not really meaning it, not thinking Polly would be that mad. But Polly didn't respond, and so Luca thought, *Shit, I really pissed her off*, and she tried texting again but Polly still didn't answer.

And as Luca sat there on the edge of Madison's bed, she felt—swore she felt it, could still remember the exact chill that had knifed down her spine—long, wet fingers creep around her neck and press, tight, only for a second.

When she looked, her sister and Madison were still fast asleep.

Luca takes a slow breath now and lets it out, a gentle rush that blends with the breeze up here.

"We were supposed to hang out," she says, leaving out the rest. "I was late. I texted her, called, and she didn't answer, so I went to meet her anyway but she wasn't there. And then she kept not answering, and it got later, and nobody had seen her, and it was like . . ." She waves a hand through the air, cutting a spiral into nothing. "Like she vanished."

"And how—" Naomi shifts, her voice soft. "How did they find her?"

Of course Luca told Detective Charles about the place

below the bridge, she told the cops and her parents and Polly's parents too, about every place they used to hang out. "You know what was funny?" she says to Naomi, although of course she isn't smiling. "I told them about this spot we used to go to, where we liked to hide away from the world together, right under the bridge. I told them about that, and about everywhere else I thought she maybe could have gone to, but they never actually looked in any of them. It was like they had decided, already, that she was gone. And then on the third day someone calls from a spot on the other side of the island. Says they think there's a body in the water."

Three days, out in the ocean. Lungs filled with cold salt water. Slices on her thighs, the backs of her hands. Broken vertebrae, her neck snapped like a piece of glass. Luca has memorized the autopsy report, the one that of course no one outside the Parris PD was supposed to see, but Jada had her ways, as the head of the department's daughter.

The damage, like Polly had been mauled. By the ocean, maybe, or by a beast.

Or by somebody, Luca thinks, like she always does.

Naomi rubs her hands together, like she's cold, even though the evening is warm still. "That's fucking awful. What a shitty accident. I'm so sorry."

Luca lifts her chin. "An accident?"

That was what the police had determined, what the medical examiner on the mainland had eventually determined, what everybody on the island believed. It was her own sad fault, really, for ignoring the warnings, for swimming in the rough water by herself, with no one around to see once she got in trouble.

And it was easy to believe it was an accident, if you didn't know what Luca knew about Polly. If you didn't know what she knew about the curse.

Naomi is looking at her uncertainly. "You don't think it was?"

I think the curse claimed her, Luca thinks. What she has never managed to understand is how its victims are determined: What doomed Polly, and not Luca? Why did it have to take her, and not somebody else?

Luca shrugs in Naomi's direction. "Polly was afraid of the ocean," she says. "For as long as I can remember, which is basically our entire lives, she was afraid. She never swam in it. She never waded up to her knees, she never even let the waves come up over her toes. She kept her distance, especially down there, where the waves could turn in a second. But I'm supposed to believe that on that day, she decided to go swimming? Or somehow accidentally slipped in? On *that* day, she did everything different from how she ever had before and ended up in the water?" She shakes her head, hard. "No. However she got into the water, I don't believe it was by choice. And however she got her injuries—she had injuries, you know, her neck was broken—I don't believe it was the fault of the ocean."

"So, what?" Naomi asks. "If it wasn't the ocean, then what?"

"Not what," Luca says, because Naomi has set her up perfectly, like she already knew. "Who."

That is what Luca thinks happened, what she believes. That somebody saw Polly down there, or followed her, and hurt her. Hurt her bad, so bad, and then put her in the water, the salt water filling her lungs and washing away any evidence, any chance that they'd figure out the truth of what happened to Polly.

Naomi exhales through barely parted lips. "The cops didn't look into it?"

"No." Luca lifts one shoulder, half a shrug. "Why would they? They've never had much luck solving these things." And she stands. "Come with me," she says.

She walks away from the edge and back toward the trees, but turns deeper into them, leading Naomi under low-hanging branches until they reach the hidden-away clearing, where there is one tree different from all the rest, placed perfectly in the center. It is low and reaching and studded with small, brass-colored rectangles, each of them bearing a name, a birth date, a death date.

The plaques are worn to different degrees, some shiny, some so weathered you can barely read them, and organized somewhat haphazardly: you can see where they used to be placed in neat rows, and where the pattern was abandoned when the names became too many.

Naomi walks around it, her fingertips brushing the plaques. "What is it?"

"A memorial," Luca says. Not in the center of town, or taking pride of place in the museum, or anywhere you might pass by and be forced to stop. No, it's here. Tucked out of sight, and out of so many minds. "Remember last night, when Carter was being a dick? Remember what he said, about a curse?"

"Yeah," Naomi says. "So . . ."

"So it's true," Luca says. "Parris is cursed."

Luca expects her to laugh, but Naomi only keeps circling the tree. "Cursed?"

"That's what some people call it."

"Is that what you call it?"

She could tell the truth now. Tell Naomi that she believes in the curse in a way others don't, that she has felt it, heard it.

But then there is Jada, the things she said that Luca can never forget. *Are you kidding me? You're going to blame some stupid fucking story people tell? You should have been there. If you had been there, she wouldn't be dead.*

"Yes," Luca says, and it's not entirely the truth, but it's not a lie, is it? "Parris has a history like you wouldn't believe. Bad things happen here." A simplification, but the most honest way to say it.

"Here?" Naomi says. "This place is perfect."

"You see these names?" Luca steps up beside Naomi. "They're all gone. Dead, or disappeared, or worse."

"So you think it's, like, doomed?" Naomi says. "The island? Everybody here?"

Luca finds Polly's plaque, hiding beneath sleepy leaves, and presses her fingers to it. Then she trails her hand farther up to the plaque bearing Isla Hollinghurst's name. "This girl, Isla," she says. "She's who Carter was talking about. She lived in one of the oldest houses on the island, and one day it just . . . caught fire. Started to burn. The family all got out, except for Isla. She just burned up along with everything else. And I—my mom was driving, and she stopped when she saw the fire, we pulled over and she told me to stay in the car, but of course I didn't, of course I got out and I watched the flames eat the house alive, like it was nothing at all." Standing on the side of the road, the night bright and clear and cold except for where the Hollinghurst mansion smoldered, smoke and heat haze enveloping the house.

Fire trucks had come, and people had gathered in the street, and there were anguished howls piercing the night. Still Luca stood by herself, staring up at the burning house. And then there, at the last window on the second floor, a figure. Hands pressed against glass.

Luca had watched the window until her mother came and swept her up, back into the car, saying, *Didn't I say to stay put? It's dangerous out there.*

"She was seventeen, you know."

The *just like us* hangs unsaid, and Naomi bites at her thumbnail. "Still. A curse, though?"

"People need an explanation," Luca says, "answers for questions that don't have any." *For when they don't want to believe the answers that are already there.* "The cops, they don't have a good track record of solving any of these cases. So it is what it is." She looks at Naomi then, sees the doubt in her eyes, and wonders if she has gone too far. She wants to make Naomi like her, not scare her.

So she lifts her hands and says, "Don't worry, though. It's just a story. Curses aren't real. Right?"

Naomi looks like she wants to say yes, to call bullshit on the whole thing, but she's also running her fingers across the plaques, still, and Luca can see everything she has just learned ticking through her mind.

Luca walks around the tree until she is on Naomi's other side. "You had a friend," she says. "Last night, that's what you said. Anya."

Naomi exhales slowly. "Yes."

"I told you mine."

"So, what?" Naomi says. "You wanna know how she died?"

Luca nods.

"It really was an accident, with her," Naomi says, her gaze back on the tree. "A car accident. The most boring, run-of-the-mill kind. So you win, on that front." And then it's like she hears what she said, and closes her eyes. "That was extremely bitchy."

Luca thinks back to what her mom had asked, at dinner yesterday: *Is she nice?*

"Lucky for you, I like bitches," Luca says, and then, "So that's why you don't drive."

"Stupid, I know," Naomi says. "What are the chances of it happening again, right? But I just . . . can't do it."

Luca nods. "Do you miss her?"

"Anya?" Naomi backs off from the tree, turns away from it actually, and watches Luca. "Do you miss Polly?"

And Luca feels those pins and needles rush through her again, head to toe. She can't meet Naomi's eyes, but she can't quite look away and so she just stands there, they both just stand there, and Luca says, "She is a part of me," and there's nothing more to say.

10

They drive home under an inky sky, a scattering of stars visible beyond the lights of the town. Quiet. Comfortable and uncomfortable.

Naomi tips her head to the side, staring out the window. "I never saw stars like this back home," she says. "You can't, unless you drive out for miles and miles."

"See," Luca says. "Another slice of perfect Parris."

When Luca's phone buzzes in the cup holder, she asks Naomi to check it for her. "If it's Whit, see what she wants," she says. "She gets pissy if I take longer than two minutes to text back. That's when I think, wouldn't it be nice to be an only child?"

She sees Naomi smile as she picks up Luca's phone. "Not your sister," Naomi says. "It's your dad." She pauses. "You have, like, five missed calls from him."

Luca drums her fingers on the steering wheel. "Really?" she says, ignoring the twist in her stomach as she turns onto their street. "Whatever. I'm sure it's nothing."

The words leave her mouth exactly as the police cruisers come into sight.

Two of them. Parked in the driveway in front of Luca's house. Not neatly, either, but left at sloppy angles. Like they didn't have time to be tidy about things.

"Luca?"

She is not aware that she has stopped the car but evidently she has, because she's out of it now. Walking up to the house when a feeling like the world has gone sideways takes over and she knows this feeling, she has felt this before, everything that she knows knocking off its axis because something bad has happened.

Whitney.

Hasn't heard from her all day, hasn't seen her since last night, and then Luca is inside and she walks into the kitchen and there is her father, there is her mother, there is Detective Charles and Officer Harold and there it is all over their faces, there it is in the way her dad is crying and her mom rushes over and begins to push Luca's hair out of her face, staring at her desperately, like now that she has Luca, she will not let her go ever again.

And Luca snaps back into focus. "What?" she says, even though she knows but she is pretending to herself that she doesn't. "Mom. What's going on?"

"I'm sorry, I'm so sorry," her mom is saying, "Baby, baby, I'm so sorry, Whitney—" And then she's sobbing and Luca has to step back because she's never seen her mother cry like this before. Not when Polly died, not even when her own mother died, and Luca has always counted on her mother's coolness to carry her through. Luca is the mess and her mother is the rock, but now things are the wrong way around and Luca looks at Detective Charles standing there.

"What?" she says again, the word almost blank. "Where is my sister?"

He has the grace to look uncomfortable and Luca thinks, *good*, she thinks, after all he didn't do for Polly, he should be burning with shame to be standing in their kitchen about to tell her that her sister is dead.

That's what you're here for, right? she thinks, and then she feels a hand on her elbow, and when she looks, Naomi is there and she almost forgot about her entirely. Naomi is looking at her oddly and Luca realizes she said it aloud, she must have said it aloud. "Oh," Luca says, slipping her elbow out of Naomi's grip. "What?"

"Luca." Detective Charles takes a step closer, then immediately walks it back. "Earlier this evening, the body of a young woman was discovered on the grounds of the Lansdowne estate. We still need to make a formal identification, but—" He pauses, swallows around the hot air in the room. "At this moment in time, we do believe that the body is that of your sister. We believe it is Whitney."

The air crackles for a moment, Luca hears and sees or thinks she hears and sees, because now somebody has said it. Somebody has put into words what she knew the moment she saw the cars outside, and she is both surprised and not because didn't she feel it coming? Last night, felt it pressing close around her, and she told herself nothing bad was going to happen but she was wrong, she's always wrong, and it is happening again—

First Polly floating in the water and now Whitney killed on the Lansdowne estate and—

Now somebody has said it, she thinks, and then she thinks that she should be better at having the world break apart around her but it does hurt, it is a sharp knife in the space beneath her ribs and her sister is dead, Whitney is dead Whitney is dead Whitney is dead Whitney is dead Whitney is dead Whitney is dead Whitney is dead Whitney is dead Whitney is dead—

11

Luca accepts the plastic cup of water with shaking hands.

She has been trying for the past thirty minutes to make them stop, to steady herself, but she's remembering: there is no real way to calm the feeling that floods you when you have to look at the dead body of somebody you love.

Last time it was her knee. Bouncing, constantly, couldn't stop it. And now it is her hands, as she raises the cup to her mouth and drinks.

"Thank you," she says to the officer in front of her, when the water is drained. "Can I have some more?"

The officer—white and balding and blandly handsome, in the exact same way that every Parris cop is—takes the cup from her and disappears through the swinging double doors.

Empty now, her hands shake more than before. Luca twists them into her sweater cuffs as if binding them, muting their movement. *I need a minute,* she said to her parents before she ran out and landed here in this hallway, but now she's alone and it feels worse this way. Or it would feel worse, if she could feel.

Through the doors at the other end of the hall there's a

set of stairs, and down those stairs there's a room, and that is where Whitney's body lies.

Her parents had tried to keep her out, but Luca held fast. *I'm not a child,* she'd said, *I do not need to be protected from the truth, because if Whitney is really dead, I want to see it for myself, I have to see for myself.*

(I should have listened to them.)

Detective Charles had led them into the room. The Parris police station is small, no real morgue. A holding space for bodies and then the coroner comes from across the bridge, or they send the bodies the other way, into the nearest city, which has a real morgue and a pathology lab and everything needed to deal with a murder.

Those are things the Parris PD should have, Luca thought as she avoided looking at the sheet covering the steel table and what was underneath it. A place like this, filled with death as it is? Of course they should have a morgue and their very own coroner and everything needed to deal with a murder, but she supposed it is like all public institutions, underfunded and overworked. It's just that in Parris, they aren't used to relying on public services, don't know how to manage in situations that can't be fixed by throwing money at them.

You can't fix this, Luca thought, as Detective Charles peeled the sheet down just far enough that they could see Whitney's beautiful face, her beautiful slack dead face. Her dark curls like Luca's fanned out around her shoulders, her brown skin sallow under the fluorescents, dappled with deep dark bruises on her chest. Her pretty pretty eyes so gone.

Luca's mom stopped crying but she couldn't seem to talk, so her dad was the one who said, so quietly, "Yes. Yes, that's Whitney."

In the hallway now, still alone, Luca is thinking about how long her sister has been dead. She is trying to think of the last definitive moment that she saw Whitney—was it when they were dancing with Beth and Naomi, or after? She's sure she saw Whitney laughing at something some boy was saying to her, but maybe that was a different party, a different night, and maybe that boy was Carter, actually, but she doesn't know, she can't remember, everything got blurry after her third drink.

So did Whitney die while Luca was still drinking, still dancing, still at the party, or was it while she and Naomi were walking home? Was it later than that, still?

When Luca called her, was she already gone?

What did she do to deserve this, to make the curse take her?

The double doors explode open and it's Madison running through them. "Luca!"

Luca looks up at her and watches Madison's face fall. *Jesus, I must look exactly like my sister is dead*, she thinks. *What do I look like now that my sister is dead?*

"No." Madison shakes her head, her long, white-blond braid whipping around her. "Luca, no. I refuse to accept this. I can't—I don't—" And then Madison sinks into a crouch, pressing the heels of her hands into her eyes. "She's dead?"

Luca lets Madison cry for a minute, the sound a strange kind of soothing.

"How did you know?" Luca asks when Madison stands up again.

"How do you think?" Madison wipes roughly at her nose. "Nothing's private here."

Then she comes over and sits in the chair beside Luca. "Where are your parents?"

"With Detective Charles." Luca knocks her head back against the wall. "So everybody knows?"

Madison doesn't answer her. "Are they sure it's her? Are you sure?"

"I saw her, Madison." Luca swallows. "I saw her. It's really real."

They sit in silence, the clock high up on the wall tick-tick-ticking. Luca doesn't know what happens next. Do they just . . . go home? How can they go home, when Whitney isn't going to be there? But there's nowhere else. Their house, their island. This is where they've always been, and Luca remembers all the times Whitney talked about leaving Parris without ever meaning it, because why would she want to leave? But now she has no choice.

Luca reaches a still-shaking hand out to Madison, who takes it in her own and looks at Luca with red-rimmed eyes. "I don't know what to do," Luca says. "What do I do now?"

Madison raises their joined hands and presses a kiss to Luca's knuckles. "I don't know," she says. "But we can not know together. Okay?"

Luca inhales sharply, like she's about to cry, but it never comes. She just hangs on the precipice, like she always does.

She hasn't cried since Polly's funeral, as if something broke in her that day. As if she cried a lifetime's allowance on that day and now she's left with nothing. "Okay," she tells Madison. "Okay."

The sky is still dark when they return home.

Luca is so tired, down to her bones, but it's not enough to mask how unbalanced the house feels when she walks inside.

From four down to three.

It's that hour that's not quite morning but not night, either, and her parents look lost. She's waiting for them to tell her what to do when she realizes that they are doing the same thing.

Luca tries not to laugh. Look at them: waiting for her to say something that will make this make sense, or maybe they are waiting for her to fall apart so they have something to do, a next crisis to briefly focus on.

But she isn't about to fall apart; she's too numb for that.

So Luca goes into the kitchen. She walks over to the cabinet above the sink first and takes out the pills she had for her sprained ankle, the ones that made her drowsy. Then she opens the freezer and pulls out the vodka, and walks back out to find her parents, and presses both items into her father's hands. "You should both sleep," she says, not quite meeting his eyes. "Try to sleep."

She leaves them there and makes her way through the living room, dragging a blanket from the pile by the fireplace and a cushion from the nearest couch. She takes them outside and down to the pool, where she lies on a lounger and turns on her side.

She'll sleep out here. She has to sleep out here, because going upstairs means seeing Whitney's room, and being in the unbalanced house is making her want to claw her skin off.

Except Luca knows she won't sleep. She knows she's going to think about Whitney's blank dead face in place of sleeping, and if she does manage to cross over, those thoughts will become her dreams, so either way, she won't get any rest.

That's the last thing she remembers thinking, and the next is that somebody's cold hands are touching her.

Her eyes open and the sky is no longer dark, dawn filtering in. The face in front of her belongs to Naomi, who holds her cold hands up. "I didn't mean to scare you," she whispers in the morning hush. "I didn't know if you were awake or not. I wanted to come see you."

Luca says nothing and Naomi bites her lip. "I'm sorry," she says. "Jesus, I'm sorry, Luca. Are you okay?"

Am I okay?

She will never be okay.

"I told you," Luca says, and her words are sleepy-soft but clear. "Cursed."

12

I'm so sorry for your loss.

The thought plays on a loop in Luca's head, background noise that she cannot escape. It's all anyone has had to say to her for the past two weeks, and she is sickened by the sound of it, the carefully constructed expressions of sadness people paste onto their faces when they say it. *So sorry*, like they didn't know this was going to happen to somebody sometime. *So sorry*, like they haven't done all of this before.

"Can I get you another drink?"

Luca snaps her head up. A server holding a tray of empty glasses stands in front of her, eyebrows gently raised. "What?"

The server gestures at Luca's empty glass. "Something else?"

"Oh." Luca shakes her head. "No. It's fine."

She sets her empty glass on the server's tray and turns away, forgetting the reason she is facing the piano: the photograph of Whitney, blown up too large, and placed where it seems like her eyes can follow you. "Stop it," Luca says under her breath, staring the image of her sister down. "Weirdo."

This was her father's idea, this memorial. A time for people to come and say goodbye; a time for their family to say goodbye, he'd said.

What if I don't want to say goodbye? Luca had said, staring at her parents across the dining room table.

I don't want to say it either, her mom had said. *But she's gone. And perhaps, if we do this now, it will keep her in people's minds. Could keep her in the minds of the police, too, and then we might get closer to finding out who did this to her.*

A hand lands on her shoulder, and Luca jumps, but it's her mother in the flesh. "What are you doing standing in the corner?" she asks gently. "Are you okay?"

Everybody's favorite question. "I'm doing what you asked," Luca says flatly. "I'm being the grieving sister."

She expects her mom to sigh at her, but instead Emilia stands beside her and watches their friends and acquaintances milling through the living room and kitchen, talking in hushed tones. "You're doing a good job," Emilia says. "What about me? Do I look like the perfect grieving mother?"

Luca glances sideways, surprised by her mom, this new black humor. "Just about," she says. "Yes, I think we're making everybody very sad."

One side of her mother's mouth lifts, but her eyes are still flat, red and glossy. "I can't stop thinking about Kara Stern," she says. "How we stood in her house, three years ago, doing the exact same thing for Polly."

Luca plucks at the sleeve of her dress, the only one she has that wasn't too short or low-cut or semi-sheer for an occasion such as this. It itches like a motherfucker. "I need air," she says, choking on the memory of that other day. "I can't breathe in here."

She leaves her mother standing there, staring at the picture of Whitney.

When she's outside, she stops and pulls in a deep lungful of air. The garden is empty, except for the two figures she sees far off at the end of the yard, staring out at the ocean beyond.

Luca kicks off her shoes and walks down to Madison and Naomi, soft steps across the manicured lawn. "Thank god," she says. "I was wondering where all the sane people had gone."

Madison glances over her shoulder and it's obvious that she's been crying, but even so, she looks beautiful. One of *those* girls, those golden glowing girls. "Escaped the parents?"

"Finally."

Naomi offers her a glass of something clear. "I think it's gin," she says. "You want it?"

Luca's stomach turns. "No thanks."

"You want something else?" Naomi's hand dips into the top of her dress and she pulls something from her bra—a vape pen.

Madison gives one breath of laughter. "Wow," she says. "Huh. Is it wrong to get high at your best friend's memorial?"

"Only as wrong as it is to get high at your sister's memorial," Luca says, although she's only pretending. She doesn't like to get high anymore; it never made her feel good, only more jumpy.

"Would she care if you did?" Naomi asks, not mocking but

a genuine question that makes Luca smile without realizing she's doing it.

"Not at all," she says.

Naomi twirls the pen through her fingers but nothing more. "I know I only met her that day," she says, "but—I really liked her. She was . . . I don't know. Fun. God, that sounds so stupid. Is that all I have to say about her?"

Luca begins walking a curve around them, the grass cool on the bottoms of her aching feet. "It's hard to summarize a life," she says, concentrating on her steps. "It's especially hard at one of these things, when everyone's watching for what you're going to say. Waiting for it to be so profound, so sentimental." She stops and looks over at Naomi, her dress with soft gray flowers sketched across it. "What did you do for Anya?"

The vape pen slips out of Naomi's fingers and she swears. "For Anya?" she says as she crouches to pick it up. "I—I don't even know, really. I think I've wiped all that time from my mind."

"Anya?" Madison looks between the two of them. "Who's Anya?"

"A girl I used to know," Naomi says. "She died too. Car accident."

Madison shakes her head. "Fucking death," she says. "Can't we be left alone?"

There's a noise from the direction of the house, and when Luca turns, she sees Beth and Carter coming down to them. "Gang's all here," Luca says drily.

"We were looking for you," Beth says, and she catches Luca in a hug. "Sensible girl, escaping."

"Trying my best," Luca says.

Beth takes a pack of cigarettes from her clutch and lights one with a shiny gold lighter. "You probably want to stay out here as long as possible," she says, with the cigarette in the corner of her mouth. "Detective Charles is in there."

Madison raises her eyebrows. "For real?"

"Brought the kids, too," Carter says, taking the cigarette pack from Beth. "I always forget Jada exists."

Jada is in my house.

Naomi touches Luca's wrist, a warm spot. "It's okay," she says quietly, so only Luca hears, and it must be written on her face. "Whatever it is, it's okay."

Beth's twisting her hair up on her head and saying, "Do you think they're going to do it this time? Figure it out? Charles and them, our illustrious police department."

"Feels like they're trying, at least." Madison accepts a smoke from Carter. "They brought us all in to get our statements, didn't they? They're probably going to do an autopsy at some point, right?" Here she looks at Luca. "Did they say? When they're going to do it?"

She's holding out the cigarettes to Luca, and smoking is another thing she doesn't do that much but right now all she can think is Jada is in her house, Jada is walking through her home like she used to, as if she hasn't been absent from it since Polly died and she cut Luca off, and her skin is pulsing where Naomi touched her and so she takes a cigarette, lights it, inhales. "I have no idea," she says. "Charles said they have a backlog in the city. He said he'll try to get them to prioritize her, but—" Without the autopsy they have no cause of death, not an official one. But Luca has heard the cops talking to her parents, telling them about the damage to her sister's skull.

She's been picturing it every night as she tries to fall asleep, her distraction from the emptiness of Whitney's room down the hall and because fixating is what she does best. That's what she's doing, fixating on what or who happened to her sister to cause that damage to her skull.

Could have been somebody inside her house right now, she knows. Could be that the person who did it is eating crab cakes from the caterers and pretending to grieve with everybody else. Could be that they are one of the people who told Luca how sorry they are.

"That's what they always say, that they'll *try*." Beth gestures with her cigarette, the end glowing as she circles it through the air. "While the fucking freaks try to blame it on some made-up story."

Carter exhales a spiral of smoke. "Curse bullshit," he says. "Jesus, I don't want assholes talking about her like she's a joke."

Luca has to bite her tongue to stop herself from reminding Carter that he's one of those assholes, that he loves nothing more than using the curse for a laugh. To stop herself from telling Beth that she herself is one of those *fucking freaks* and it's not about blame, it's about truth.

She feels the vomit rise without warning and drops her cigarette without putting it out. "I have to go," she manages to say, and Madison calls after her as she rushes up to the house, a hand clamped over her hot mouth.

She is inside and she can make it upstairs to her own bathroom, she thinks, but at the bottom of the stairs stands a white girl with a pixie cut and knockoff sunglasses and a look like she's been caught somewhere she shouldn't be. "Luca," Jada says, not the least hint of any kind of feeling in her voice. "I'm sorry about—"

Luca bends over and throws up at Jada's feet.

13

The water seeps out of the corners of her mouth and Luca finally spits into the sink. Rising up, she wipes at the corners of her mouth with a towel, the mint of her toothpaste burning on her tongue.

Then she smiles. That's one way to clear out a memorial.

She comes out of the bathroom and Naomi's sitting on the edge of her bed. "Better?" she asks, a small smile like Luca's own playing on her lips.

"Much." Luca sits next to Naomi and she can see half their faces in her dressing table mirror: hair and eyes, her curls and Naomi's straight, her almost-black eyes and Naomi's warmer brown.

Their eyes meet in the mirror and Luca looks away first. "I've never been very good at this," she says.

"What?"

"Mourning." Luca twists her fingers into her pure white bedsheets. "Not with my grandmother, or Polly, or my stupid bunny that only lived for a year."

Naomi laughs at that. "I can mourn," she says. "You know,

one side of my family is Filipino, and the other is Irish. That's
a lot of Catholicism, okay? Mourning is in my blood. But when
it comes to the actual feelings—" She shrugs, the movement
rippling into Luca. "Repress, repress, repress."

"I kind of got that," Luca says. "The way you talk about
Anya. Or don't talk about her."

"Yeah, well." Naomi shrugs again. "Like I said, it was a long
time ago."

Luca goes back to watching their reflections and listens to
the sounds of the caterers leaving. "I don't remember the last
thing I said to Polly," she says, exhaling with the confession.
That's what it feels like, a confession of this thing she's always
been too ashamed to say aloud. "Face-to-face. The last actual
words from my mouth to her. I have no idea what they were."

Naomi tilts her head so she's looking at Luca instead of
the mirror. "What about Whitney?" she says.

"I left her a voice mail," Luca says, and closes her eyes. "But
she never listens to her voice mail. I used to do it to annoy
her, but it still made me feel closer to her. So no, I suppose I
don't know what I said to her, either."

Then the words are rushing out: "Sometimes I try to pick
something. Decide that yeah, it was when I left Polly on the
beach the day before and all I said was goodbye. Or that it was
later, and we were out, and I asked for a bite of her sundae.
But maybe it was none of those, and maybe I just told her to
shut up. I don't know. I can't pick. Because no matter what I
choose, it's not real. I'll never know exactly what I said. And
she's buried in the ground now, so she can't even help me."

And Whitney's waiting on a slab and did Luca call out that she was going to get a drink, and did Whitney call back, *Bring me a beer*, or was her telling Luca to dance the last thing?

It's hitting her now, that the two people who knew her best in the world are gone. The only ones to have ever known her fully without judging her, who accepted her and her crazy and her queer and her body like she deserved to be treated kindly. Who does she have left now?

Naomi is quiet for a moment, picking at the hem of her dress, splayed across her thighs. "I don't remember Anya's voice," she says suddenly, haltingly. "I can't remember what she sounds like anymore."

"You're just saying that."

"No," Naomi says softly. "I'm telling you that you're not the only one."

Luca looks at Naomi. Her hair hangs in front of her face, and Luca wants to push it aside, hook it behind Naomi's ear so she can see her face fully, the shape of her.

Luca swallows. "You can't remember her voice," she says. "I can't remember her words. This is the part no one tells you about. How you're left behind to feel like the worst sister— friend—because who the fuck doesn't remember the most important parts of a girl they claim to have loved?"

"What did you say to Whitney?" Naomi pushes her straight black hair back exactly the way Luca wanted to. "In your voice mail. What did you tell her?"

Luca has tried not to think about it too much, but the words are right there. "That she was the worst sister," she says.

"And I didn't mean it, I was only fucking around, and I know she didn't hear it but—" She shakes her head so violently dizziness overtakes and she thinks she might throw up again. "Don't repeat that," she says to Naomi. "You're the only one who knows. You can't tell anyone what I said to her."

"I won't," Naomi says. "You can say that to me. You can tell me about her, tell me the worst things. You don't scare me, Luca Laine Thomas. I get it."

Luca tries to smile but it won't come. "You should be scared," she said. "Don't you know I'm crazy?"

"Did you hear what I said?" Naomi leans in. "I get it. I get you. Like you get me. That's it."

The world around Luca unbalances a little more, axes shift. "That's it," she says.

14

Luca has always known every inch of their house, every soft sound of settling, every flick of a light switch. Used to wander downstairs in the dark when she was younger, keeping her eyes half-closed so as to block out any moonlight, and find her way to the kitchen, get a glass and fill it with water, judging when the glass was full enough only by the weight of it.

That's why her eyes fly open as she lies on her bed in the middle of the afternoon, some days after the memorial. She is sure that the noise that snapped her into alertness was the creak of Whitney's bedroom door.

She gets up and leaves her own room, and there, at the end of the hall: Whitney's door, open for the first time since—

Luca turns away from it, the wide yawn of the space pulling at a similar chasm inside her chest, and scrapes her hands over her face. "Mom?" she calls.

A noise carries up the stairs. Voices, loud ones. Ones not belonging to her parents.

She pulls her hair over her shoulder as she makes her way

downstairs, twisting the curls into one single spiral, and calls out again. "Mom? Dad?"

And then she slows, because there in the entryway is Officer Harold, and as Luca watches he picks up a stack of boxes and carries them out of the open front door.

"*Mom—*"

"In the kitchen," comes the reply finally, except it's from her dad, and when Luca walks in, her mom is sitting with her back to the room, staring out the glass doors.

Her dad, though, sits at the kitchen island, and standing across from him is Detective Charles. "Hey," her dad says when he sees her, and he sounds exhausted, but they all do, Luca has noticed. "I was about to come get you—"

"What are they taking?" Luca interrupts, and she looks at Detective Charles. "Are you taking Whitney's things?"

"It's routine," Detective Charles says. "To help with the investigation."

But I don't want you to, Luca wants to say. Not that she doesn't want them to investigate, of course she does, but— they're in Whitney's room, and Luca hasn't even been in there since Whitney died. What if they're messing it all up? What if they're in there pulling apart the world that Whitney had so carefully built around herself?

She lifts her chin. "What are you looking for?"

"Anything that might help," Charles says, and he picks up the coffee sitting in front of him but doesn't take a sip. Under his arm he's holding a thin folder, pressed to his side. "Like I said, it's routine."

Luca says nothing to that, but her dad reaches up to put a hand on her shoulder. "Luca, Detective Charles has some questions he wants to ask you. It's nothing to worry about, okay?"

"More questions?" She's already given her statement, her account of that night. They all had to: everyone at the party. Carter and Beth and Madison, Naomi, every other person Luca was busy paying zero attention to.

Charles sets the coffee down. "It would be helpful if we could talk." He glances over his shoulder. "In there, perhaps?"

For a second Luca feels outside of her body, like she's watching a play, carefully rehearsed: there is the way Detective Charles moves his prop around, the deliberate words from her father, her mother stage right drawing a quiet, intense attention.

Then she comes back to herself and nods. "Okay."

She follows Detective Charles into the formal dining room, where they have those family dinners, one-two-three-four around the warm wood table.

Not one-two-three-four now.

Luca sits at the table and lays her hands flat, fingers spread wide.

"Now." Detective Charles sinks into the chair beside her, setting the folder in front of him, and it surprises Luca, how he isn't sitting across from her but next to her. "We're just trying to piece things together. That night—" He pauses, his gaze flicking up to the ceiling as he seems to be deciding what tack to take. "What can you tell me about Whitney's drug use?"

Whatever Luca had been expecting, it wasn't that. "Drugs?" she says, unable to keep from smiling, but it's a confused, *what the fuck are you talking about* smile. "Whit?"

"Yes."

Whitney did not do drugs, not in the way she knows Charles means right now. Maybe it would seem like it, maybe it would seem like of course they all partied as often as possible, being that they ran with Carter. But Carter's business, when he had it—it had always fallen outside the group. He sold pills and powder; they smoked up, if anything. *A good dealer never uses their own product,* Carter used to say.

So she shakes her head. "Whitney wasn't into that. I mean, like . . ." She folds her arms. Defensive? Maybe. "Maybe she smoked some weed every once in a while, but that's all."

Detective Charles shakes his head. "That's not what we've heard."

"Then you've heard wrong," Luca says.

"So the reports we have of Whitney using drugs that night," he says, "they were wrong?"

Luca snaps her fingers. Yes, *wrong*, obviously. "Who said that?"

He watches her for a moment, his concentrated gaze a lot to bear, and then he flips open the file. "Take a look at this for me," he says, "and then think about what you want to tell me."

Luca ignores the dip in her stomach and pulls the file toward her.

Inside is a sheet of paper, an official police-looking report, and she thinks at first that he's giving her the statements, so that she'll see it for herself. But then she sees the part that says DUI, right before she sees her sister's name.

Wait.

What?

Luca opens her mouth, but the way Detective Charles is watching her take this information in stops her from saying anything.

Instead she reads the report, not once but three times, just to be *sure.*

It's from the police department in Whitney's college town, dated January two years ago. Says she ran a red light, no collision. Was pulled over and tested positive for narcotics, MDMA and cocaine and something else Luca can't pronounce. A small amount of coke in her bag, and some pills, too.

Whitney got a DUI? is not the thought loud in her head. More *Whit didn't tell me about this? Whit got in trouble while she was at school and kept it a secret from me this whole time?*

"Okay." She pushes it away and folds her arms again. "What am I supposed to say to this?"

"See, this tells us that what people reported seeing her doing on that night is likely true," Detective Charles says. "And so I'm asking you, Luca, to tell me what you know about your sister and anything she might have taken, at the party or before it, or at any other time, actually. Do you know who her dealer was? How often would you say she got high?"

Luca shakes her head. "I'm telling you, she *didn't*," she says. "And what would it matter if she did, anyway? It's not like she OD'd. I mean—" She sits up straighter. "Why are you asking me this? You have her body. You can test for that, right? So test her. You'll see."

"We will." Charles leans forward. "But I'm giving you a chance to let me know, before. If there's anything that might . . . impact the investigation. Change what we should be looking for, where we should be looking."

Luca shifts slightly, digs her nails into her upper arms, a small amount of pressure. She's not stupid. She can hear what he's not saying.

Maybe, if Whitney was high out of her mind on something, this whole thing was an accident. Or maybe whoever she was getting high with was responsible, which partly makes Whitney responsible, because she should have known better than to keep that kind of company, right?

Charles is staring at her and she's not sure what more she expected from the man who was so quick to write off Polly's death as an accident, make it all disappear. And Polly was white, younger, more innocent. If he couldn't get it together to help her, then what chance does Whitney have?

The curse—it doesn't change the fact that someone did this to Whitney. It doesn't absolve them of any guilt.

But she knows, also, how this investigation is going to go. Shouldn't be surprised by it at all, and she isn't, really, not as much as she is tired. Exhausted, actually, by this curse and having to live beneath it, of feeling like there is no way to resist it.

Luca rubs her thumb across her bottom lip. Maybe—

Maybe there is a way to try, at least. Maybe there is a way to use what momentum there is, and finally decipher how the curse works. *If I can figure out why it chose Whit, and Polly, Isla Hollinghurst, and Laney on the yacht and Evelyn who was assaulted—*

If she can do that, then maybe Luca can know how to make sure she is not its next victim.

"So this is it?" she says, eventually, slowly. "This is the direction you're going in?"

Detective Charles raps his knuckles on the table. "This is the direction the investigation is taking us," he says. "We have to follow all leads. And whether you choose to believe it or not, your sister had a history. All I'm doing is my job, Luca."

He stands, straightens his tie, and Luca shoves the DUI report at him. "Don't forget this."

"You keep it." He nods at her, so magnanimous, as if he is doing her a favor. "And call if you think of anything that might answer my questions."

He walks away, and Luca is left with the report in her hand and the feeling that the curse has not had its fill of the Laine Thomas girls.

Not yet.

15

It does not take Luca long to decide on her plan.

She needs to trace Whitney's night, that night. She needs to know exactly where she went after Luca last saw her, and who she was with, and what she did or didn't take, and— whatever else happened. That's where she will start, and along the way, she hopes, she'll find something. A phrase her sister uttered, or a particular path she took, or perhaps— perhaps—

I don't fucking know, Luca thinks, sitting on the edge of her bed and running her fingers over the DUI report for the millionth time. *There must be something. There has to be something that marks them for death. And I'll know it when I see it, with Whit, and then I will do the same thing for Polly, and then I'll have to move on to the others, Isla and the rest, and further back, until I find the pattern.*

Until she knows the truth of the curse.

So yes, she's going to track Whitney's steps on the night of her death.

Luca leans over, to slide the report beneath her mattress.

The one thing she's stuck on already, though, is the idea of Whit using that night—using in general, like a habit. If that's for real, then she kept it a pretty good secret, because Luca never had any clue.

She catches herself in the mirror. *You know who might, don't you?*

Luca exhales.

She picks up her phone and dials. Listens to the ringing against her ear, impatient.

"Hey," Carter answers eventually, and he sounds surprised, which is fair because when is the last time he and Luca just chatted casually? "What's up?"

"Hey," Luca says. "Are you busy? I need to ask you something."

Whitney and Carter had ended up at the same school, although Whitney slyly attributed Carter's presence there more to his family's *very* generous donations than to his academics. But he had been there alongside her, and Luca can't ignore that, not when she thinks about his previous . . . career.

"Hold on." There's noise in the background, a girl's voice, and Luca can picture him leaving Beth while he steps outside. "All right. You okay?"

"I'm fine," she says, and then clicks her tongue. "Well. I mean—"

"I know," Carter says. "But you wanna ask me something?"

There's a knock on her door, and before Luca can even say, *Leave me alone, please*, her father opens it.

Luca puts her hand over the speaker. "Yes? What?"

He looks around the room before his gaze settles on her. "Are you on the phone?"

"Yes. So?"

"Who are you talking to?"

"What does it matter?" Luca says. "What, I'm not allowed to talk to people now? Do I have to run it by you first?"

He narrows his eyes. "Watch your tone."

"I'm in the middle of something," Luca says. "Can whatever this is wait until later?"

Her dad hovers there, and for a split second Luca feels guilty, like she knows all he wants is to be able to make sure his remaining daughter is okay, is present and alive.

But the annoyance wins out, because while he's acting all protective, she's the one actually trying to do something about it.

"Dad," she says. "Do you mind?"

And he sighs. "Fine," is all he says, and then he closes the door.

Luca waits a moment, until she hears his footsteps retreating, before putting the phone back to her ear. "Sorry," she says to Carter. "My dad . . . whatever."

"It's fine," Carter says. "So, question?"

Luca stands and starts to walk a slow path around her bed. "So Detective Charles was just here, and he was asking me about Whit and how often she gets high and I told him she doesn't, not really, but then he showed me this report, this DUI she got a couple years ago, and I told him I had no idea about that and even if she used to mess around with shit then, it doesn't mean—"

"Wait, wait," Carter says, cutting her off. "Slow down, all right? Did you say she got a DUI?"

"Yeah."

"Huh." There's a moment's silence and Luca pictures him again, staring up at the early evening sky. "Well, she kept that quiet."

"I know," Luca says, shaking her head. "She should've told me. I don't know why she didn't." She pauses. "Unless—"

"Ah," Carter says. "Unless she really *did* have a habit, the kind bad enough that she wouldn't want you to know about it at all, and so you're calling me because you want to know if I used to sell to her. Is that it?"

Laid out like that, it makes her sound like an asshole, but—"Yeah, that's about it."

"I get your thinking," he says. "But Whit was never a customer. And before you go there, that's not some slick way of me acting like I didn't supply her when I did and she just didn't pay. I never gave Whit anything but weed, and she never asked me for anything else. You know that wasn't her thing."

"Right," Luca says, spinning in front of the wall and retracing her path around the bed. "Except she has this DUI and the record says she had coke and other shit in her system, so maybe I *don't* know."

"Didn't you say it was years ago?" Carter says. "It was *college*. I'm pretty sure if Whit was using, I'd know about it. I may not be in the business anymore, but that doesn't mean

I don't still stay in the loop." He pauses and there's the click-crackle-burn of a cigarette being lit. "What does this have to do with anything anyway? Shouldn't Charles be out looking for whoever did this to her, not interrogating you over her Friday-night habits?"

"You would think." Luca stops and sits again, not saying anything, and neither is Carter, but she can hear him smoking and it's comforting, for those few minutes. At least he cares, at least Luca has him and Madison and Beth on her side.

"Okay, I gotta go," he says eventually. "But—don't keep thinking about this. You'll stress yourself out."

Luca wants to do exactly that, to go back over every inch of that report, *again*, and then think herself into a spiral.

But she's had enough therapy to recognize that this is not the best plan.

No. The best plan is the one she's already made. All she has to do now is carry it out.

"I won't," she says. "I know what I'm doing."

16

The next day Luca finds herself at Jada's house.

She has never been to Jada's house, which is strange, when you really think about it, think about how braided together the three of them were. There was barely a day that they didn't see each other, but it was always at Polly's or Luca's. Because they lived next door and it was easier for Jada to come to them, they all used to say, but the real reason also hummed beneath that: because Polly and Luca had money, and Jada did not. Not that she was poor—her dad was a high-up cop, after all—but in Parris, poor is relative. You don't have the ocean view and the museum benefit list and the housekeeper who you never actually see?

Then you're not rich.

Luca looks at the house she has found, closer to the bridge than the beach, and thinks it is fine. More than fine: charming, even. White fence and rosebushes in the front yard and the door painted sea-foam green. Luca wonders who's responsible for that—did Jada do it, or was it something her mom did, before she left them? Has Jada been keeping it up since then, a decade of painting and pruning?

It's almost noon now, the sun beating down, but she had to wait until Jada was alone—or at least, until she saw that her father was gone. Could be that Jada isn't even at home. Maybe Luca will knock on the door and find only silence.

Last night, when she told Naomi what Charles had said, Naomi said, *You should find out. Who's saying it, what they said.*

And Luca said, *That's exactly what I was thinking.*

She straightens the strap of her dress before she knocks, three sharp raps on the green wood. From behind it she hears the music that was playing stop, and then footsteps. They come closer, closer. Stop.

The door swings open and Luca takes a step back. "Isaac," she says, trying not to sound too disappointed. "Hi."

"Luca," he says, but he's surprised. "Uh, hey. What are you—" He stops, his cheeks reddening. "I mean, hi. How are you? I'm really—" Here his voice drops, the appropriate level of solemn. "Really sorry about Whitney."

I'm sure you are, Luca wants to say, *even though you only really knew her as Madison's best friend, even though she was the one who had to break it to you that Madison not answering your texts or calls anymore meant she was through with you. And oh yeah, even though you called her a bitch, at the coffee shop, like, not even that long ago?*

Asshole.

Isaac's standing there, running a hand through his hair, which looks like he just woke up, but then he always looks like that. "Listen," Luca says, "is your sister here?"

He raises an eyebrow but turns back toward the inside of the house. "Jada!" he calls. "Someone here to see you." He turns back to Luca. "Well. Guess I'll leave you to it. And I'm—"

"Really sorry," Luca says. "Yeah, I know."

He ducks his head but turns, leaves, to the sound of footsteps coming down the stairs and then he's gone and then Jada's there, eyes wide, and Luca steels herself and Jada—

Slams the door shut.

There's a peephole above the brass number on the door and Luca looks right at it. "*Really*, Jada?"

A moment of silence, and then, "What do you want?"

"I want to talk to you," Luca says. "Don't you think it's about time we talked? It's only been three years."

"You threw up at my feet the other day."

"I don't know about you, but I don't consider that 'talking,'" Luca says. "Besides, what did you expect? You show up in my house, at my sister's memorial, and you *don't* think I'm gonna vomit all over you?"

"We have nothing to talk about."

"Open the door, Jada. You're so stubborn, I swear to *god*."

There's another minute of silence and then the door swings open. Jada's in cutoffs and a tee of some band Luca's never heard of, her short, usually straight hair curling like she recently got out of the shower. "I'd invite you in," she says, "but I don't want to."

Luca looks behind her, inside the house. It's much the same as the outside, from what she can see of it: small, clean, bright. But to Jada she says, "I see why."

Jada barely even rolls her eyes. "Why are you here?" she says, and then, "I'm surprised your new bestie isn't with you."

"You mean Naomi?"

"Oh, is that her name?" Jada shrugs. "So what, is she just your bestie, or is she your girl?"

Luca stares her down. "You don't get to ask me that," she says, and at the same time she's trying not to think of the all-consuming crush—no, *crush* is not the right word; it is bigger than that, more intense, a force of feeling so rough and so sudden that it almost kicks Luca off her feet every time she catches Naomi watching her, like she thinks Luca isn't looking.

Or maybe she doesn't care if Luca sees.

(That's the part that takes the ground from beneath her every time.)

"Convenient for you," Jada says, and she leans against the doorframe. "Polly left that house all ready for her to move in and become your new follower. You don't even have to try. It's like the universe puts them in your lap, good little girls who'll do whatever you want them to."

Luca stiffens. "You know my sister's *dead*, right?"

Jada doesn't miss a beat. "I was at the memorial," she counters. "So is that what you came here for? To tell me off for not being nice enough to you now that Whit's gone?"

And the way she says it—it's so quick, that *Whit*. But it's a reminder of the before time, when Jada was close enough to call her that.

She wonders when Jada found out what had happened.

Did she cry? Did she sit in the dark of her bedroom and listen to that sad song she always used to play them, did she find a long-ago photo on her phone and stare at it like if she focused hard enough, Whitney would take a breath again?

"It's about Whitney, yeah," Luca says. She can feel the sweat building at the small of her back. Should not have bought this dress, in all its rayon stripe glory. "Your dad, he came to talk to me. He asked me if Whit was into drugs—I mean, 'asked' is putting it generously. He thinks she was fucked-up when she died."

Jada's eyebrows rise. "Okay," she says slowly. "And I care about this why?"

"Because I need to know if it's true," Luca says. "So I need to know who said it."

"Throw a dart," Jada says. "You know it could've been absolutely anybody who was at that party. Why does it even matter who said it?"

"Because whoever it was, I need to talk to them," Luca says. "So they'll set shit straight. Because if they don't, everybody will be looking in the wrong direction. Your dad and the rest of the cops will be looking in the wrong direction, and I'm not about to just watch while they file her away as an 'accidental' death too."

The *like Polly* goes unsaid.

Luca ignores the twist in her stomach. Yes, this is manipulative, and she is playing on Jada's grief, but what other choice does she have? Jada doesn't need to know that this is not entirely about getting justice for Whitney. She doesn't need to know that Luca is doing this for selfish reasons, to protect herself as well as her sister's memory, or anybody else. Luca can't tell Jada that she's trying to understand how the curse works, because Jada doesn't believe in the curse at all.

A car passes by on the street, crackly seventies rock filtering out the open windows, and Jada waits for it to pass before she says, "Whatever it is you want me to do, I'm not doing it. One, I don't break into my dad's shit for free anymore, and two, why would I do *anything* for you?"

"Because it's not for me," Luca says. "It's for Whitney. And she never did anything to you." She's gripping her phone and can feel it buzzing, but she ignores it. It'll only be her mom, or her dad, or Naomi or Madison or maybe Beth or—none of them matter right this second because Jada is looking at her like she's out of her mind for even *considering* asking for this favor and isn't that funny, isn't that *hilarious* when Jada is the one acting like she doesn't know exactly why Luca's here.

Jada takes a step back. "Let me get this straight," she says. "When Polly died, it was a curse. And now that it's your sister, you want somebody to blame? What, it wasn't a *curse* that killed her too?"

Of course it was, Luca wants to say. This is what everybody gets wrong, this is why they can't see it as clearly as she can: to them, *curse* means something inexplicable, working on its own. They don't understand that it's more than that. The curse didn't snap Polly's neck, but it picked the hand that did, it picked her to be the one broken like a doll. The curse didn't cave Whitney's skull in. But it chose her to die. It chose the one who killed her.

Luca can't leave without getting Jada to agree. "She's my sister," Luca says finally, her breath hitching as she catches herself. "She *was* my sister. Now she's gone. And I know you, Jada. We aren't friends anymore and you're different now, I know, but you're also not, because you belong to Parris in the same way I do, and you don't grow up here without hearing the stories. I don't want Whit to become another ghost story." *And I do not want to become a ghost story.* She takes a step forward. "I know you don't really believe Polly's death was the accident your dad decided it was, and I know it kills you to sit in this house with him while you think about how quickly everyone accepted that story. I don't think you want to let it happen to Whitney, too, watch them following bullshit leads and writing her off while whoever did this to her slips away. So I need you to help me, I need to know who said that about her, so I can make them unsay it and make the cops do their fucking jobs."

So I can figure out how not to be the next one to die.

She presses her knuckles into her chest, like she can ease the knot of guilt that has built behind her sternum.

Jada's staring at her but her usual hostility is gone, replaced by something else. Maybe pity. Maybe fear.

Maybe recognition that Luca's right, that ever since Polly died Jada has slowly been dying inside too.

Jada tugs on her earlobe and sighs. "Okay," she says quietly. "I'll see what I can do. But don't hold your breath."

How can Luca explain that she hasn't properly exhaled in weeks?

Instead she nods. "Thank you."

Jada shuts the door in her face without another word; Luca goes back to her car.

17

Luca scrunches her feet into the velvet of the couch she's sitting on. It's the palest pink, a perfect match to the detail on the geometric rug running between Madison's bed and the doors that hide her walk-in closet. Her whole bedroom, actually, is done in shades of pink and pearl and the softest off-white. Luca has always thought of it like the center of a just-blooming flower.

It is nice to feel something familiar.

"Here." Madison has come back in with Diet Cokes and a crystal bowl of strawberries, which she sets on the table before sitting, her back against the arm of the couch in a mirror of Luca. "I think my parents told the housekeeper not to get groceries while they're away. Either that or she's trying to starve me."

Luca picks out a plump strawberry but can't quite put it in her mouth, because its soft redness only makes her think of a heart, her teeth sinking into flesh.

She puts it back and tries not to look at her pink fingertips. Instead she looks past Madison and points at the garment bag hanging from one of the closet doors. "It's all finished?" she asks.

Madison turns and sighs in the direction of her wedding dress. Couture, from a small designer in Milan, where she had to go for initial fittings and FaceTimed Luca and Whitney from, allowing them peeks of soft tulle. "Yeah," she says. "I don't know what I'm going to do with it. Feels wrong to put it in my closet and leave it with the rest of my things, but . . . I guess that's all there is."

"It's only for a few weeks," Luca says, and Madison looks back at her, her dark blond brows pulling together.

"No," she says, as if she thought Luca already knew. "I mean, because the wedding's not happening."

"What?" Luca sits forward. "You're canceling?"

"What else am I going to do?" Madison says. "I can't have a, like, big obnoxious *party* while all this is happening." She pauses, and when she speaks again, it is quiet. "I can't get married without my best friend there."

Luca slips a finger inside the rip at the knee of her jeans, pushing her nail as deep into her leg as she can and then scraping it back. It's the only way she can push back the sudden hit of grief that comes from realizing that her sister won't be at her own wedding. She's never thought about her own wedding before, even, because picturing herself marrying somebody would mean picturing a person who could love her queerness and all the sharp parts and crazy strange brain that she is and who in this universe would ever do that?

Maybe Naomi would marry me. The thought comes unbidden and Luca digs the pointed end of her nail deeper.

See, this is more crazy. Naomi looks at Luca in her own particular way a few times and all of a sudden Luca's marrying them off, some future version of themselves, which is funny because right now Luca can't see more than a day ahead at a time.

Then Madison's hand is closing over hers, stilling her. "It's okay," she says gently. "It's only a wedding."

Luca nods but— "If the only reason you're not doing it is Whitney," she says, "then I think you should do it."

"What?"

"She's dead." Luca says it fast, blunt, the only way that feels right. "She's gone. So she won't be at your wedding now, but she won't be there if you do it next year, or ten years from now. She's never going to be there, for anything, ever again—" She snatches her hand away from Madison and uses it to cover her eyes. *Fuck.*

She feels the couch shift and the absence of Madison, and then her perfume from right in front of her face. "It's okay," Madison says, and it sounds like she's crying too. "No, it's not okay at all, but—"

"You should do it." Luca shakes herself clear and uncovers her eyes to look sideways at Madison, crouching by the couch. "Don't cancel the wedding. Get married. Tell this island to go fuck itself."

Madison laughs a little at that, even as she sniffs. "A screw-you wedding," she says. "Isn't that so Whitney."

She stands and walks over to the closet, running her hands down the front of the garment bag. "You really think it would be okay?" she asks. "Won't everybody think I'm heart-less, to carry on like nothing's happened?"

"So what if they do?" Luca says. "It's 'screw you,' remem-ber? Besides, they'd have to really care about Whitney to think anything at all."

Madison turns and leans against the doors. "Have you heard from the cops at all? Do they have anything new?"

"Oh yeah, I heard from them," Luca says. "They came over and took things from Whit's room. And then Charles—" She stops for a second. Does Madison know about the DUI already?

That she's even questioning it feels strange. Whitney told Madison everything, just like she told Luca everything. Except she didn't tell Luca about the DUI so maybe she didn't tell Madison either, and she knows it's wrong but a big part of her is hopeful that that's true. If Madison doesn't know either, then they're the same, still.

"Charles what?" Madison says.

Luca pushes her hair behind her left ear and sighs. "He asked me if Whit had a drug habit," she says. "And he told me about the DUI she got. A couple years ago. While you were at college—"

She stops because Madison is biting her lip and it's clear to Luca. It's so clear. "But you already knew about that."

Madison lets her head drop back against the closet doors, staring up at the cloud-painted ceiling. "I'm sorry," she says, and she sounds mournful.

(Don't they all, now, always?)

"She made me promise not to tell you about it," Madison's saying now, and she closes her eyes, smiling a tired kind of smile. "She was embarrassed. I mean, yeah, it was stupid, I get it. But I always told her you wouldn't think less of her or whatever."

Luca's trying hard not to tug too tightly on that piece of hair behind her ear, an old habit. But it stings, of course it stings. Whitney didn't tell her but Madison knows all about it, and Madison didn't do what Luca would expect and go behind Whit's back to keep Luca in the loop. No secrets from each other, that was how they worked.

Or how they had worked, anyway, and she's being child-ish, maybe, but if you can't be a little petulant in the wake of your sister's murder then when the fuck can you?

"I get it," Luca says, only partly a lie. "It's okay. She asked you to keep it a secret, and you did."

"It hit her kind of hard, I think," Madison says. "Nothing happened, but she did get caught, and then I think she got stuck on the fact that something *could* have happened, it could have been so much worse. What if she'd hit somebody? Hurt somebody? She learned her lesson." She moves back to the couch and sits opposite Luca again. "Didn't use again after that. So I don't know why Detective Charles would bring that up like it's relevant."

"Somebody at the party said they saw her getting high."

"What?" Madison shakes her head. "Bullshit."

"That's what I said." Luca shifts. "Naomi said I should find out who said it."

"Naomi said, huh." Madison taps a finger on her knee. "You like her?"

"Sure."

Madison looks at her, deeper. "You trust her?"

Trust?

You don't scare me, Luca Laine Thomas.

"Yeah," Luca says, and Madison almost looks relieved.

"Good," she says, nodding. "It's good that you have her. It's good that you have a friend."

A friend, Luca thinks, and she smiles. "Sure."

Of course Madison thinks of Naomi only as a friend for Luca, not anything else. It's not that Luca is ashamed of her sexuality or anything, but—it's not the easiest, here. It's not the easiest when only three people have ever known and two of them are dead, and the other one hates her.

She knows Jada doesn't hate her because of her queerness. It's far more complicated than that. It's about Polly and the hole she ripped between them, and it's about how one day it just hit Luca, that she loved Jada differently, and it's about how that love couldn't bridge the distance between them.

And honestly, since then, Luca hasn't been sure about anything. She'd had feelings for Jada and then it fell apart and then there was nothing, no one, nobody who made her feel any kind of anything and she thought, *Maybe I'm not built that way* when she listened to Whitney talk about how she became infatuated with somebody new every day at college. She thought maybe love was not meant for her.

Until Naomi, with her stare and her fearlessness. Right here, when Luca needs somebody the most.

"She gets it," is all Luca says to Madison finally. "She had a friend who died too, remember?"

Madison makes a face. "Worst kind of thing to have in common," she says. "But I can see how that helps." Then she looks over her shoulder at the garment bag again. "Well," she says. "I guess we're still doing it, then."

"Can I see?" Luca holds a finger up. "One look."

A real smile spreads across Madison's face. "Okay," she says, "but don't tell Beth. She's been begging me to show it to her."

Luca places a hand over where her heart is. "Promise," she says. "I won't say a word."

So Madison disappears into the closet with the dress, and even though Luca offers to help, she insists on getting into it by herself. When she comes out, she's in a gown with a top of raw silk, millimeter-thin straps and a sharp V of a neckline, and a swirl of skirts on the bottom, layer upon layer of organza, and between those layers, flowers trapped there, flowers that Luca is sure she's supposed to be breathtaken by but as she watches Madison twirl, it only reminds her of the cemetery and she wonders if silk rots too.

18

On Thursday Luca and Naomi are in the pool.

Well—Luca is in the pool, while Naomi sits on the side, leaning back to bask in the sun as she kicks her legs through the water. Sharply pointed toes that make Luca imagine her on a balance beam, steady and sure.

Luca swims back and forth, trying to stay underwater longer and longer with each lap she does. Their house is icy cold and quiet; outside is the only place where it feels safe, warm in the sunlight that never fails.

Through the water she sees Naomi kicking her feet, causing a small hurricane of bubbles around her.

It has been a month since Whitney died, which means it is also a month since she met Naomi, but it feels like forever. Still, Naomi always comes to Luca's side of the wall. Luca avoids going to Naomi's, because she isn't ready to see the Stern house stripped of everything familiar and replaced with everything the Fontaines have brought with them. Without Polly's room covered in dance shoes and leotards, without her mom's vintage pinup artwork decorating the halls.

When her lungs are burning, Luca finally surfaces, pulling in a deep breath of warm air. She wipes her sodden curls out of her eyes and catches Naomi looking at her. "What?"

"What's your sign?"

"Cancer."

Naomi nods like this is the right answer, and Luca feels absurdly pleased for a moment, like she's satisfied her. "Water baby," Naomi says. "That's what I thought."

Luca swims over to the side and holds on, looking up at Naomi cast in shadow. "Wanna know something?" she asks.

"Always," Naomi answers.

"I made a therapy appointment," she says. "I'm supposed to be there right now."

Naomi frowns. "Why aren't you, then?"

"You ever been to therapy?"

Naomi pauses a moment and makes a kind of faraway face and Luca thinks—remembers—that not everybody is so cavalier about discussing their mental health as she is.

But then Naomi nods again. "I'm going here, actually," she says, and her shoulders sag, but she's smiling. "Shit. I'm going to therapy."

Luca smiles back. "Yeah?"

"I never said it out loud before," Naomi says. "Even back home, I never told anyone."

Luca won't ask why, although she can guess—Anya, the grief of it all. Same reason she made her appointment, the one she's not at.

But then Naomi says, "It helps, doesn't it? Talking to someone about them."

"Sometimes."

"But you bailed today." Naomi swings her legs through the water. "You don't like it?"

"I like it as much as anyone can like someone digging around inside your brain," Luca says. "I haven't been since last year. I didn't really need to. And then all of this, and I know I should go because that's how I stay middle functional, you know? I take my meds and I go to therapy when I need it, but also I don't want to right now. I'm sick of telling people how it all feels."

"You tell me, though," Naomi says. "Does that mean I'm allowed to come inside your brain?"

"You're already in there," Luca says, and ducks back underwater.

When she surfaces again Naomi has her eyes closed, her face tipped up to the sun. Luca watches her for a moment, her exposed throat, her body in her emerald-green bikini, the way her stomach folds so soft and inviting that Luca wants to lay her head there, and maybe she'd sleep well for once.

Naomi is so unselfconscious of her body that it bleeds over into Luca, too. Not that she is ordinarily self-conscious: she knows who she is and what she looks like, she knows she is a fat Black girl and that her hair is maybe her defining feature and that she has a face people like to look at. But she's still a girl, spending a lot of time in an array of bikinis in view of the girl she has rapidly become beyond infatuated with, and she wants Naomi to want her. Is that so bad? That she should want Naomi to desire her, for her brain and her body, the same way Luca desires her?

When Luca looks up again, Naomi's chin is tilted down, her sunglasses angled so she can watch Luca watching her. Neither of them say anything for a minute, and then Naomi pushes her glasses up and tips her head back again. She sighs, so overwrought that it's clear she's performing, and Luca has to bite her lip because she likes the idea that Naomi wants to put on an act for her. "I can feel myself burning," she says, even though Luca saw her putting on SPF 30 this morning and her skin is an even, burnished sand.

"Swim, then," Luca says, but her phone chirps where she left it on her towel and they both snap to attention to look at it.

See, all of this is just killing time, really, the laps and the sunbathing and the endless conversation. It feels strange and slightly wrong to be hanging out and planning where to go for dinner and all the rest, but what else is there to do? It's only been a few days, but until Jada gives Luca what she needs, she is in limbo.

In danger.

Luca knows this and Naomi knows at least part of this and now they're both staring at Luca's phone and Naomi gets up, pads on wet feet to the lounger, and picks it up.

"Well?" It's probably not Jada, it's probably Madison with something about the engagement party for the wedding that is definitely going ahead now, or maybe Beth—

Naomi holds the phone up. "It's Jada."

× × × ×

They're waiting in the parking lot of the organic grocery store, leaning against the bumper of Luca's car.

Got it, Jada's text said, and then where to meet. Like she didn't want Luca anywhere near her house again, which was laughable, considering how Jada had put herself right inside Luca's home.

But fine—if this was the way she wanted to play it, Luca would do her part.

Her hair's wet from the pool, still, dripping down her back and her neck, and Naomi reaches over. Without saying anything at all, she presses her thumb into the base of Luca's throat and chases a bead of water away across her shoulder and Luca has no time to react because Jada's car swings into the parking lot right at that second.

She cuts across the lot, empty as it is where they've parked at the back, and stops one row over. When she gets out, Luca sees she's wearing the Chloé sunglasses Luca's mom gave Luca for her birthday last year, except even from this distance she can tell they're knockoffs.

"It's about time," Luca calls as Jada saunters over.

"Patience," Jada says. "I know you're used to everybody being at your beck and call, but I'm not on your payroll or up your ass, so—"

Luca rolls her eyes. "Do you have it, then?"

But Jada looks at Naomi. "Are you going to introduce us?" she says.

"Why?" Luca says. "You know who she is."

Naomi folds her arms across her chest. "And I know all about who you are."

The barest flicker of—*what is it?* Luca wonders: annoyance? Or betrayal? She can't quite tell. Whatever it is, it flits across Jada's face and then she's back to careful closed-off boredom. "Which version would that be?" she says, not hiding how she looks Naomi up and down, from her gold sandals to her dark hair scraped up into a knot. "The one where she did nothing wrong, ever, at all, and I'm the bitch who cut her off instead of trauma bonding with her?" Jada slips her sunglasses onto the top of her head. "Or the one where Luca tried to blame Polly's death on a story?"

Luca pushes off the bumper. "You ever think that maybe the reason no one likes you is that you're such a sad, bitter little girl, Jada?"

"Bitter?" Jada laughs. "I guess maybe I am bitter, sure. But I don't give a shit if people like me. I just think it's *fascinating* how everybody tries so hard to pretend that the *reason* they don't like me is because I'm a bitch, without ever considering the fact that they made me this way. We all know why they don't like me. Don't we?"

She pauses and the silence hangs there, and Luca stares, and finally Jada sighs.

"Fine," she says. She holds out her fist and uncurls it, revealing a tiny flash drive in the palm of her hand. "This has all the statements they took from everyone who was at the party. Whatever you want to see, it's on there."

"How did you get them?" Naomi asks.

Jada gives a tight smile. "None of your fucking business," she says, and looks at Luca.

"I only did this because of Whitney," she says. "You know, you said the other day that I belong to Parris in the same way you do. But you know and I know that it's not true. We're both from here, but that's where it ends. I think Polly got that, but you didn't, and you still don't."

"Sure, whatever," Luca says as she reaches for the flash drive, but Jada snaps her hand closed.

"I'm serious," she says. "You don't ever think about what it is to live on this island without money, or without a mom to play nice at all the charity crap, or with a cop dad who's supposed to keep this place safe but can't handle it. You're always pissed at me because I didn't give you the attention you wanted and I didn't believe what you wanted me to, but you never think about what it's like to be *of* Parris but not good enough for it."

Birds wheel in the sky above them and Luca watches them for a minute, catching the wind and swooping and lifting high again.

This is where Jada's wrong. Not about how people view her, or that she hovers on the outside looking in, because yes, that's true, of course it's true. But even with the money and the family name and the ideal house, Luca is an outsider too. She is queer on an island where girls still kiss in front of boys for entertainment, she is mixed race on an island full of uptight old-money white people, she is crazy on an island where whenever a new bad thing happens the talk is always *insane, what kind of mental illness, some people are really just psycho I guess.* That's what Luca meant when she said they both belonged, but of course Jada doesn't see it that way, because as outsider as she might be, she's still white and in Parris, where people claim not to see color at all, that means Jada fits fine.

"Okay," Luca says, because she doesn't have the energy to tell Jada any of that when she knows she still wouldn't get it. "Sure. Can I have it now?"

Jada bares her teeth and tosses the flash drive high, so it turns end over end.

Naomi snatches it out of the air before it can hit the ground.

"Sorry," Jada says, anything but. "My hand slipped."

Fuck you, Luca wants to say.

Instead she nods as she takes the flash drive from Naomi and holds it tight. In this is the person who is twisting up the truth of what happened to Whitney, and now that she has it, she can fix it, and then maybe she'll be closer to escape—

Not *then* yet. Only now.

"Thank you," she says, as sincere as she can, and Jada's lips part, the surprise there before she can cover it.

"Don't expect anything else," Jada says, but the uncertainty in her voice undercuts the point.

And it doesn't matter anyway. Because Luca's already in the car, feeling the corners of the flash drive bite into her skin she's holding it so hard, and then Naomi joins her and they drive off, leaving Jada fading into the background where she's so afraid to be.

19

They split the list.

Back at Luca's, in her mom's office, which hasn't been entered in weeks. Luca can tell by the closed door. Inside everything is in its place: the design books artfully arranged on the low table, the pillar candles that are yet to be lit, the pile of embossed envelopes with Madison's wedding invite sitting on the top. Her parents aren't home, because unlike Luca, they have been going to their therapy appointments. Grief counseling, like before, except this time they're looking for advice not on how to deal with their daughter but on how to deal with themselves.

Luca sits at her mom's gleaming glass desk and begins reading through her share of the statements from the flash drive, while Naomi does the same using Luca's laptop, sitting cross-legged on the navy couch.

There's an electricity running through Luca now. Feels likes she's *doing* something, and that's a better feeling than the nothing that fills her daily.

She clicks and reads through everyone else's statement,

and her breathing gets a little more ragged with each one and it seems like the walls are shrinking in. It's just being back in the moment, reading about that night.

I spoke to Whitney around ten, but I didn't see her again after that.

I think I saw her as I was leaving, but then I heard these girls fighting and I got out of there, because I always get dragged into these things and you know I could not deal with that—

I saw Whitney and Luca together outside, I don't know what time. It was late, though, I think?

We—me and my friends—we were sitting by the pool and I saw her go inside, and I remember because I thought her shoes were really cute and I wanted to ask her who made them, but then my boyfriend threw me in the pool and I kinda forgot all about it.

Of course I remember seeing her. Everyone always remembers seeing Whitney Laine Thomas. But she did look mad when I saw her.

Luca thinks about Beth storming off and Whitney going after her, the way she so often had to, fixing Beth up after Carter made her cry. That was what this person saw, right, had to be.

She starts reading again:

She was with her sister and Madison and all of them, but that was like normal.

No, I didn't speak to Whitney, but I did talk to Luca. She was being kind of a bitch, actually, but then again, it was the anniversary. Of Polly Stern, you know?

That asshole. "Tiff fucking Lancaster," Luca says under her breath. *She's got a lot to say all of a sudden.*

We were dancing, and then she went to get a drink and I went to the bathroom, and later I saw her but I didn't speak to her again. It wasn't unusual. It was a party. That's how things go at parties. I don't know when she left. I didn't even know she was gone until I left later. I looked for her for a minute and I figured she went home already and then I went home too. Like I said, it wasn't unusual. I didn't think anything was wrong at all.

Luca finds herself running her fingers across the screen, over those words. They belong to Madison, and Luca can almost hear herself in them: *It wasn't unusual. I didn't think anything was wrong.*

Luca can't find what she's looking for. All she sees is how spoiled and vapid they all sound in these pulled-apart pieces of one single night, and she wants to believe that they aren't really this way, that it's only a consequence of slicing things up but maybe they are.

"Okay." Naomi closes the laptop with a tired sigh. "I'm done. Nothing."

"I still have one," Luca says, clicking to the next, but the desperation is obvious in her voice. Even she can hear it. "You think this is really all of them, though? I mean, there could be more. Or maybe it was, like, saved somewhere different and—"

She stops. Stops, because she'd been half reading the last statement and now she needs to fully read it to make sure it says what she thinks it does.

We were all hanging out and then, I don't know, we went our separate ways. It was a party, you know? I didn't see her leave, but I don't know if she was still there when I went to bed. Yeah, I stayed there, it was my girlfriend's party.

"What?" Naomi's looking over. "What is it?"

Carter.

"Come here," she says, and Naomi lets the laptop slide onto the couch and comes to lean over Luca's shoulder, her perfume a dark floral wash over the both of them.

"What is it?"

Luca points with one sharp red nail. "Carter's statement," she says, and now she's thinking less about some person she barely knows telling the cops about Whitney getting high and much more about Carter. About the questions she asked him the other day and how she believed his answers and now about this lie he's told, right here in his statement.

Naomi shrugs as she peers at the screen. "So?"

"So he told the cops he slept at Beth's house." Luca sits back and digs that same nail into her bottom lip. "But he didn't. Remember? He was being a dick, and Beth got mad?" She moves her hand from her mouth and finds a piece of hair to pull, twisting the curl of it around her fingers. "She texted me in the morning. She was still pissed at him. She told me he didn't stay over."

bring Whit and also a list of new boyfriend options bc i think i dumped mine last night.

god knows whose bed he slept in last night but it sure as shit wasn't mine.

Luca takes out her phone and scrolls past the dozens of unread sympathy texts she's received until she finds her thread with Beth and there it is, black and white on the screen. sure as shit wasn't mine.

And yet—

She looks up and finds Naomi staring not at her but at the computer still, reading Carter's statement, and Luca watches her, tries to think of some logical reason why Carter would lie about that.

People lie about where they were when they don't want anyone to know what they were doing and where they were doing it, a voice in her head says softly, a quiet threat of truth. *People lie about being with their girlfriend when they need that girlfriend as an alibi.*

Naomi taps her nails on the desk. "So he's lying." She tilts her head to the side. "Or Beth is. One of them isn't telling the truth."

"Beth?" Luca shakes her head. "No. One, it's Beth. And two, Carter—"

She spreads her hand flat on the desk, absently noting her raggedy nails. Those things that fall to the bottom of your importance list. *Carter lied in his statement. Why? If he lied here, was he lying to me when we talked the other day? What's he hiding?* And she is thinking about Carter being the boy she's known, trusted, since she was a kid but if Whitney had secrets, then Carter certainly fucking could too.

Naomi's waiting. "What?"

Luca rubs her fingers on the desk's slick surface. "I asked

him about Whit using, and he said she didn't, not that he knew of. But he was talking about the past. Everything he said—" *Whit was never a customer. I never gave Whit anything but weed, and she never asked me for anything else. Didn't you say it was years ago?* "He never said he didn't give her shit now. He was very careful not to say anything about now." At least, that's how it seems to her, remembering it. How it seems knowing that he has told the cops a different version of that night than the one Luca knows.

Luca yanks the flash drive out of her mom's computer and shuts everything down before getting up. "Come on," she says, tugging Naomi to her feet. "We're going to go talk to Carter."

They're a couple of steps from the door when Naomi pulls back from Luca. "Wait," she says. "I can't."

"What?" Luca turns in the doorway, catching the strap of her dress falling off her shoulder. "What do you mean, you can't?"

"I mean I can't." Naomi shifts, and the green of her bikini is visible through her white tee. "I have—someplace to be."

Luca lets out a sharp bark of laughter without meaning to. "Someplace to be? Where? I'm the only person you know here."

She says it, and it takes a few seconds for the bitchiness of it to echo back at her.

Well. It's true, she thinks, already defensive. *What's she doing and where's she going if it's not something and somewhere with me?*

Naomi hooks her hair behind her ears and looks away. "Maybe," she says flatly, "but remember earlier? Therapy?"

Oh. "Shit, I'm sorry," Luca says, and she's trying her hardest to soften, not to still feel the burst of irritation she'd gotten when Naomi said she couldn't come, but.

It's still there.

Fuck therapy, she wants to say, *this is important.*

Except she can't tell Naomi to bail, she can't tell Naomi that her own grieving somehow means more than Naomi's. So out loud she says, "Okay. You go do that. I'll talk to Carter."

"Yeah?" Naomi looks unsure. "You don't want to wait? I can come tomorrow—"

Luca taps her knuckles against the doorframe and gives Naomi half a smile. "No," she says. "I can handle it just fine."

20

Luca drives across the island, to a house belonging to a kid whose name she can never quite remember—Kyle or Chris or Kevin, one of them. The name isn't important, only that Kyle/Chris/Kevin is having a party, and where there's booze and music and an opportunity to piss off Beth, Carter will be.

She parks down the street and heads inside. She has made herself party presentable, as if that will stop people staring: all black, hair up, red lipstick.

Luca feels the ripple as she passes through the house. Eyes briefly on and then off her, the whispers that follow, the pointed way people smile at her.

What, she thinks as she stares back at them, *I'm not allowed to be here? You all are. My sister was murdered a month ago and here you all are, back to your normal lives. Is this how it goes?*

She slips through the party, out of the house and back inside, upstairs and down to scan the gardens, but there is no sign of Carter, and Luca's beginning to think she got it wrong, again, when—

There.

Carter's kissing Beth, has her pressed up against the low wall that surrounds a small fountain, and Luca's breath catches.

She's supposed to be focused, she knows, and she's supposed to be pissed at him right now, but for a moment all she can see is the way he's kissing Beth so hard and the way her hands are clutching at his waist and she can't breathe, suddenly, with how much she wants somebody to hold on to her with an equal desperation.

Not somebody. Naomi.

She watches Carter and Beth separate, and Beth swats at him as she saunters off and Carter watches her go.

Looks like they're on again.

But then Carter heads inside and Luca rushes to follow. He passes through the kitchen, exchanges a few back slaps and head nods with people on his way, and Luca realizes: he is leaving.

She follows him out and through the mess of cars on the driveway, and sees Carter get into his, no one blocking his way.

He's going to leave. *And what are you going to do, follow him?*

Luca moves out of the driveway and along a little ways to where she parked earlier, gets in, and barely lets the door close before she revs the engine and reverses, then slams on the gas and burns down the street.

No, not follow. She has a better idea than that.

She sees the other car edging out of the driveway and they're a second away from colliding—

But Luca brakes hard right as the other car swerves, and

she grinds to a stop at an angle, blocking the other car in, and she looks to her right to see Carter behind the wheel.

What the hell, she sees him mouth, and then they're both of out their cars and he says it again. "What the hell, Luca?"

She squares up to him, and he's so much taller than she's ever fully realized. "Sorry," she says loudly. "Did I get in your way?"

"What is wrong with you?" he says. "Do you have a death wish?"

It hangs between them for a moment, Carter grimacing as he realizes what he's said. "No death wish for me," she says. "But for you, maybe."

"What?"

"It's the only reason I can think of why you'd lie," Luca says. "You know. How you told the cops that you stayed over at Beth's that night, but actually that was a lie? Yeah," she says when he takes a step back. "Yeah, that. So I need you to tell me, Carter, where you really were and what the fuck else you've lied to me about."

He pales. Luca actually watches the color fade right out of his face, and he tightens his grip on his open car door. "Or what?"

"There is no 'or what,'" Luca says, and she points at their cars, frozen inches from collision, him with no way to go anywhere. "So get in. Now."

He hesitates, a second or two, but long enough for Luca's fear to spike. Maybe he won't play along. Maybe he's about to laugh at her and her attempts to intimidate him.

But then he sighs, and without saying another word he's folding himself into the passenger seat of her car.

Luca exhales and holds her hands up where Carter can't see, which she is glad for because they're shaking. *Stop it,* she thinks, *stop it right now*, and clenches her fists. Then she gets into the car without even glancing at Carter. "Better get your truth straight," she says. "Because if you lie to me again, I'm going to hurt you. Clear?"

Carter says nothing, and Luca pulls away.

21

Luca drives north, up to the hills.

They are silent the whole way, the only sound the music playing low and the wind through her open window.

They climb up and up, until the car crunches over gravel and Luca stops.

She gets out, and smacks her palm on the roof when Carter doesn't do the same. "Come on."

Usually she doesn't stop here. Usually she walks up to the top, closer to the memorial. But tonight she stays here in the stretch of uneven gravel that passes for a parking lot, leaning against the hood of her car and tipping her head back to look at the clear sky, pinpricked with stars.

"You're good," she says without looking at Carter.

"What?" He sounds impatient now. "Look, ask me your questions and we can be done."

"Done?" Luca pulls her gaze away from the stars. "I'll never be done. I was supposed to have an entire lifetime with Whit, and now she's gone, and how does that end? Do you think I'm going to forget about her? Do you think there's going to come a magical time where I just . . . move on? I don't think you get it, Carter. I don't think you get how it feels to have somebody ripped away from you so completely."

"I didn't mean—" He sighs. "Yeah, okay. I get your point."

She pulls out her pack of cigarettes and then clicks her teeth. Looks up at Carter. "Light?"

"Smoking again?" Carter says. "You always used to tell me how terrible those things are."

"My sister was murdered," Luca says. "Is that okay with you? If I smoke, while my sister's dead?"

Carter flinches. Boys always do that when Luca speaks. Actually, everyone does it, with the exception of her therapist. Naomi, now, too. Luca can't ever work out if she's really that jarring to listen to, or if people are just not used to a girl who looks so soft being made of so many razor-sharp pieces.

He says nothing now but hands her his lighter with the **CM** engraved on the back.

Luca lights her cigarette and inhales twice before she starts. "I know you weren't at Beth's," she says. "She texted me, you know, the morning after. So I know you didn't stay at hers except you told the cops that you did, didn't you? Which made me really think, like—if you lied about that, there must have been a reason, and all I can think is that wherever you *were*, you couldn't let the cops know about it. And it made me think, too, that if you lied about that then you're probably lying about other shit, like how I came to you and asked if Whit had a habit and you told me, 'No, no, not at all!' But you see how it's hard for me to believe that now?"

"Luca," Carter says, and then he makes a pained face. "Just say it."

The glowing end of her cigarette hovers somewhere between them. "You left," she says. "You left the party and where did you go?"

"Home."

"By yourself." It's flat, no lift to her words, but her meaning is clear: *I don't believe you went home all alone.*

Carter's looking somewhere beyond her, down at the spread of the island, and she watches the fight on his face.

And then he seems to sink, his whole body an exhalation. "I left," he says. "I left with Whitney."

It's what Luca's been expecting, but it's still a knee to the ribs, stealing her air. *Here is the first solid new entry in Whitney's night. She left the party with Carter.*

It's hard to keep her brain still, though, to not keep picking at this thread until it unspools and she can spiral with it. She turns away from Carter, throws her cigarette down and grinds it out under her heel.

"You left with her," she says. "You left Beth's with Whitney and then a few hours later she's dead, so what did you do?" She whips around. "You don't deal anymore, sure. Let's say I believe that still—"

"Why wouldn't you—"

"But you're still in the loop, right? That's what you said." She steps up closer to him, acting unafraid even if she can't feel it. "I've been thinking that whoever said she was high that night was wrong, but now I'm thinking what if they weren't? Because maybe you don't sell anymore, but maybe you still have your own supply, and maybe Whit comes to you when she wants something or maybe it's just another party and she feels like something extra, so off the two of you go and then—" *Then what?* "It goes wrong, somehow. Whatever she takes is bad, cut with something, and you—" She falters because she doesn't like what she's saying but she has to say it, because it might be what happened or at least close to it and she needs to know. "You make it look like something else because then no one will suspect you, right? So you—"

"Jesus *Christ*, Luca, *what*? I bash her head in to cover my tracks? Are you fucking serious?" Carter's eyes are bright with something like anger. "You think I took her somewhere to kill her?"

Wouldn't that be easy, if all I have to do to stay safe is to avoid this boy? And no, she doesn't want to think that he killed Whitney, but he was with her, and he has lied to Luca, and—

"Fine." Carter rubs at his neck and makes a sound somewhere between frustration and grief. "She—we were—"

He stops, the silence around them full, and her mind gets there a second before her body does, the swoop in her chest chasing the words in her head. "Fucking," she says bluntly, and then she's laughing. Luca laughs in disbelief, entirely the wrong sound to come out of her, but it's all she can do because *her sister* and *Carter* and there is no way, there's no way— "Oh my god," she says. "No. That's not possible. I would have—"

I would have known is how that sentence is supposed to

end, but hasn't she already discovered how good her sister was at keeping secrets?

Carter's shaking his head. "It wasn't like that," he says, and for a moment things are right again, Luca feels steady again, but then he speaks again and it's quiet this time.

Raw.

"I loved her," he says, at last. "I still love her."

22

The words drop into the air, a true weight to them that keeps them spinning for a minute, two, more.

He says it so simply that Luca—she feels it. He loves her. He says it in a way he's never said it about Beth; he sounds like he has never sounded talking about Beth.

But Luca is spinning along with the words, because if it's true, then that means he and Whitney had a whole secret *thing* happening and this isn't the point, she knows it isn't the point, but Luca feels stung.

She can only think of the times Whitney went out without saying where she was going and was she with Carter? When she told Luca about the boys she'd been hooking up with in empty bedrooms—was that Carter? How long had it been going on and what did it mean to Whitney and how come she hadn't trusted Luca enough to tell her about it?

"You loved her." Luca has to say it again to make it feel even a fraction right. "You *loved* her. Okay, sure, fine. Let's say you did." She pauses. "Did she love you?"

She is waiting for his answer and he is looking up at the

sky, and Luca thinks she heard that people always look up when they lie.

But then Carter looks back at her. "Yes," he says after a minute, and then he rubs at his neck again. "I loved her. She loved me. We—it started when we were still at school. I don't know how, really. We were hanging out a lot, and I didn't think too much about it because we always did, but somehow it felt different. And then one day it just—happened. And it was easy because Beth was back here and neither of us thought too much about her or what we were doing." He shrugs. "Then we came home, and me and Beth, we were— like we always were."

Luca bites down on her tongue. He can never do it. He can never call Beth his girlfriend when it matters, and Luca always wonders why Beth puts up with it, but whatever. "So you were cheating on Beth," she says. "You and my sister."

"Whitney liked it at first," he says. "The secrecy. Hiding. She used to say it was nice to have something nobody else knew about, like she felt she was holding something over everyone."

Something nobody else knew about.

"She liked it," Carter went on, "but then she didn't. She started saying she felt bad for Beth and that I should tell her, because it wasn't like me and Beth were official or anything, so I should stop stringing her along. She said until I did it, me and her were done. And she meant it, you know. She didn't talk to me for almost an entire month."

Luca scratches at the inside of her left wrist, a long, deep press with her nails. "When was this?"

He has the decency to look ashamed. "Around Christmas," he says.

Now Luca laughs for real, because he and Beth have been on and off so many times since then that she's lost count, and judging by the kiss she witnessed earlier, he has no intentions to make it a permanent *off*. "So you didn't do it," she says. "Wow! Brave."

"Listen, you don't know," he says sharply. "Beth is—you know how long we've been together?"

"But you're not!" Luca shakes her head. "You're *not* together, not really. You *just* said that."

"We have history, still," he says. "Or, I don't know—fine, I'm a coward, I couldn't do it, I never really loved Whitney. Pick one. You're writing this story, aren't you?"

He's almost yelling now, but it's only them around to hear, them and the trees and the sky.

"If you and Whitney weren't happening, then what was it, that night?"

Carter begins rocking back and forth. "I was going to end things with Beth," he says. "For real, for good. So I wanted to tell Whitney that. And then we . . . we drove around for a while. We talked for real, like we used to. That was what I loved doing with her, talking about nothing at all, how I could say something completely ridiculous or really real and she'd give both of them the same weight." He swallowed. "I know I'm kind of an asshole, but Whitney always called me on it. And I felt—like I was someone different with her."

That part, at least, is something Luca can believe, because she's never heard Carter talk like this, and there's an openness in his face that's new.

This is what Whitney did to him. This is what she made him into, by wanting him. By loving him.

"So you drove around," Luca says. "Is that it?"

"That's it," Carter says. "We went back to the party. We carried on with our night. Things wound down, I went home, and then . . ."

Luca finds herself nodding, nodding, nodding. "Then she was dead," she says, and she has to turn away.

She puts a hand over her mouth and tries to keep her pained moan inside. She had thought she was talking to dealer-Carter, someone who might have known the dirtier things Whitney did, someone who might have helped her do them, but in fact he turns out to be the boy who loved her.

Luca does believe that. She does believe he loved, loves, Whitney, if only because Whitney was magnetic and hard not to love, if she let you.

She pulls herself together, swallows the emotion of it all and turns back around. "But you didn't tell the cops," she says. "You lied."

"I'm not stupid," Carter says. "I know how it would look, I know how it works. They always look at the boyfriend first."

Luca snaps her fingers. Like a gunshot in the quiet. "You know why that is, right?" she says. "You know that boys kill girls they supposedly love all the time? Even here in perfect Parris."

Carter holds one hand up in front of his chest, pushing against the air like he can push the accusation away. "You think what you want," he says. "It doesn't really matter, does it? I wasn't the last person to see her. I took her back to the party. She was with Madison after me, and Beth, and god knows who else. So, you know, yeah, maybe I was being selfish, or a coward. Whatever you want to call me. But I didn't kill her."

Then he pulls in a loud breath, and he puts that same hand flat against his chest, and Luca thinks he might splinter into a thousand golden-boy pieces. But instead he says, "I should have waited. I should have taken her home myself. Every day I think about how it was the last time I saw her and how I can't even really remember that last moment and I think, if I'd known that would be the last time I'd ever see her, I wouldn't have let her get out of my car. I wouldn't have taken her back to the party. We could've said forget everyone else and gotten out of this place, over the bridge, somewhere better than Parris. I would have kissed her again and told her that I loved her but—"

Carter cuts himself off and looks up, toward the trees. Toward the memorial, where Whitney's name is not. "Doesn't change anything, thinking about her," he says. "She's still gone." And then he turns his bright blue eyes on Luca. "I am sorry, Luca. I know you won't believe me, but I am. I should have told you before now. I loved her," he says, as he did before, raw. "I love her."

Luca feels for the familiar half-moons on the inside of her wrist, the pressure points of relief, release, and she knows it is not the time, but god—

If somebody could love me in that same way—

Luca nods at Carter, waiting there to be absolved. *I love her.* "Yeah," she says. "I love her too."

23

She drives back to where she found him, his car abandoned at an angle.

He opens the passenger door and noise from the house filters in, and Luca knows she needs to refocus, remember what she's supposed to be doing here. *Trace her steps. Discover the truth. Unravel the curse. Protect yourself.*

"Wait," she says, turning her head to look at him. "You still think she didn't have a habit?"

Carter breathes a laugh. "Here's the thing," he says. "A *habit* and getting high at parties are two different things. I told you what I thought before, and I believed it, but I guess she could've hidden it from me. I mean, she hid me from you. She hid the DUI from all of us."

Good at hiding, good at lying. *How good?* Luca thinks.

"Beth," she says. "She didn't know? She still doesn't?"

"I never told her."

"That doesn't mean she didn't know," Luca says. Was Whitney that good, slick enough to keep from one of her closest friends that she was sleeping with her boyfriend? Luca thinks of that night, Whit going after an upset Beth. Was she good enough to comfort Beth, not giving away how she really felt? "Are you sure?"

He looks at her like he knows what she's pushing at, but only says, "I never told her."

For a long minute there's only the sound of the party and then Carter says, "I see her. I think I see her, every day. I don't know if that's better or worse than never seeing her at all."

He gets out, leaving Luca with that, and walks over to his car. She watches him get in and sink his head into his hands, sit curled over like that for a moment or two.

Then he pulls himself together and drives off without looking back.

24

Luca drives home with an argument in her head.

She cuts the engine and waits as it quiets down. It's late now, the house dark. She knows, though, that her mother will be listening out for her, will only let herself fall asleep once she knows that the daughter she still has is safe inside.

She's sitting there when the passenger door opens and she jumps. "Jesus—"

"It's me!" Naomi slides in and shuts the door. "Sorry. It's just me."

Luca presses a hand to her pounding heart and turns away. She's still mad at Naomi, she thinks, for not choosing her instead of therapy. Or maybe not. Maybe she's mad at everyone and everything and Naomi is the closest person to her, now, so it's safe to be pissed at her.

Naomi speaks first. "What did Carter say?"

"You would know if you had been there."

She thinks Naomi will tell her not to be such a bitch, but she only says, "Well, I wasn't. So are you going to tell me, or not?"

Luca sighs and shifts so she can face Naomi, rubs her lips together before she speaks. "It wasn't drugs," she says.

And then she tells Naomi what Carter had to say, everything.

When she's done, Naomi sits there for a minute, and then she nods.

"He loved her." Naomi says it softly, as if to speak any louder might shatter something in the air. "That's what it was. He loved her."

Luca drops her head back and sighs. "That's what he says."

"What?" Naomi looks at her sideways. "You don't believe him?" But it's barely a question, and Luca knows why. Naomi is smart. She knows the statistics. Knows about the curse.

Her pack of cigarettes is in the cup holder and Luca takes one out, taps it in the palm of her hand. "Of course he could have loved her, she was Whitney. But he was sleeping with her, and now she's dead," she says, and she lights the cigarette and inhales. *Are we ever safe?*

She exhales and thinks about the *we*. She, and who? *And Naomi, of course*, she thinks, the most obvious thing blooming for the first time. *Naomi*. She is a part of Parris now, isn't she, which means she's as much at risk as Luca, and it hits her, suddenly, violently, how much she wants to protect her from this, too.

Luca looks over at Naomi. "You know, I used to think we were the same, me and Whit. She never treated me like an annoying bratty little sister. She treated me like I was her friend, and I told her my secrets, and she told me hers. Or I thought she did."

Naomi knocks her hand against the window. "You think Beth really never knew? You think she still doesn't know?"

Luca closes her eyes and brings up that night again. They're dancing, her and Naomi, Whitney and Beth. They're dancing and Beth's laughing, and Whit's spinning her around, and shit, if Beth knew, then she was a *really* good actress.

She opens her eyes. "I don't think so," she says, finally deciding. "Beth's not—she doesn't take things lying down. She likes a little drama, you know?"

"Hence the on and the off," Naomi says.

Luca nods. "If she'd found out about Carter and Whit, god, I don't think there's *any* way it wouldn't have been all over the island immediately."

"Maybe." Naomi reaches for Luca's cigarette. "You know, smoking's bad for you."

"Thanks for that brand-new information."

"You should quit."

Luca looks at the cigarette in Naomi's hand, the smoke drifting out of her parted lips. "So should you."

"I don't smoke."

"Just because you smoke my cigarettes doesn't mean you don't smoke," Luca says. "Come on, Naomi."

She doesn't mean to but those last three words come out so heavy, so full of bone-deep exhaustion that she almost feels embarrassed. Like she's shown Naomi too much.

Naomi is watching her, she's always watching, and it's overwhelming. Like earlier, how much Luca wanted to be held by her. Now she wants to take Naomi's hand in hers and feel grounded, know that there is somebody in the world, somebody sitting right beside her, who sees her.

She is beginning to burn under Naomi's watch, and yet she can't find any words to shift things back to how they were.

Keep moving, then. Move, move, move.

"I should talk to Madison," Luca says. "She'll know if this is real." And she's about to turn the key in the ignition when Naomi puts her other hand on Luca's knee.

"Not now," she says. "It's late. You need to sleep sometime."

Luca closes her eyes and feels Naomi's fingers burning through her dress into her skin. "I can't," she says. She can't sleep, not any true kind.

"Okay," Naomi says, and she winds the window down, flicks the cigarette out. "You don't have to sleep. But you have to stop, for a while, at least. You're gonna burn yourself out."

Luca watches the dark house. She doesn't want to be alone. It's so quiet up there, knowing Whitney isn't down the hall, isn't going to come rushing out in the morning in a whirlwind of perfume and necklaces, shoes hanging from her fingertips as she yells, *I'm late, I'm late, I love you, see you later!*

"Will you come up?" she asks Naomi without thinking about it too much.

That's the important thing, when dealing with Naomi, all that she feels. *Don't think about it too much, it's not a big deal, it's nothing at all, really.*

"Come up?" Naomi repeats.

"It won't be so bad if you're there."

"You mean like, sleep over?"

No. Yes. *Yes? Shit.* "If you want."

Luca listens to the sound of Naomi breathing, and the hand that Naomi can't see digs into her thigh, and she thinks, *Stupid, stupid, you are so stupid.*

And then Naomi says, "Sure, okay. Let me grab some stuff from my house. I'll be back in ten."

Luca is dreaming, half a memory of the beach and bicycles and Polly still alive, when something pulls her out of it.

It takes a second for her to adjust, to realize she's awake and it's still the middle of the night and that it was only a dream.

There's a movement next to her and Luca looks at Naomi, fast asleep with her back to Luca. That's not a dream, though.

Maybe this is too much, she thinks, pressing her hands into the sheets. *Maybe this is crossing a line.*

But she can't say she doesn't like it, having Naomi here with her. This is what friends do. Sleep over, and braid each other's hair, and watch movies. Not that they did any of those things tonight. Luca got changed and talked to herself in the bathroom mirror, and when she came out, Naomi was back and brushing her teeth on the end of Luca's bed, and then Luca turned out the lights and put on a movie and pretended like she didn't notice Naomi playing with the end of one of Luca's curls as they lay down beside each other.

She looks at Naomi now and wonders what it would be like to lie down right behind her, tuck her chin into Naomi's shoulder, her knees into the back of Naomi's knees.

She doesn't do that. She stares up at the ceiling instead and thinks about Polly on the beach, and Carter being in love with her sister, and about the things her sister hid.

Is that why the curse came for her? Because she had secrets?

Luca digs her teeth into her bottom lip. *So it's her own fault now, is that it? Am I really blaming Whit for her own death, like she brought it on herself?*

And another part of her whispers back: *Isn't that what you've been doing all along? Retracing her steps, finding out what she did so you can make sure to do the opposite—because she must have done something to bring this on. Right?*

Luca swallows the guilt. Selfish, selfish, selfish.

If secrets are what this is about, then Luca is already doomed. All the things she keeps to herself, because she's afraid of people knowing her, that they'll judge her and find her wanting. The thoughts she keeps inside, afraid of what people will think of her because of these things she can't control.

Luca's fingertips itch, and she rolls onto her side, her back to Naomi now as she folds her hands together and holds them between her knees.

It's not that she thinks Whitney was somehow responsible for her own death, *jesus*, no. It's just that—there must be a reason, she thinks. There must be *some* kind of logic or pattern or *something* to the curse, because that's how they work, right? In every other story Luca has ever heard, every myth and legend and fairy tale. A spell from a wronged witch, a punishment for an old crime, vengeance for eating the fruit that wasn't yours. That's how it always goes. But the stories of Parris have never had that element, are always missing the key to the *why* of it all, and—

Luca is afraid. Always, always afraid, but more so now than ever, because if there are no rules to this, then how can she ever keep herself safe, and if there are no rules, then *why* is Whitney dead, why is Polly gone, why did it happen to them and not anybody else?

And none of it makes sense, Luca thinks. The more questions she asks, the more she finds out, but it's like every new piece of information she gets about her sister leads away from the curse, deep into some long-hidden part of Whitney's world.

The small, whispering part of her brain echoes at her: *Maybe you're wrong. Maybe you have this all wrong.*

A sigh sounds from behind her, Naomi in sleep.

Not for the first time, Luca wishes for the results of the autopsy report to actually come through. Then she'd have it all laid out, a definitive catalogue of her sister, what killed her.

Strange, to be thinking so much about your sister's body being sliced open and what it can tell you. Strange, to be dreaming of her being retraumatized in death.

She lies still in the dark, feeling the air from the cracked-open window ghosting over her body. She feels it coming like a slow wave, and for a second it overwhelms her, what is about to happen, and then she is crying.

Quietly, carefully. The only way Luca ever cries, and it's half a relief, because she hasn't cried since she found out

Whitney was dead and sometimes she thinks she's broken but this is proof she's not, right?

But it is half—no, more than half, a whole swallowing part—painful aching knot in her chest. It is her sister being gone and her best friend, too, and the first girl she maybe loved who hates her now and her parents still not knowing how to handle her, and the girl next to her, who she is, she's pretty sure, falling in love with but what even is love?

She makes a sucking, gasping noise and puts a hand over her mouth so she doesn't wake Naomi.

There is a shift behind her, though. Luca stills, tries to keep herself steady, and then there is a hand, Naomi's hand, on her hip. She feels the uneven terrain of Naomi's gymnastics-scarred palms on her bare skin, only for a moment, and then Naomi reaches over and takes Luca's hand.

Naomi laces her fingers through Luca's and Luca hiccups. The air is warm and sticky and Luca cannot stop this crying but she clasps Naomi's hand tight, an anchor. Naomi's arm is warm around her, through the thin cotton of her shirt, and Luca gives up any prettiness, any hiding.

They stay that way until Luca, wrung out from weeping, falls asleep.

25

On the morning of Madison's engagement party, Luca resolves to put everything away for the day. All emotion, all fear. Fold it up tight in a little box and lock that box and swallow the key, burn it in the acid in her stomach.

It's a sunny Saturday evening, like they all are, and her house is quiet when she leaves.

She carries her heels in her hand; Whitney always used to drive in her stilettos, but Luca goes barefoot and puts them on after. One more way that Whitney was infinitesimally cooler than her.

She's tossing her shoes in the backseat when a hand nips at her waist. "Boo."

"Naomi." Luca spins and slaps lightly at Naomi's hand even as Naomi's laughing at her. "God, I could get so sick of you."

"I know," Naomi says, but it's not true at all. "Come on. I'm dying to meet this mysterious man Madison is soon to be marrying."

Luca rolls her eyes. "He's exactly like every other boring cis het rich white man you've ever known," she says. "Trust me."

She's met Mr. Peter Martin van Wyle (that was how the invitation named him, below Madison's name in gold cursive lettering) only a handful of times. He's pretty, like Madison, and well raised, like Madison, and wealthy, just like Madison. "His parents *insisted* on throwing this for us," Madison said to Luca upon delivery of the engagement party invitation. "I said it was so close to the wedding, what's the point? Peter's mom said 'You're not even having a bridal shower! We have to do *something!*' So fine. But let's be real—it's just a chance for them to remind everyone that even though my parents are paying for the actual wedding, they too are filthy rich and don't you forget it." And then she smacked Luca's shoulder and said, "But we can get wasted in pretty dresses, so at least we'll have that."

Naomi looks at Luca now and says, "You look nice." And then, a teasing lilt to her voice, "Hollywood."

Luca touches a hand to her hair, which she has left long and loose except for the victory rolls she's spent far too long crafting, two spirals of hair carefully pinned at her crown. "You look nice too," she says, which is an understatement. Naomi looks like the only thing Luca wants to see for the rest of her life, in a strappy red dress and matching red lipstick and her warm brown eyes glittering with gold. She's glittering all over, actually, some kind of bronzer that makes every visible inch of her summer skin shimmer with even the tiniest of movements. A gleam on her shoulders, at the hollow of her throat.

Luca has to swallow and force herself to look away, to pull her car keys from her clutch. "Ready?"

At the Rivers estate, a valet takes the car, and Luca leads Naomi inside. They make their way through the house and follow the hand-lettered signs directing them to the lawns that have been transformed for the day, crowned with Madison's and her soon-to-be husband's initials constructed out of wildflowers, almost as tall as Luca.

Outside she sees Madison, flitting around, and there's Beth laughing with somebody by the dessert table, and Carter heading in Beth's direction, and more people she knows, everyone she's grown up in this place with, and she's supposed to not be thinking about any of the bad shit today, but all she can think is, *What else don't I know about them?*

Thought she knew every little thing about her sister. Wrong. Thought she knew Carter too well to be tricked. Wrong again.

She is not as smart as she thought, she is not as right, and it feels like the ground is slipping out from under her.

She sees Madison turn and wave at her, but then Naomi taps her on the wrist, and Luca looks over, and Naomi says, "Are you okay?"

There's a server passing by and Luca snags a glass of something golden, downs it all in one. "Super," she says. "Shall we?"

When it is sunset-late, Luca goes to the bathroom, fixes her lipstick and her one victory roll knocked askew, a lean to it like the way Whitney used to drape herself on anyone, anything, vertical when she was happy drunk.

She shakes her head. *Stop.*

No matter how much she tries, it's always creeping in. Whitney's always in her head with her.

On the way back she grabs another drink—water, this time, sparkling with that metallic bite to it that cuts right through the baby buzz Luca has. Maybe if she's more focused, less blurry, she can control herself. Control her mind.

She's about to step back outside when a hand grabs her. "Luca!" Madison grips her wrist hard, her eyes wide and relieved. "Thank god. I cannot talk to one more of my parents' friends about grad school or London or whatever else they keep droning on about."

Luca laughs. "It's your party," she says. "You're supposed to entertain. This is what married life will be, you know, you and your *husband* doing all the society things that you claim to hate so much."

"It's not a 'claim,'" Madison says indignantly. "And you hate it as much as me. All this pointless posturing and who's on what board and who donated what to their kid's school, around and around just like their parents did, and their parents before them, and so on and so forth."

"That's Parris," Luca says, a little sharper than she means to, and Madison raises an eyebrow.

It's how Luca is starting to see Parris now, anyway. A place she's lived her whole life, thought she knew and understood, but the more she digs into things, the more it shifts in front of her. Becoming something different, something Luca isn't sure she wants it to be.

"Come on," Madison says, tugging Luca away from the

purple dusk and toward the back staircase out of the kitchen. "Come hide out with me for a minute."

Luca hesitates for a moment, wondering if she's abandoning Naomi, but then she thinks Naomi's a big girl who can more than handle herself. "Okay," she says. "But only for a minute."

So Luca follows Madison up the stairs, hushed steps on soft carpet.

They are halfway up when the noise from outside suddenly disappears, like Luca's ears are on mute. It makes it easier for her to hear the creak behind them, as if somebody else is following.

When Luca whips around, there's no one—nothing—there.

And then her hair lifts around her face, as if tossed by ghostly hands that then slide over Luca's shoulders and start to pull her back.

Luca feels the moment her balance falters, as she begins to tip off-kilter.

No, she thinks, and finds herself mouthing the words like it—the curse, the *curse*—can hear her. *Not here, not now. Leave me alone. Leave me* alone.

"Hey."

Madison's single word snaps Luca back: the stairs solid and still beneath her steady self, the noise present again, her hair falling over her shoulders just like before. Madison's looking down at her, the slightest furrow between her arched brows. "You all right?"

Luca nods without looking over her shoulder. She isn't sure what she's more afraid of: that if she looks, someone will be there, or that she'll only see the same emptiness as before. "All good."

They wind up in Madison's bedroom, in their usual places: Luca in the corner of the couch, Madison drifting around the room. From the open balcony doors sounds of the party drift up, and Madison turns her back on the noise. "Typical that my parents are home for this," she says. "Graduation? Well, they couldn't leave Italy in time. When Peter proposed? The yacht was already on its course and what were they supposed to do, right?" She rolls her eyes. "But this? Sure. Only when they have a chance to check in and make sure everyone's aware that the Riverses are still *very important* here and everywhere else they go."

That's one thing that sets the Riverses apart from most in Parris: they spend as much time away from the island as on it, and have done since Madison first went to college. It has the air of them being better than everyone yet again, Madison's right: it's very *well, of course we love our home, but staying in one place all the time is so . . .* small, *don't you think?*

"At least they'll be here for a little bit," Luca says, because it's all she can think to say. "For the wedding, and after—"

"They're not even *staying* after!" Madison snaps. "They said since Peter's flying back for work in London right away and I'll be 'busy' getting ready for the 'honeymoon' that there's no point in them hanging around. Like they don't know I'm not flying out to meet him until September." Madison picks up a silver hairbrush from her dressing table and stands there as she begins running it through the ends of her freshly colored hair. "But whatever. How are *your* parents?" she says, softer now. "How are things at home?"

Luca lifts one shoulder. "Okay," she says, and then laughs. "No, of course things aren't okay, but . . . I don't know. They're trying, I think, to be as normal as they can. There's no fucking guide for what you're supposed to do, you know. When your child dies. When your child is killed."

Madison stops brushing and her glossed lips pull into the slightest of frowns. "Well," she says. "Are *you* okay? What I feel can only be half of what you feel, and Luca, I feel like a part of me got sliced right out. Especially on days like today—" She stops and shakes herself, like she's shaking the sadness away somehow. "So tell me, for real."

The paper straw in Luca's sparkling water is already disintegrating, but she takes another sip anyway, leaving a red lipstick print on the paper.

What she learned first time around, the Polly time, is that when people ask if you're okay, they only want to hear *yes.* You can dress it up, or tease it out—*you know, it's hard, but I'm taking it day by day* or *I just try to think of what she would want me to feel, and I don't think she'd want me to be sad forever*, that kind of saccharine shit.

What you are not supposed to say is, *Don't worry, Madison, don't worry for a second, yeah sure my sister's dead bloody body was found only weeks ago but I'm totally fine!* You are not supposed to say, *The other night I cried so hard I woke up the girl in my bed* or *I'm beginning to think that I'll break before I understand the curse, before I ever know who killed Whitney.*

Madison is watching her intently and the rest of the world feels so far away and the locked box comes undone. "Tell *me* something, for real," Luca says. She pushes her hair off her shoulders and sits forward, caught somewhere between interrogation and plea. "Did you know about Whitney and Carter? Did you know they were together?"

Madison blinks her doll eyes once, only once. "What?"

Luca's not sure whether the surprise is feigned, surprise that Luca knows or because this is something Madison didn't. "Whitney," Luca says, and from outside a cheer goes up and the harp music is replaced by a swing-band noise. "And Carter. They were together, before she died. When she died. Did you know?"

"*Him?* And her?" Madison drops the brush with a clatter and then stares at her empty hand for a moment before looking back at Luca. "Who told you that?"

"Carter."

Madison's eyes close and her whole face twists, like she's working to fit this together, piecing out whether it is true or some twisted prank. "Oh my god," she says after a moment, and outside an insistent drumbeat starts up. "Oh my *god*. No, I didn't know that. She—" She opens her eyes and lifts her hands like she doesn't know what else to do, an all-encompassing gesture of bewilderment. "Jesus. How were they together and none of us knew? I mean, he's with Beth. And she's—she was with whoever she felt like, whenever she felt like it."

Madison moves over to Luca now, sits beside her, the beading on the bodice of her slip dress—like a drowned corps dancer in *Giselle*—gleaming in the evening light streaming in. "What is 'together'? Like they hooked up a couple times? Because *maybe* that I can see—"

"He says he loved her." Luca cuts across Madison with this news, this new world. "He says she loved him."

"For how long?"

"Months," Luca says. "Since last year, at least."

"Last year?" Madison exhales. "*Carter*. What, she was bored with everyone else? She had to pick one of our best friends to fall in love with? The one who's been dating our other best friend for like a hundred years? It's not some random guy at college with a girlfriend she didn't know. It's *Carter* and it's *Beth*." She scrapes a painted nail across the velvet of the couch, leaving a scar in the softness. "Goddammit, Whit," she says quietly, and now it's like she's speaking to herself, a terseness to her words. "You always picked the shittiest thing, didn't you? Couldn't just mess things up a little. Had to go for the nuclear option." Then she looks back at Luca, like she's remembering Luca's there, and her eyes clear. "Okay. Tell me."

Luca pulls the straw from her drink and begins tearing it into pieces, saturated fragments on the pristine couch. "They left the party together," she says softly. "For a while, anyway. They went out there together, the two of them, driving around so he could tell her he was going to end it with Beth for good, for real. Then they came back to the party and acted like nothing was different, like nothing at all was going on, the same way they'd been acting for months, and I guess they were good because I never knew. And you never knew." Luca looks up through her lashes. "Right?"

Madison shakes her head no. "He told you all this?"

"Yes."

"Huh." Madison plays with one of her straps, tied in a bow at her shoulder. "So what, he just came to you with this? Out of the blue?"

Luca pinches at the inside of her elbow, sticky from the heat. "Kind of," she says. That's a lie, of course, but she can't tell Madison that she's basically investigating her own sister's murder. She can't tell Madison that what started as a way to discover who killed Whitney and unravel the curse feels like it's becoming less about saving herself and more about the secrets her sister kept.

She looks at Madison sitting there, so bride-beautiful and pink-cheeked. "I guess he felt like he needed to confess," is all Luca says. "Or something like that."

"Guilty conscience," Madison says, and arches one eyebrow. "Or something like that."

"Maybe."

There's another loud cheer from outside and Madison sighs. "I suppose we should get back," she says. "Or else I'll be in trouble for not playing my part right."

"Tell them you were dealing with a crisis," Luca says. "Everyone loves it when I'm in crisis."

Madison laughs at that, and they make their way back

downstairs and into the garden, now lit up with hundreds of tiny pinprick lights, and people are up and dancing.

They're about to step fully back into the fray when Luca grabs Madison. "Wait," she says. "One other thing."

"Yeah?"

"Are you sure," Luca says, and she thinks for a second that she shouldn't ask, should stop now and be done with it all, but it's like she told Carter: she can't be done, not while the truth is something she doesn't know. "Are you sure about Whit, and the drugs?"

Madison is quiet for a moment, only looking up at the sky, and then she shakes her head. "Did Carter say something?" she says sharply. "Did he tell you that, too?"

"No. He told me the opposite, actually. But—"

"But you don't believe him?" Madison says. "And you don't believe me."

"It's not that—" Luca holds her hands up. It is that, though. She doesn't believe it when Madison says it, or when Carter says it, or when she herself thinks it, because why should any of them think they knew every single little thing about Whitney now? "You know, there's the DUI, and I was thinking maybe I was wrong about—"

"Listen." Madison comes close and locks eyes with Luca, an intensity there that she keeps reserved. "I don't care what people say about her and neither should you, because they didn't know her and we did. The cops want to act like because she liked to get high sometimes that she *deserved* to die? *Fuck* them. Like yeah, okay, maybe it got a little out of hand for a while there, but she got it back. She hadn't used since college, not at all. And so what if she had? People make choices, and sometimes those choices are a mistake, but they shouldn't follow you around forever," she says, disgust curling her lips. "It's such *bullshit*."

Luca is still, a little shell-shocked from Madison's anger, and she wants to think that Madison's right, that she's always right, but.

What if.

To Madison she gives only a tight smile, though. "Right," she says. "Fuck them."

By the time she finds Naomi again, the sky has deepened to navy and the music has begun to grate.

Naomi's sitting on her own, watching Carter spinning Beth on the dance floor, and she looks up when Luca approaches, her eyes soft focus. "Guess they made up," she says. "Until the next time."

Luca looks to the two of them dancing and imagines how everyone would look if it were her and Naomi up there, together. The rush of whispers through all her parents' friends, the pointed not-watching.

Suddenly she's tired and irritated and wants nothing more than to be at home, out of this dress and away from all the artificial joy she was so wrapped up in earlier. Now it seems obvious, the falsity of it all. She's about to say so when Naomi shimmies her shoulders, skin glittering. "Hey," she says. "Look what I have."

From under the table she produces a bottle of champagne, gold label gleaming, and Luca tries to look stern but can feel herself failing. "Stop stealing things," she says, no conviction to it.

"Call it a party favor," Naomi says. She stands and leans close, whispers in Luca's ear. "I'm bored. Can we go now?"

Luca's skin hums where Naomi's breath passes over it, and she steps back. "You read my mind."

26

Naomi pops the champagne and laughs as it spills on her dress. "I've never gotten the hang of that."

"It won't stain," Luca says, and Naomi frowns down at herself.

"It better not," she says. "This dress is very expensive."

Luca watches as Naomi lifts the bottle to her lips and drinks, a long, greedy gulp. The dress may be expensive and it may have been worth it, for the way it sets Luca aflame to look at Naomi in it, but it doesn't compare to the overall image of Naomi drinking champagne from the bottle and kicking off her heels at the same time. *How come everything she does looks effortless?*

"You want some?" Naomi proffers the bottle. "You don't have to."

Luca says nothing but takes the bottle, tips it up to her mouth, and the dry taste of it is sharp but the bubbles are soothing. She wrinkles her nose anyway. "Yum."

Naomi laughs. "That's three hundred dollars a bottle," she says, and steps up to the edge of the pool, balancing with her arms out wide. "You don't like it?"

"What can I say?" Luca lies on her side on the lounger, ignoring the way her position and her dress make her breasts spill over in a dramatic way. "I'm a cheap bitch at heart."

Naomi laughs again, long and loud in the quiet of Luca's backyard, only them and the lights. "Sure," she says. "Sure."

Luca sits up to take another drink anyway, the golden liquid spilling out the corners of her mouth, and then she stands and joins Naomi at the water's edge. "When I was little, I used to pretend there was another version of me who lived down there," she says. She crouches to set the bottle down and then sits, dangling her feet into the water, pulling her dress into her lap so it doesn't get ruined. "At the bottom of the pool. And she had her own family and her own world beyond the pool. But the only place we could see each other was in there. I would always tell Whitney about her, make her swim down to the bottom with me so we could meet the other me. But she'd never be there and then I'd tell Whitney that she scared her away or the other me must have been busy out in the ocean or a hundred other things."

Naomi copies Luca, leaning on Luca's shoulder as she lowers herself down. "There was this park my mom used to take me to," she says. "After the divorce. Between school and going to the gym, we'd go there. There was this bridge that went over nothing, but every time we crossed it we would run, like there was a monster underneath who would get us if we were too slow, and we would be *completely* hysterical laughing as we did it."

Luca watches the shine of the moon on the water. "When do they stop being believable? The stories?" she asks.

"When they stop being made-up and start feeling real."

That is the difference, Luca thinks, *between me and everybody else.* When the curse started feeling more real to her, she started to believe it more, not less. When she was younger, watching the Hollinghurst mansion burn, seeing that hand pressed against the windowpane. If she was like Jada, like Madison, like everyone else she knows, she would have let the curse be a strange and unreal story about their home, something to thrill. But why was it so easy for them all to let it go, to remain rooted in reality? In perfect Parris.

Lately, though, Parris isn't feeling so perfect. At least not to Luca. The faults and flaws of the island are creeping through, being unveiled. The secrets Whitney kept, Carter's cheating, the way that Luca looked around the engagement party today and saw beauty, yes, but also the gross indulgence of it all.

Naomi plucks the champagne up then, and drinks more, and when she's done she wipes her mouth with the back of her hand, seemingly oblivious to the way she's smearing her lipstick.

Luca leans back, takes a deep breath. "That monster under the bridge," she says, a little cautious, testing. "What if you still believed in it?"

There's curiosity in Naomi's face when she looks at Luca. "What do you mean?"

Luca pauses, half of her afraid to say it, the other half

hungry for someone who might understand. But after earlier, that moment on the staircase when she almost believed that was it, that the curse was about to take her down—her hunger wins out. "The curse," she says after a moment. "I don't think it's just a story."

There is silence, a long enough moment that Luca thinks, *Fuck, I've done it again* and all she can think of is Jada, three years ago, looking at her with such revulsion.

But Naomi isn't looking at her with anything other than that curious smile, still, and she nods. "Not a story," she says softly. "Something real."

It is so quiet here, and for the first time in weeks Luca feels a kind of relief, knowing that Naomi does not think she's lost her entire mind. "Right," she says. "My whole life. While everyone else was moving on, ignoring the curse, I never did. Because I can *feel* it, you know? I can always feel it, and so—" She shakes her head. "All of this. Finding out about Whit, the drugs, the statements, Carter—I wasn't straight with you. I wasn't trying to just, like, figure out what happened."

"Then what were you doing?" Naomi asks.

"I wanted to figure out how the curse worked," Luca says. "So I could understand. Keep myself safe from it." *And keep you safe,* she thinks.

Naomi says nothing, only nods again.

Luca laughs, a forced sound, to break the silence. "Now you really do think I'm crazy," she says.

And Naomi arches an eyebrow. "Oh, this? You think *this* is what's gonna get me there? Oh, we passed that a long time ago," she says, but the lilt in her voice is teasing, and then she shrugs. "Shit is hard," she says, softer now. "Losing someone— it's all so fucking hard and we get through it how we can. So if that's what you're doing, then—I'm still in."

Luca shakes her hands out, unsure what to say. So she says nothing, and they just sit there then, comfortably quiet, only the gentle wash of the water against their legs and the clink of their jewelry on the bottle as they pass the champagne back and forth. Luca rolls her head to one side, a slow, long stretch of her aching muscles. "I'm so tired."

"Okay," Naomi says. "Let's go to bed, then."

Naomi says it so casually, the words slipping from her mouth as easily as the champagne bottle meets her lips again, but Luca's skin prickles all over.

Some line *has* been crossed, she knows. The other night, her crying and Naomi holding her—before, they were in one place, and now they are in another. Maybe Naomi didn't feel it, maybe she didn't notice, but Luca did.

And maybe it all would have been nothing if they had talked about it at all, if they had woken up and laughed it off that morning. But instead Luca had rolled over to face Naomi and neither of them had said anything. Only watched, breathing quietly, their sleepy morning gazes on each other until Naomi's phone had made a noise and the real world had clawed its way in.

Luca looks at Naomi now, one strap of her red, red dress falling down, her slick skin. *It should not be possible for one person to be so beautiful.*

A slow smile spreads across Naomi's face. "Stop."

"What?"

"Staring at me."

Luca's face warms and she looks away. "I wasn't."

"You were."

Caught.

Luca was not lying before: she is tired, but not just from her sister's death. From this, *god* from this, she is exhausted from trying so hard not to feel what she does. Not to show it too much. And so she says, "Don't you like the way I look at you?" She lifts one shoulder. "I see you, too, you know. You watch me. I see."

For a second she can't believe she has said it: it is so brazen, so obviously flirting, and Luca doesn't flirt, doesn't even know how that came out of her mouth.

(No. She knows.)

(That dress. That smeared lipstick, that smile.)

"Am I wrong?" Luca's voice sounds so certain and clear that it is like she's hearing herself from far away. Hearing some other, blunter girl, saying what is in her brain without filter for once. "Am I?"

Naomi looks away for a moment, and then back at Luca, her smile fading. So serious. "Maybe I watch you," she says. "So what if I do?"

"So you watch me," Luca says, "and you talk to me, and you sleep with me, and you hold my hand in the middle of the night like it's nothing at all, except it's not nothing to me, Naomi." She says it and she means it and she wants Naomi to know she means it, means it, means it. "Does it mean anything to you?"

"That's what friends do," Naomi says.

"You're not only my friend."

"I'm not?"

"I don't want you to be." Luca is hot, her blood burning, and she might ruin it all but she is so sick of swallowing what she wants to say, always, to this girl. "It's all I can think about, when I think about you. The way you look at me and the way it feels and the way I don't want to be the girl whose bed you sleep in like it's what friends do, because the way I feel about you is not how *friends* feel about each other and if that's all you want, then fine, but you can't look at me like that anymore. You can't say, 'Let's go to bed.' I don't want you to be my 'friend.'"

She reaches out and pushes Naomi's hair behind her ear, the gesture she's avoided so many times because it always felt like crossing the line, but if the line's already been crossed, how much hurt can this one thing cause? "That's all," Luca says, quieter now, slower. "So I said it. So you know."

They hang in the moment, Luca's words in the air, her hand on the side of Naomi's face. Luca's chest rises and falls rapidly. Naomi's eyes don't leave hers, fixed in a way that makes Luca ache like she's a raw nerve and Naomi is pressing on her, just to see how she might move.

"Fine," Naomi says after the quiet spills over. "Then let's not only be friends."

Luca kisses her.

It's nothing more than a soft press of lips on lipstick-smeared lips, because Luca is not practiced in kissing people, has never kissed anybody or been kissed. Has never really wanted to up until this moment, when Naomi was looking at her and Luca felt such greedy want in the pit of her stomach.

She kisses Naomi once, and in the split second their mouths are apart she thinks, *Fuck fuck fuck, what if this was all wrong?* and *What do I do now?* but then she doesn't have to think about it because Naomi takes over.

Naomi kisses *her*. Naomi moves closer, and her hand moves up Luca's thigh, and she is kissing Luca and her teeth are scraping Luca's bottom lip and Luca ignites.

She pulls away, hand to her mouth, covering how hard she is breathing. "Naomi," she says.

"Luca," Naomi says quietly, her hand still under Luca's dress. "Is that what you meant? Not friends?"

Luca laughs because she doesn't know what else to do. She laughs, a peal in the night, and ducks her head. "I don't know," she says, and then, "Yes. I just didn't—"

"What?" Naomi says. "Didn't think I'd do it?"

"Maybe," Luca says. "I don't know. I don't know why you would ever like me."

Naomi tips her head to the side. "Look at you," she says. "Have you ever seen yourself? Have you ever listened to yourself?"

Have I seen myself, heard myself? "I'm fat and I'm crazy."

"Sure," Naomi says, "and you're smart and you're mean and you—you know why I'm always watching you? You do things so sexy and you don't know it. When you smoke, when you put on lipstick, when you do this—" She puts her thumb on Luca's bottom lips and drags, slowly, the way Luca knows she does so often when she's thinking. "Holy *shit*."

"Stop," Luca says, looking away now.

"You said you don't know and I'm telling you. So you know," Naomi says. "See? I can play this game too."

Luca kisses her again, hungrier now, and somewhat disbelieving still. Nobody has ever called her sexy. Before this moment, she would have gagged at the thought, because before now *sexy* was sleazy and gross, but now it is—still sleazy, but in a hotter way, from Naomi's lips. "Okay," she says when they break for air, into the space between their mouths. "Not friends."

27

In the morning, Luca rolls over in bed, hand between her legs.

It's early, too early with her champagne headache really, but she's alone already. Naomi is gone: she woke Luca up from her shallow sleep to say she was leaving, early therapy appointment. Kissed her on the shoulder and said hi.

Now she's gone, but the smell of her is still there and Luca is there with one hand working inside her underwear and the other at her mouth. And it's usually not like this, not this scalding intense rush that comes faster than she expects, little warning. It is usually not like this, but she is usually not thinking about a girl who turns her on, a girl who slept last night with her leg hitched around Luca's, a girl who touched her middle finger to Luca's lip before she left and smiled, wicked.

Luca makes herself come three times in the dawn light and lies there afterward, a little stunned, and as she catches her breath she replays what Naomi said to her before she fell asleep, the light of the old movie Luca had put on illuminating her: *If this island is cursed, then what are we?*

It can't touch us, Luca said. *It can't touch what we are.*

But they both knew she was lying.

It's later, and she's out on the patio, drinking down the water she hopes will hydrate the hangover right out of her.

"Luca?"

The call comes, tentative, and Luca looks up to see her mother approaching. She's wearing a blue dress that trails on the ground, her hair loose, and it makes her look younger, some prairie woman walking wild. A sharp change from her usual weekday wardrobe of slick sheath dresses and heels, but those are for the office and her mom hasn't been into work since Whitney died. Takes meetings at home, some days, but doesn't go into the office, and Luca isn't sure if that's because her mom isn't ready or because neither of her parents wants to leave her home alone.

"Hi," Luca says, closing the book that she wasn't really reading. "You look nice."

Emilia waves her off as she sits, leaning her elbows on the table. "I was thinking," she says, "it would be nice to go out for dinner tonight. Just you and me, actually in a restaurant. What do you think?"

What Luca thinks is that she had planned, tonight, to forget about everything else and spend hours learning how to kiss as good as Naomi does. But it would be nice to spend time with her mom outside the house, like they used to, before everything. "Sure," she says, and her mom brightens. "Naomi can find something else to do, I'm sure."

"Oh," Emilia says, "you have plans?"

"It's fine, we'll just hang tomorrow."

Her mom shakes her head. "No, no," she says. "It's okay. You go be with Naomi. It's good for you to get out. Be with friends. We can do dinner another night."

"You sure?" Luca frowns. "She won't mind—"

"It's okay," her mom says again, and she reaches out to smooth Luca's hair. She sighs, a gusty exhale. "They're going to find the person who did this."

The abrupt shift is jarring, but Luca keeps still as her mom plays with her hair.

"I know time keeps passing," Emilia says, "and maybe you feel like nothing's happening, no one's doing anything, but they are. They're going to find them."

Luca nods slowly.

Are they?

Am I?

"I know," Luca says after a moment, searching for something that her mom wants to hear, even if she doesn't believe it exactly. "Someone's going to pay."

Her mom sighs again. "I don't know about that," she says. "What is paying? What is justice, anyway? None of it's going to bring her back—" She stops, looks away.

"Mom?"

Emilia clears her throat and smiles brightly as she turns back to face Luca. "I have a work call in a second," she says. "I'll be upstairs, if you need me." She taps her thumb against Luca's cheek and then rises. "I love you. Okay?"

"Okay," Luca says softly as her mom walks away, and there is something about the shape of her mom's shoulders that makes Luca want to weep.

The stinging sensation rushes through her, but—no, not weep. *Burn.*

Look what someone has done to her family. Stolen her sister, broken her mother.

I'm going to figure this out, Luca wants to call after her mom, suddenly so sure. *I'm going to make sure somebody really does pay.*

But she only watches her mother leave.

28

Luca meant what she wanted to say to her mother.

I'm going to make sure somebody really does pay.

That's why on Monday she is sitting in her car, parked across the street from Jada's house.

It has been weeks since Whitney died and she is no closer to understanding the curse.

So she is starting over, from the beginning again. Back to the pills and powder or *whatever*, because she knows for sure now, from Madison, that once upon a time that *was* Whitney's shit. And maybe all those things she accused Carter of—a deal gone bad, the wrong kind of pill, a crack on the skull to keep Whit quiet—maybe those things did happen. Just at the hands of another.

But to find out who that might have been, she needs Jada.

Luca taps a pattern on the steering wheel. After she and Naomi talked about everything last night, Naomi sat there in the bed and said, "You think she'll help you again?"

"I don't know," Luca said. "I don't know where else to go."

168

"Last time she couldn't even get you the information you wanted," Naomi said. "None of those statements had anyone who said anything about Whitney using."

(Which is true. Luca has looked back over them, like she might have missed something the first time, missed it by getting caught up on Carter, but there was nothing.)

"That was my fault," Luca said softly. "I was looking in the wrong place."

"And you think Jada knows the right one this time?" Naomi lay down, her head on Luca's thigh. "What is it with you and her?" Then she looked up at Luca. "Or maybe it's not her. Maybe it's just you and your tendency toward bitches."

Luca allowed herself a fraction of a smile. "Maybe."

It's not lying, that she hasn't told Naomi that she was once in love with Jada. It's not lying, so much as protecting what she and Naomi have. She is not going to risk losing the one person who sees her, not now that she has her. She is allowed to be selfish about that, since the island already took two of them from her.

Besides, she was fourteen. Jada didn't love her back. And was it even love? (Yes.) Wasn't it just her awakening, becoming aware of who she is and who she wants? (Yes, but.)

"What are you going to ask her, exactly?" was Naomi's last question, and sitting across from the house now, Luca still isn't sure, but then the car she has been waiting for comes speeding down the quiet street, and she is out of time.

She steps out of her car right as Jada pulls into the driveway. "Hey!"

Jada looks out the open window, face hidden behind sun-glasses so Luca can't see what she's sure is irritation.

Her strappy sandals slap against the ground as she makes her way across the street and toward Jada, who is unfolding her long legs out of her car. "You stalking me now, Luca?"

"I need your help."

"Didn't we already do this?" Jada rises to her full height and flicks her hand in Luca's direction. "Didn't I already tell you not to expect anything else?"

"Jada."

"Luca." Jada says her name in such a precise imitation of Luca and the pleading tone she's adopted. "I don't know what you want. You wanted the statements, I got them for you. What else are you expecting from me?"

Luca folds her arms across her chest. "You know every-thing about everyone," she says. "Isn't that your thing now? You, always getting into people's business, always wanting to find out people's secrets."

Jada pushes her sunglasses on top of her head. Her hair looks darker than before, if possible, the snipped-short ends of her pixie cut feathering across her forehead. "Look, I'm sorry about Whitney. You know I am, okay? But we're not thirteen anymore and I don't just do what you tell me to."

"I'm not telling, I'm asking—"

Jada laughs, so hard Luca can see the pink inside of her mouth. "You never ask," Jada says, her shoulders shaking. "None of you do. People with money, you expect to get what you want when you want it, and the rest of us are supposed to deal with it. You're here right now to tell me to do something. Admit that much, at least."

The rest of us, and hasn't that always been the unsaid issue between them? Luca and Polly were rich girls, and Jada was not. They tried not to acknowledge it, make a big deal of things they had and Jada didn't, but they weren't that good at it, Luca had always known. That was why she and Polly had started hanging out on their own, sometimes, so Jada wouldn't feel left out.

Stupid, Luca thinks now. They excluded her so she wouldn't feel excluded. Nice.

Besides, it was pointless; in the years since Polly's death, the gulf between Jada and everyone else has only widened. In superficial ways—their new cars, hers used from over the bridge, their parties and vacations and gossipy whispers, her circling the edges of it all, trying to find a foothold and in ways that matter: their Ivy applications, bolstered by legacies and donations and expensive SAT tutors, Jada left behind as always.

Luca looks Jada up and down. "Fine," she says simply. "Yeah. I want what I want. But I don't want it because I'm some spoiled rich bitch. I want your help, *again*, because it's been a month and I have no answers and I'm not going to stop until I get some."

Jada looks past Luca, eyes narrowed like she's thinking.

Once upon a time Luca would have known exactly what was running through Jada's head. Now, not so much.

"Okay," Jada says after a minute. "You want my help? Fine. But I want something too."

Now Luca does step back. "Really?" she says. "You're really gonna make me pay you?"

Jada rolls her eyes. "It's called a favor," she says. "Quid pro quo. I do something for you, you do something for me, you understand."

Luca presses her palms together. "What do you want?"

"Madison Rivers is getting married," Jada says. "I want to be there."

"What?" Luca begins to laugh, an echo of Jada moments ago. "You want me to get you invited to Madison's wedding?"

"You're tight with her," Jada says, and she starts playing with the necklace she's wearing, running her thumb along the inside of the silver chain. "You ask, she says yes, I'll get you whatever it is that you want. Deal?"

Luca takes Jada in, her pale white skin, her dark, dark hair, one eyebrow always cocked, always questioning. The strange thing about loving Jada was how unloving her happened in the same exact way: one day, it was gone. Now when Luca looks at her she only sees the girl she used to know, a pretty girl, an angry girl. "It's just a wedding," Luca says, and Jada's lips press into a tight line.

Luca's only pushing her. She knows it's clearly not just a wedding, not to Jada.

"Will you do it or not?" Jada says. "It's simple."

And Luca nods. "Okay," she says. "I'll make it happen."

Jada slips her glasses back over her eyes and pushes past

Luca, toward her house. "Let me know when it's done," she says over her shoulder.

Don't let her go so easy. Get what you came for. "Dealers," Luca calls.

Jada stops, turns. "What?"

"That's what I want to know," Luca says. "Who deals in Parris, from here or over the bridge. Who might have sold to Whitney."

There's silence for a minute, and then Jada sighs. "Fine," she says. "Leave it with me."

29

"You want me to invite Jada Charles to my wedding?"

Today they are on the patio by Madison's pool, mimosas sweating in front of them. Luca hasn't touched hers; she is not a champagne girl, she has decided, unless that champagne is being fed to her by Naomi.

"Come on," Luca says. "It's not that big a deal."

Madison shakes her head. "Okay. I have one very simple question, which is, are you high? Literally. You're asking me to invite the girl you hate the most in the world to my wedding? I cannot wait to hear the reasoning for this, because truly, it must be something beyond belief. Come on. Out with it."

Madison's staring at Luca over the top of her mirror sunglasses, and Luca doesn't know what to say other than *Jada has her uses.* There's not much she can say to Madison to get around the fact of her and Jada's fractured friendship, because Madison was there, of course, and Madison has heard her go on and on about Jada being a bitch.

So because she can't fool her, and because it's all she can think of, she says it: "Jada has her uses."

"Like what?" Madison sits back, arms folded across her chest, black gingham bikini peeking through. "I'll bite. Tell me about these 'uses' of hers."

"She's helping us. Me," Luca says. She reaches for her glass and picks it up, just to have something to do.

"Helping you what?"

The condensation on the glass makes it slippery, cold, and Luca switches it from hand to hand so her fingers touch that coldness equally, so she is balanced. "Find out what really happened to Whitney."

Madison's eyes are hidden behind those sunglasses, and the rest of her is so still that Luca can't gauge her response. The only hint is the tapping of Madison's foot in the air, her gold sandal hanging off, almost vibrating with the movement.

The silence drags on a minute longer, and then Madison comes alive again, shaking out her hair and unfolding her arms. "Tell me you're not serious," she says. "Please, tell me you're not seriously doing this."

Luca sinks, a crack in her certainty. "I—it's not like I can sit around and wait for Detective Charles to figure it out. You know how it goes here," she says. "I thought you'd understand. I thought you'd get why I'm doing this."

Madison rips off her sunglasses, and behind them she is blazing. "I get it," she snaps. "Of course I get it. I'm talking about the *Jada* of it all. How is she helping you, exactly? How are you *trusting* her with this?"

"Who else am I supposed to trust?"

"You haven't spoken to her in years and now you're relying on her?" Madison says. "God, that would be like *me* asking *Isaac* for help."

Luca can't say the thought hasn't occurred to her before now, but now that Madison brings it up—

She sits up. "Would that really be so—"

"Luca, don't even." Madison rolls her eyes. "What would you want me to do? Call him up like hey, I know we haven't spoken for a while but remember how we dated for like a month a billion years ago and you were really intensely into me and it was creepy because I was *not* that into you so I had to end it and then you wouldn't leave me alone and I tried to ignore you until we went to college and now I'm back and I'm getting married? Well, do you think you could do me a favor and ask your dad what's going on with finding out who murdered my best friend?" Madison leans close now, so Luca can see the line where her foundation is not quite blended into her hairline. "Yeah, I don't think that's gonna work."

"It worked well enough with Jada," Luca says. "I asked her for some information. And she gave it to me. The statements from the party. It was all I wanted, then, to see what everyone said. But you know it's more than that now, and if I ever want to know what really happened, I need more from her." Luca wets her lips. "So I asked her for more. And she asked me for this."

"My wedding." Madison sits back and clicks her tongue against her teeth. "Oh, sad little Jada. Is that really the best thing you could think of?"

Luca plays with the tie at the waist of her dress. All in black today, all the way down to the polish on her toes. Something about black makes her feel powerful, always, like the femme fatale in the moment when she strikes the match and the flame illuminates her face, her entrance into the dim bar and the protagonist's sorry life. "It's what she wants," Luca says now. "So I'm going to give it to her."

Madison tips her head back, her neck stretching out long, the cluster of chains around it shining as she stays that way for a minute or two, breathing in the quiet.

Then she looks back at Luca. "You're sure you want to be doing this?" she asks, her tone altogether more serious now. "Have you thought this all the way through? What happens when—*if*—you find who killed her? This is not a game, Luca." Her voice softens slightly. "I can't deal with something happening to you, too."

It won't, Luca thinks, almost believing it. Even though she is no closer to knowing how to protect herself, even though it feels like even as she turns away from the curse, it circles ever closer, day by day.

It won't.

Luca shrugs, a nonchalance she doesn't feel. "I'll be careful," she says. "I promise."

Madison still looks unsure, her teeth pulling at her bottom lip. But after a minute she exhales loudly and shakes her head, blond curtain falling around her face. "Okay," she says, even though she sounds regretful already. "If it'll get us closer to knowing—okay. She can come."

Luca smiles, wide and brilliant, and stretches to pull Madison close to her.

"Nothing's going to happen to me," Luca says, and tries to ignore how it feels like she has invited doom in.

30

On Thursday morning she and Naomi sit in the parking lot of the organic market, waiting for Jada to show, exactly where they were one week ago.

Luca holds on to the invitation given to her by Madison— thick card stock, glossy finish, Jada's name inked in calligraphy on the envelope.

She's checking her phone every minute, and in the passenger seat Naomi shakes her head. "Relax," Naomi says. "She's not even late yet."

"She should be early," Luca says. "She's the one making me do this farce of an exchange. She could have just emailed me the info, and Madison could have just had this dropped off at her house. I can't tell if she wants us to look ridiculous or if she has some kind of delusion that we're doing something really bad."

Naomi shrugs. "She is stealing from her dad's police files," she says. "So . . ."

"Don't take her side," Luca snaps. But then they pause as

another car drives in and parks a few spaces down. "I think this is her."

Sure enough, the door opens and Jada climbs out, looking decidedly casual for once in leggings and a black T-shirt, eyes hidden behind those same sunglasses she's always wearing.

They get out of Luca's car and cross the few spaces between them. "You have it?" Luca says.

Jada reaches back into her car and comes out with another flash drive just like the first. "All here," she says.

Luca eyes it hungrily. She feels like she's in a dream, and on that flash drive will be everything she wants to know: the name of Whitney's (possible) Parris dealer, and maybe a statement from Beth about what she did that night, just to soothe Luca's brain, and some kind of proof that Carter has been telling the truth, that he really does love Whitney and that his love was the kind that wouldn't have harmed her.

Like she said, a dream. Reality is far closer to a nightmare, though. More the moment when the spindle pricks the princess's finger than when the dragon is slayed.

Jada spins the flash drive through her fingers. "And my invitation?" she says, pushing her glasses on top of her head.

Luca hands it to her and watches the way Jada looks at it in awe. Like a little kid getting their favorite toy, eyes widening in joy as she takes the invite out of the envelope, turns the paper over in her hands and traces a finger across the embossed border.

It lasts only a few seconds, as long as Jada ever allows her mask to drop these days, and then she snaps back to her usual self. "Thanks," she says, bored almost, and Luca would buy it if she hadn't seen that look on her face.

Luca would buy it if she didn't remember the girl Jada used to be.

"Here," Jada says. "The numbers are on there. So we're even now. No more favors."

"Oh, won't need any," Naomi says boldly.

Luca snatches the flash drive from Jada's outstretched hand. "Not if you've done what you said you would."

Jada glances at Naomi and then looks back at Luca. The small smirk on her face tells Luca how *amusing* she finds Naomi and Luca's double act. "Have I ever lied to you, Luca?"

Jada asks the question but Luca doesn't answer, and she knows Jada doesn't want her to. It's all *fun* for her, whatever she's doing. All just another way to pass the time. Another way to know people's secrets, be part of Parris.

"See you there, I guess," Jada says, and she slips back into her car and rolls up the window and peels out of the parking lot like she was never even there at all.

31

Naomi disappears to spend the afternoon with her mom—
"She calls it 'nonnegotiable mother-daughter bonding time,'
and I call it shopping"—so Luca is alone when she puts the
flash drive into her laptop. She almost expects it to be empty,
for Jada to be screwing with her. But no—there's a document,
and a list.

A very short list, three numbers, but they're there, at
least. So maybe Jada has done something good for her for
once, maybe Jada is not always the complete and utter bitch
she pretends to be.

Luca taps her nails on the keyboard and exhales slowly.
She has never bought her own drugs before. That whole thing
with not really being into them, and also that whenever she's
gotten high in the past—those limited times—she was with
other people. Got their weed from Carter, their whole group,
or from someone Jada's brother was friends with, the one
time Jada, Polly, and Luca smoked together. She has never
had any need to do this, and she does not know what to say.

So she constructs a message to send: *got this number*

from Kendall, said you were cool. just looking for something fun. help me out?

And Luca sends the message to each of the numbers before she can fixate on how seedy it all feels, grime clinging to her skin. But that is how everything is starting to feel to her lately, almost as if she could peel the surface of anything away and see something dark and wet beneath.

This will work, she tells herself. *They will meet with me and maybe none of them are the right person, but if they're not, they'll know somebody who is. I will find out who Whit's dealer was and then, and then, I will find out if they killed her.*

That evening: she and Naomi are sprawled across Luca's bed watching a movie; or Naomi is watching, and Luca is half-asleep, listening to the sound of Hedy Lamarr breaking a heart.

But when her phone buzzes, she snaps wide awake.

"Who is it?" Naomi is watching her, fully aware of the plan Luca has put in motion, knowing what Jada gave them.

Luca sits up, grasping for her phone where it's buried somewhere in the heap of bedcovers. "Probably Madison," she says. "Or Beth." Or anybody but one of the strangers she's reached out to, because that would be too much to ask, that they could get back to her so quickly, or at all. And Luca knows now not to look for luck.

She brings her phone closer, though, and there's no name on the screen. Only a number.

Luca hesitates, hand hovering above the screen, and all

she can think is that she is in desperate need of a manicure, something to fix her cuticles turned raggedy from chewing on them.

"Not Madison," Naomi says, and when Luca looks up from her phone, Naomi's looking at her with bright, curious eyes. "Not Beth. So . . ."

Luca opens the message.

517 heath lane, tonight

& tell kendall if she keeps giving out this number, she's cut off.

Luca reads it twice and then turns her phone over to Naomi, so she can see for herself. "Heath Lane?" Naomi says. "Where is that?"

"East side of the island," Luca says, and she closes her eyes, her heart pounding. Suddenly this feels a little too real. Like before was one thing, questioning Carter. She knew him, *knows* him. This person, though?

Whoever's on the other end of this number could be anybody at all, could be someone from Parris or someone from over the bridge.

Could be the person who saw Whitney last, who knows what happened to her.

Hurt her, maybe.

She senses Naomi's hand coming to her cheek before she feels it, and she leans into the softness of her palm cupping Luca's face. "Hey." Naomi's voice is quiet. "It's okay. We can do this."

"I know."

"You look like you don't."

"I look like this person we're going to meet tonight could have killed my sister." Luca opens her eyes and stares Naomi down. "That's how I look."

Naomi pulls her hand back. "All right," she says, and swings her legs off the bed. "All right."

And Luca sighs. Sometimes she feels incapable of saying the right thing. Not letting the first thought in her head be the one that slip-slides out of her mouth, even though she knows those thoughts are always the ones that cause her the most trouble.

But then sometimes she thinks she is so tired of not saying the first thing, of rewriting her words before she's even said them.

"Okay," Luca says, and she reaches out toward Naomi. Puts a hand on the space between Naomi's shoulder blades. "Are you coming or not?"

And Naomi looks over her shoulder, eyebrows sloping together. "Do you really have to ask?"

32

They pull up and find somewhere to park on the long, wide street.

So many cars around, music coming from the house at the top of a long set of steps.

Luca stands at the bottom and stares up. It's not like she hasn't already seen how fast things have returned to normal, how easy it is for everybody to carry on like what happened to Whitney means nothing to them.

But where before it made her tired, now it sparks her rage.

"Who lives here?"

Luca startles. "What?"

"Who lives here?" Naomi asks again. "Or you don't know?"

"I don't know." Luca shakes her head. "Does it matter?"

"I suppose not," Naomi says, and she wraps her fingers loosely around Luca's left wrist, like another question.

Luca shakes her off and checks her phone for another message from the anonymous dealer.

There's one. **Last bedroom on the left, third floor**

Luca shows it to Naomi. "Come on."

They walk through the party and Luca is so *angry*, she has been through this kind of night so many times before, too many times to count, really, and so many of those times she was at her sister's side and it all feels so empty now.

That is all she thinks when she sees people she knows, people she's known all her life, playing out the same scene as any Friday night. There, Tiff Lancaster dancing all up on Siobhan East. There, Jada's brother, Isaac, passing a joint to one of his friends. There, Jasmine Donovan taking three shots, one after the other. When Luca was with Whitney, when it was the before times and they were the ones dancing and drinking, it was *fun*. Luca never felt like she fit in more than when she was holding court alongside Whit and Madison and Beth, the center of attention. Now, though, she doesn't know if she'll ever be that girl again. It seems so plastic and pointless. Pathetic prettiness.

They find their way to the third floor, to the hall spreading out to the left, to the last closed bedroom door.

Before Luca knocks, Naomi takes her hand—for real this time, no questioning, no hesitation. "Wait," she says, her fingers lacing tight between Luca's. "What are you going to say?"

"I don't know." Luca rolls one shoulder. "Maybe I'll ask if they killed any girls lately. It's worked well for me so far."

Luca smiles, but it's forced and wrong, she knows, and Naomi only looks blank in response.

So Luca pulls her hand free and uses it to rap sharply on the door.

A voice calls out, "Come in."

Luca makes her spine steel, her face icily composed, before she twists the handle and opens the door and steps inside—

She stops short, Naomi bumping into her, and all she can think to say is, "Are you fucking kidding me?"

And there's a girl there, sitting on the edge of the four-poster bed, and she freezes mid hair toss. "Luca?"

"Beth?" Luca stares at Beth, Beth sitting on the bed, Beth with the phone in her hand. "What—"

Then Beth's eyes narrow and she is back in motion, except it's with a kind of edge Luca's never seen from her before. "If this is some kind of setup," she says, "you two are dead."

33

"A setup?"

Luca repeats it and then she blinks until the room is blurry Until Beth, the dealer they've arranged to meet tonight, the dealer she was planning on questioning about Whitney's death, is blurry. It's the only way she can face her, because this cannot be right or real.

Shouldn't you know by now? a voice in the back of her head says. *Everything you thought was real is wrong, and everything you never thought could be right is true. When are you going to get it?*

Luca turns to Naomi, illuminated in the doorway. "I didn't even need to go to Jada," she says, her first somewhat coherent thought. "I could have just asked Carter all along. What a waste of my time."

Behind her Beth laughs, and Luca whips back around. "What's so funny?"

Beth covers her mouth until she is composed again and shakes her head. "You thinking Carter has a single clue about me," she says. "God, Luca. I thought you knew me better than that."

"I thought I did too," Luca says. "And yet, here we are. You sell, apparently. You sold to my sister, apparently."

Beth ices over. "No," she says, getting to her feet, sticking a finger in Luca's face. "I never sold to Whit. I'm not that stupid. Don't mix business and pleasure, all that." And she steps back. "So, what? What exactly is it that you're here for?"

"Luca—"

Naomi's hand is on her back but Luca shrugs her off. She feels like there's something here, something scratching at the edges of her brain. Something that knits together Beth and Carter and her sister's bashed-in head, but this is Beth, *Beth*, and is this how it is? Is it real, that everybody Luca thought she knew so well is a completely different person and everything she believed to be steady beneath her can shatter and collapse at any moment?

"Whatever this is," Luca says, "you can tell Carter I'm not—"

Beth lets out a pained groan. "Jesus. Did you not hear me? Carter has nothing to do with this. He has *zero clue* what I do."

"Sure." Naomi walks around Luca, around Beth, hand trailing along the baroque wallpaper. "Your boyfriend, the former dealer, has no idea that you now deal. Yeah, I buy that."

"Again, I'm not that stupid." Beth pulls a hand through her dark curls. "Like I would let Carter know I'm the one running things now. He'd have a heart attack."

She moves back to the bed and sits, crossing her legs so that one of her pristine five-hundred-dollar sneakers taps against the linen sheets. "He still thinks I'm that sweet airhead he liked so much when we first got together, and it works for me that he thinks I'm still her, so no, he doesn't know what I do. And he *certainly* didn't have anything to do with you two being here. God, I just thought I was getting some new business and then it turns out to be you two screwing me around." She clicks her tongue. "Unless you *actually* want to buy something. Is that it, Luca? You finally off that holier-than-thou kick about pills being the devil?"

"It's not about that and you know it," Luca says.

"All right then." Beth stares at her. "So, what? You want to question me like you did Carter?" One corner of her mouth picks up. "Oh, yeah. He thinks I don't know, but as established, there are a lot of things Carter thinks that are really not correct. Come on, then. Ask me what you want. But I gotta say—I don't know what you think you're ever going to find out that will help you. All of this? It's only going to bring you more hurt. When are you going to learn, Luca?"

When are you going to learn?

And Luca thinks—*never*. Not when *learn* means turning away, shutting her mouth, letting the horror of this place run unchecked. *Curse or not,* she thinks, *I'm in it now.*

Luca stares Beth down. "When did this start?"

Beth smiles. "Remember back when Carter came home from college and took up his spot at his dad's company? His big moment. No more drugs, no more stupid shit, he was going to be a *good* boy from now on, do what his daddy wanted. Except that left a space in the market and I thought—I'm sick of the men in my life taking control of everything. And so *I* took control. I took his business and I made it my own and I'm doing a great job, thanks for asking."

"Oh," Luca says, harder now. "Well, that's great, Beth. I'm glad your drug empire is going so well! Congratulations!"

"Don't be a bitch," Beth says, and she shifts, crossing her legs the other way. "You're like everybody else, you know that? It's so easy to make you believe I'm just the fun girl who drinks a little too much and wears her skirts a little too short and drives a little too fast. But I have ambitions. I have things I want to get done. Maybe in a place far from here, where people don't patronize me constantly and my boyfriend doesn't cheat on me right under my nose while thinking he's getting away with it."

It hits Luca like a punch to the gut, and she exhales a noisy breath. "You knew?" she says. "About Carter and Whitney, when it was happening? You knew?"

Beth looks at her, a little pityingly now. "Of course I did," she says, and her voice is softer too, like she needs to be gentle with this part. "He always thought he was being so slick with it, but a girl like me knows, right?"

"So you knew your boyfriend was cheating on you with one of your best friends." Naomi speaks up. "You knew one of your best friends was screwing your boyfriend. And then that girl ends up dead and we're supposed to believe—"

Beth springs to her feet. "You wanna keep that pretty hair, you think carefully about how you finish that sentence," she says. "You wanna accuse me of murder, you better be ready to back that up, because I didn't touch Whitney.

I would never. Carter Muszynski is *not* worth that much to me."

There's a small overstuffed couch in the space between the bed and the window, and Luca sinks into it, her shorts riding high on her thighs. "He's worth something," she says, staring at her feet, and then she lifts her head to look at Beth. "You're still with him, after all. He means *something*."

Beth shrugs, and Luca looks away. *And so I took control.*

"It's really about the drugs?" she says. "That's why you're still with him. For the business?"

A smile spreads across Beth's face. "In the beginning, sure," she says. "Now I just keep him around for fun. I don't even need him anymore. But he's Carter, you know? He'll do."

"In the beginning," Naomi says. "It was different, then."

"Of course," Beth says. "See, it's not the easiest thing to roll up and call yourself the new sheriff. But people trusted Carter, and so they trusted me, too. It was easy to tell them he was busy working and I was keeping things running for him, and then they started to trust *me*, and now people don't even remember his name. It's all about me."

"Oh." Luca looks away from the single peeling corner of wallpaper she's fixed her gaze on and begins to laugh, watching Beth watch her back. "It's all about you. Okay." She gets to her feet. "So sorry to have bothered you and your business, Beth. Just trying to find out what happened to my sister. You know, Whitney? Your friend?"

Beth lets out a breathy laugh. "My friend," she says, "who was sleeping with my boyfriend. Who went behind my back to screw *Carter*. What kind of friend does that?" She rakes a hand through her hair. "You know what annoys me the most about all of it? It's how Whit was still so good to me. Held my hand every time Carter treated me like shit, and didn't let him get away with it. Maybe it was out of guilt, maybe not. But it was still better than anything he ever did for me. I always thought a cheating boyfriend was supposed to turn on the charm, right? Be extra sweet so the stupid girlfriend doesn't suspect a thing. Carter couldn't even bother with that."

"Isn't that terrible," Luca says flatly. "I'm so sorry you didn't get your flowers and diamonds or whatever the fuck else. God, I don't know what's worse, what *you* went through, or what Whit had to."

"Luca—"

Beth's hand grasps Luca's wrist and Luca tenses. An icy freeze that says, *Take your hand off me or lose it.*

She glances down at Beth's fingers and Beth lets go. "Luca," she says again. "Don't be like that. You know no matter what, I loved Whitney."

"That's what everyone keeps saying," Luca says. "Weird how the more I hear it, the less I believe it."

"I'd help you if I could." Beth slides her hand down the front of her black dress, the fabric shimmery under the low lights. "But—" She stops, and lifts her shoulders.

"But this is more important," Luca says, flicking a hand in the direction of the bed and Beth's bag on it, the glossy leather hiding who knows what. "Can I ask you one thing, though? How many people do you think will suspect you when they hear how *your* boyfriend was cheating with a girl who's dead now?"

She doesn't wait for Beth to respond. Just takes Naomi by the hand, the way that irritated her so much not thirty minutes ago, and leads her out of the room, away from Beth's lies.

34

They're back in the thick of the party and it feels louder, more crowded, sweatier than before, and Luca is trying to get through without dropping Naomi's hand, and it feels like they are pushing against the current but then Luca tastes air and they are outside—

And all Luca can think about is how she had wanted to throw herself at Beth and rip that shiny hair out of her head handful by vicious handful, could imagine each hard yank so clearly, she could almost feel the ache in her shoulders now, could see Beth's red-raw scalp glowing bloody. All Luca can think about is how she would have stuffed that torn hair in Beth's mouth, deep down her throat until she choked, because then she wouldn't be able to talk any more shit about Whitney.

Luca inhales deep, more cherry smoke and perfume than the fresh, clean taste she wants, but at least she can breathe out here, at least the smoke clouds the thoughts for the moment, at least they are nearly free—

And then the music stops, cuts out, and there's a ripple across the bodies in the backyard—*cops*, someone says, an urgent hiss that snakes back into the house, Luca hears it slither by her.

She looks over her shoulder at Naomi. Naomi looks at her, confused. "What's wrong?"

What Luca is wondering too, because she's never known the cops to bust a party here, because what's the point when everybody's parents and everyone in power knows exactly what goes on at these things?

That is why Luca knows, when she sees Detective Charles step into the space that has suddenly appeared as the yard empties out, that he is here for her.

35

These chairs are the most uncomfortable chairs in existence, Luca thinks. Strange that they are the same all throughout the station: the one she sat in after she saw Whitney's body, and the one she sat in to recall every minute up until the moment she didn't meet Polly, and now the one she is sitting in while Detective Charles stares at her from the other side of the table.

"Aren't I supposed to have a parent with me?" Luca says. "Isn't it very against the law for you to be questioning a minor on their own?"

Questioning. What Detective Charles said back at the party, and Luca thought about the last time he'd asked her a few "questions," and she thought about telling him to fuck off but—

She wants to know what he has to say.

So she allowed him to lead her out of the party, everyone watching. Why not be their entertainment, one more night, one more time?

So she followed him to the station in her car, Naomi

sitting beside her silently. As if she knew that nothing she said was going to stop Luca from going in there.

In the interrogation room—gray, blank, one of those mirrors across the far wall—Detective Charles smiles. "Relax," he says, and leans back, folding his arms across his chest. He's rolled up the sleeves of his button-down and taken off his tie, as if to show how worn out he is from trying so hard to solve Whitney's murder. "It's just a conversation, Luca."

Nothing is just a conversation, not in a place like this. "Okay," she says lightly. "What do you want to talk about?"

"I want to go over the events of the night of Whitney's death again," he says. "Nail down some details. Unless you don't want to do that, for some reason."

He's building to something. Luca can tell; well, he's barely subtle, Detective Charles. And she wouldn't be here if he didn't have something to say.

She fights the urge to say, *Haven't we been over this a hundred times?* and sits up straighter. "That's fine," she says, pulling her hair over one shoulder. Okay. Back to the fucking beginning. "We went to the party at Beth's—"

"We?"

"Me and Whitney, and Naomi."

"Who you had met that day."

"Yes," Luca says. "She moved in next door."

Charles writes something down on the pad in front of him and it's all such an act. "Continue," he says.

"We got there around nine. We hung out with some people for a while, and then I lost track of Whitney."

"This was at eleven or thereabouts?"

"Sure," Luca says, like she has a hundred times. "I don't know exactly, but it was a couple hours later, I think."

Charles glances at her. "You're not sure because you were drunk. Correct?"

Luca shifts. This is beginning to feel like an interrogation.

And they are in an interrogation room.

This was a bad idea, she thinks. "But you already know all this," she says. "And I really think that if you want to ask me something, you can do it some other time. Like with some legal representation here too."

Luca stands and takes her bag off the back of the chair, but Detective Charles doesn't move. "Here's the thing," he says. "I just thought you might want a chance to explain why you didn't tell us about the disagreement you and your sister had that night. You know, before I bring anybody else into things."

She stills. "The what?"

Charles is staring at her now, the note-taking pretense abandoned. "You and Whitney," he says. "Outside Ms. Palermo's house, at around midnight. Having a loud argument about something. That part that you forgot to mention in your recounting of the night."

Luca drops into the chair again. "Because it didn't happen," she says, spreading her hands flat on the table. "We didn't get into a fight. I didn't even see her after eleven."

"Eleven, or thereabouts," Charles corrects. "But you're not sure of the exact time because you'd been drinking."

"I—" She knows what he's trying to say, that it could have been then or it could have been later, and how would she know? Stupid drunk little girl. "We did not have a fight. If somebody told you that we did, then you have somebody telling you lies. Okay?"

Charles nods without taking his eyes off her. "I thought you might say something like that." He gets up and goes to the door, raps on it twice. The door opens and Officer Harold steps in, hands him a tablet without paying Luca any attention.

"It's all ready to go," Harold says, and Charles thanks him, shuts the door.

Comes back to his place opposite Luca. "We've been going through your sister's phone," he says. "Why don't you take a listen to this?"

Luca resists her instinct to squeeze her eyes shut. She is hyperconscious, suddenly, of every little movement, and she doesn't know how she's going to stay still once it comes.

And then it starts, her voice playing out into the gray space. "As always, you vanished off the face of the earth. You are the worst sister. But it's fine, whatever. Naomi's cool. I think maybe she could be my friend. I don't know. But please don't do what you did tonight and try to, like, flirt on my behalf, okay? I mean it, Whit. Do it again and I'll kill you, I promise."

Charles taps the screen and it cuts off, but it echoes in Luca's head.

I'll kill you, I promise.

You are the worst sister.

I'll kill you.

"So, what?" Luca rubs her thumb over her bottom lip and then remembers that she is supposed to be still, drops her hand. "This is so clearly nothing. You know that, anyone who heard me saying that would know I was—"

"Threatening to kill your sister," Detective Charles interrupts. "And then, strangely enough, Whitney is found dead."

Luca is silent for a minute, calculating what to say, what to say, what to say.

Finally she stands again, her hands still on the table, leaning forward like maybe this will make Charles hear what she has to say. "This is what you're spending your time on?" she says. "Somebody who says we got in a fight, and a message I left that means nothing at all?" She raises her voice. "This is what you think is going to help you find out what happened to Whitney? Are you *fucking* kidding me? This is *sisters*, this is how we talk, this is how we love each other, it doesn't mean I could *murder* her, jesus."

"Ms. Thomas—"

"Laine," Luca snaps. "*Laine* Thomas. And okay so, what, this is how you do it? This is how you run things here? Is that why you were so quick to call Polly's death an accident?"

"I can't comment on open investigations."

Luca makes a noise of disbelief. "Open investigation?" Polly's case has been closed since only a month after she died, when they said they were certain it was an unfortunate tragedy, *no sign of foul play, investigation concluded.* "That's bullshit."

Charles holds a hand out flat in the air and rocks it from

side to side, like she's almost right but not quite. "Actually," he says, "we're following some new avenues."

It's funny, how for so long Luca has dreamed of this. Fantasized about Polly's case being reopened and the cops actually looking, this time, to find who did that to her. Funny how now that it seems that they're doing it, now that she's heard those words out of Charles's mouth, they fill her with dread instead of hope.

Can't comment on open investigations replays in Luca's head, and she knows this is a trap but it's too late; she is fully caught. "New avenues?'" she repeats. "Like what?"

"Potential timeline discrepancies," he says. "And then, of course, there's you."

"Me?"

"First your friend dies," Charles says. "On a day when you were supposed to meet her, but allegedly never did. And then a few years later, your sister is dead too. And you were one of the last people seen with her. Seen arguing with her."

Charles leans in, and he sounds a little softer now, almost regretful, like he wishes it didn't have to be this way but he's just doing his job, right, just doing what Luca wanted, trying to solve these cases. "Polly's injuries," he says. "We chalked them up to nature. She was out in the water, alone, by the rocks. But perhaps they didn't all come from that."

Luca's breathing is ragged. "What do you mean?"

"What I mean is it's possible some of the injuries she suffered could have come at the hands of a person," Charles says. "Perhaps she wasn't alone by the water that day.

Perhaps whoever she was with is the one responsible for her death."

Luca is speechless, silent.

Yes, yes, that's it—that's what she has always believed happened. But nobody else ever did.

And now Charles is saying it, except he thinks the other person on the beach was *Luca*, he thinks *she* is the one who—who did that—

"You told us about the place beneath the bridge." Charles drums his long fingers on the tabletop. "You said it was a place the two of you used to go, quite frequently, by yourselves. Now, we've known all along that that was where she went into the water—"

"So, what," Luca says, and her voice rings loud in her own ears, "because I told you she might have gone there means I must have killed her? Do you *hear* yourself? What, you think I—broke her neck—" She has to swallow around the words. "Did that, and then—then dragged her into the water? How could I *even*?"

Charles looks her up and down. "You're a big girl, Luca," he says, with the slightest smirk.

Big girl.

Black girl.

That's what he means, too, Luca knows. That's what he won't say because of *course* he's not racist, right? That's what he would say. It's what everyone on this island would say, because to them not screaming slurs in the street equals them being the most progressive, equality-loving motherfuckers.

But they all have it, deep inside them.

Luca is hot all over and she would like nothing more than to hiss how wrong he is, how he is wasting time like he always does, how she hates him for even suggesting that she could ever have hurt Whitney. Hurt Polly.

But she knows this is exactly what he wants from her, an outburst of rage, another thing he can point at as evidence. *Big girl, Black girl, angry girl.*

She pinches her thigh. This is why she keeps so much of herself hidden. Because if on top of all that Charles knew about her mental health, if he had even a single idea about her intrusive thoughts, then she would be done for. Look: here is Charles, ready to find her guilty because of a single voice mail. There is no way on earth her thoughts wouldn't be used against her, the third strike alongside her body and her skin. *This is why I keep quiet,* she remembers. There is no *acceptance* once you step past the neat, orderly bounds of sadness and nerves that most people think *depression* means. No, then the sympathy turns to fear real quick. And fear is such a good excuse for anything, for leaving Luca demonized.

The silence around them is loud. He is watching her, and Luca keeps her mouth pressed closed so that he has to be the one to break it.

"Two girls close to you," Charles says. "Both dead. Both with you shortly before their deaths. We'd be negligent if we didn't look into it, Luca, you know that."

Yes, two girls close to her, dead, and not so long ago she believed those deaths belonged to the curse. Not so long ago she would have blamed the curse for this, too, for making it seem like she is responsible, except even she can't twist her way to that conclusion. The curse kills. Vanishes. It doesn't blame. It doesn't paint *guilty* on a back.

Luca shakes her head hard enough that her entire body rattles. No, she has done that to herself. Pulling at threads like they will unravel the truth, instead of what it seems they have done, drawing her deeper into danger. Into a place where it looks like *she* is the bad thing.

"Luca," Detective Charles says into her silence. "Sit down."

She comes unstuck and moves to the door, yanks it open, and half of her expects Officer Harold to be out there, waiting to force her back in, but the hallway is empty. "No," Luca says. "This is just a conversation, right? Fine. Conversation over." She spits the words at him. "She was my *sister*, you monster. My sister."

And she walks out, but not before she sees the way Charles is looking at her.

Like he is certain the animal in his trap is the one he has been hunting.

36

She's fumbling with her phone as she crashes out of the station doors, her breath coming fast, and she's trying to dial Naomi, but then hands grab her and Naomi is right there.

"We have to go."

"Okay," Naomi says. "What happened?"

Luca walks fast to her car, and her fingers slip on the door handle but she opens it, eventually, and climbs in. "I just really need to go."

"What did he want?" Naomi asks, and she's opened the passenger door but is just standing there.

"Get *in.*"

Naomi does as Luca says, finally, and Luca sinks into the seat's cool leather as she drives off.

Out of the station parking lot and onto the road, breezing through lights on the cusp of turning red. "What did he want?" Naomi asks again.

The roads are quiet, of course. It's late, and it's Parris. Nights are always sparse here. "He wanted me to tell him about that night."

"Again?"

Luca drums on the steering wheel. "I don't think he wanted to hear anything from me, really," she says. "I think he wanted to scare me."

There's a pause. "Scare you?"

"Yeah," Luca says. "He wanted to know about the fight me and Whitney had outside Beth's house."

She takes a corner a little too fast, and Naomi braces herself against the door. "What?" Naomi says, her rasp pronounced. "But—you didn't. Fight, I mean. I was with you, all night."

"Right," Luca says, and she is gripping the wheel now, so hard that her brown skin has gone white. "That's what I said. And he told me all about how me and Whit fought outside Beth's at midnight. So I guess—" She exhales, loosens her grip. The blood rushes back into her fingers, a sharp flush of it. "I guess that's what somebody's saying, and now Charles thinks I had something to do with it."

Charles thinks I killed my own sister.

"What?" Naomi says again, an echo of herself, but Luca can't blame her. What else is there to say to this, this story where Luca has now become a suspect in her sister's murder?

Luca's shoulder knocks against the window as she blows through the center of town, almost home, but she doesn't mind the jolt. At least this way she knows she's feeling things. "Remember that voice mail I left her?"

Sitting in Luca's bedroom at the memorial, closing her eyes as she told Naomi what she'd said. Well—part of what she'd said.

Now she tells her the part she left out, the part that Detective Charles has latched onto. *I'll kill you, I promise.*

A man like Charles wouldn't understand, wouldn't know that specific bond made between two girls when *I'll kill you* only really means *I'll kill for you.*

But Naomi does. "That's insane," she says. "That's absolutely insane—"

"Then he starts talking about Polly, how I'm the one thing she and Whitney have in common and they're both dead now and—"

She's pulling into their street now, swinging into the driveway, trying not to look at the house next door that Naomi now lives in but will always be Polly's, really.

Luca is out of the car before Naomi's even got her seat belt off, stalking up the drive and into the house.

She sees the light flick on in an upstairs window, and where she always used to feel comforted that her parents were watching out for her, now she only feels anger. *Is this all they can do? Don't they want to know what happened, the way I do?*

"Luca," Naomi calls. "Wait up."

She'll catch up, Luca thinks, because she can't slow down for Naomi, because all she is thinking now is that somebody's telling this story about her and Whit, and on her computer she has all those statements and what if she missed it? She read them all before but she wasn't looking for that, so what if she missed it what if it's been right there this whole time what if—

"Luca—"

"What?"

She's up the stairs and into her room with Naomi's call chasing her, and by the time Naomi is there, shutting the door behind her, Luca has her laptop out and the statements open already.

"Would you just tell me what you're doing? Then maybe I could help—"

She's ignoring Naomi and just reading, scanning, these words she already knows but now she's trying to see them differently even if they are all still the same.

I spoke to Whitney around ten—
I think I saw her—
I saw Whitney and Luca together—
We—me and my friends—we were sitting by the pool—
Of course I remember—
She was with her sister and Madison—
No, I didn't speak to Whitney—
We were dancing—

Luca presses the heels of her hands into her eyes, the light behind her lids blooming and fracturing, kaleidoscope.

When she opens them, Naomi is still talking, and Luca is still not listening and it takes her eyes a second to adjust, but when they do it's like the pattern slips and she sees it.

Subtle, but there.

"Shit," she says, the *T* like a shot from her teeth. "Shit, *shit*."

Take out a handful of the statements. String them together, new order.

See the story it makes.

She was with her sister—

Of course I remember seeing her. Everyone always remembers seeing Whitney Laine Thomas. But she did look mad when I saw her.

I did talk to Luca. She was being kind of a bitch, actually

I saw Whitney and Luca together outside, I don't know what time. It was late, though—

I heard these girls fighting—

It's almost nothing. But it's not quite nothing at all, and that's the problem, Luca sees. Here is the beginning of a story, and there is her voice mail, her non-threat that can be turned into a threat, and maybe there is still somebody talking to Charles, or maybe he has just decided on this new version of events.

No, Luca and Whitney didn't fight, but it's easy enough to make it seem like they could have.

And Charles is right, in a way, about Polly and Whitney. What—who they have in common.

He's building a case, she thinks, sudden and bright. *He's building a case with all these little pieces.*

"What the fuck is it, Luca?" Naomi grabs at her. "Come on—"

"Everyone's going to think it was me," Luca says. "Even if he can't ever really prove it, everyone's going to believe—"

"Luca," Naomi says, for the hundredth time, and Luca looks at her finally. "It's not going to be like that. No one's going to think any of this is—"

"Wake up, Naomi." Luca catches Naomi's chin and tilts her face up to the light, to better see the worry in her eyes. "I told you this place was cursed."

And so am I, she thinks. *I have been, this whole time.*

Naomi swallows; Luca feels Naomi's jaw working beneath her fingertips. "So what, that's it?"

Luca releases Naomi and turns away.

It's like a slow sunrise, light leaking over the horizon until suddenly it's blinding, piercing whiteness searing through. All this time she's been worried about the curse coming for her when really, hasn't it already? *It took Polly from me. Jada, too, in a different way. It terrified me so much, when I saw Isla in that window, that I haven't known a day without fear since. Then it took Whit, my sister, my greatest love. And now, a final sharp twist of a cruel knife: it's going to blame me for it all.*

She turns back to Naomi slowly, a numbness in her fingertips. "Yeah, maybe this is it," she says. "Maybe I stop looking."

"You can't—"

"Why? Because it's gotten me so far already?" Luca makes fists, nails in her palms. "I don't know anymore, Naomi. I'm stuck in this loop and things never seem to change and even if they do, what does it matter? Whitney's dead. She'll always be dead, just like Polly. So what's even the point anymore?"

She stands and brushes past Naomi, opens the door, and leaves her.

37

The days pass and the weather never changes. Luca has always wondered what it's like to mark the passage of time through the ebb and flow of warmth, sunlight, rain. Every day in Parris rolls in, same as the one before, no matter what's happening.

Instead, in her world, it's just the feeling in the air and the approach of things. Madison's wedding so soon now; the feeling Luca gets when she sets foot outside her front door.

They have nothing to back this up, Naomi has said to her, more than once. *It'll go away.*

But Luca has heard nothing from those other supposed dealers and she has nothing more to go on, and it feels like nothing nothing nothing.

It is Wednesday, and in the evening she goes down to the beach.

There's a bonfire tonight, like there so often is in summer. When there's no party to go to, no place to crash, this is where people come. The fire tonight is not so big, not so wild as Luca has seen it before. It's still hot, though, and Luca follows the call of the orange heat down the beach. There are maybe a dozen people hanging around by the fire, running into the shallows, laughing wild.

Luca sits on the sand, facing the water but close enough to the fire that she's instantly clammy under the sweatshirt and jeans she threw on over her bathing suit.

She's not sure why she came down here. She's not sure why she's doing anything she's doing anymore, actually.

Luca shifts on the damp sand and spots movement out of the corner of her eye: a new group of girls, taking up places closer to the fire. She can't quite make them out in the shade and flicker of the flames, but she can hear them fine.

"No effing way," one of them is saying. "That girl Polly drowned."

"Yeah, but her *neck* was broken too, and she was all beat up—"

"Still, that shit's hardcore. You really think Luca could have done it?"

She blinks. *They're talking about me.*

"I mean, remember that story? About the girl who was murdered on the yacht? What was her name—"

"Laney something?"

"Yes! Laney Hart! You know what happened to her, right? No? Okay, well, it was the Fourth of July, and this girl Maggie Ellory had a boat party every year. So they go out on the boat, everyone gets hammered, usual. When the boat comes back in, everyone leaves, and the crew are checking and they find Laney Hart's dead body in one of the bedrooms, and an empty water bottle in her hand. So they test the water bottle, and it comes back for—"

Antifreeze, Luca finishes in her head. That's how Laney Hart died: by suicide, poisoned by the entire bottle she drank.

The part people leave out, though, is that Laney had reported an assault, and once it had gotten out Laney had been terrorized by almost everybody she knew. Former friends, teachers, her own family, hounding her to take back her story about the trusted family friend who had raped her.

"What? What was it?"

"Antifreeze. *But* here's the thing. Why would she pick that night and that party to kill herself? It doesn't really make sense—until you realize that she had accused some old guy of rape. And that guy? He was the father of the girl throwing the party."

Luca stiffens. She's never heard that before.

"What the fuck? No way."

"Keep going!"

"So maybe she did drink that poison all by herself. But why would she even be at that party? Why would the daughter of her attacker invite Laney onto her boat?"

"To *kill* her. Oh my god, amazing."

"I mean, no one knows what happened for sure. But all I'm saying is, it can happen. A girl can be so mad at another girl that she just loses it."

"You know what I heard? The two of them got in a fight."

"What, Luca and Polly?"

"No, her and Whitney. Keep up, bitch."

"Where did you hear that?"

"Everybody heard. Keep *up*. Supposedly they were seen screaming at each other."

"Oh. So like, they fight, she gets mad, she pushes her or whatever?"

"Wait, do we even know how she died yet?"

"No, but Katherine's housekeeper's son was the one who found her. Said it was a real mess. Blood everywhere and her head—"

Shut up shut up shut up, shut the fuck up. Luca scrambles to her feet, not caring whether those bitches see her. She glances over her shoulder to where those girls still are, and now she can see them properly: Jasmine Donovan, Siobhan East, Tiff fucking Lancaster.

She is neither surprised nor hurt; she's only known these girls since pre-K, after all. What is loyalty, anyway?

Back up the beach, up the steps, toward her house. The bonfire burns bright in the background and she wishes, not for the first time, that it would burn this whole island up.

The house is quiet when she reaches it. No surprise there. It's always quiet now, she thinks as she makes her way to her room. As if Whitney were the one filling the place with all movement and light and sound.

Luca slows. Her bedroom door is ajar, light spilling out the gap.

She pushes it open slowly. "Mom?"

She's surprised to see her mom there, when she's barely seen either of her parents over the past few weeks. But here she is, sitting on the edge of her bed, Luca's laptop open in front of her and papers fanned out beside her. "What is all this?" She looks up, her eyebrows knit together in worry. "Luca?"

Luca rushes in, lunges for her laptop, slapping it shut. "It's an invasion of privacy, is what it is," she says. "I can't *believe* you—"

"Me?" Her mom holds up a sheet of yellow paper covered in Luca's handwriting, one of so many small-hours attempts to map that night out. "Luca, if this is what I think—baby, you can't do this."

"I'm not doing anything." She leaves the *anymore* off. "Besides, it's not a big deal."

Her mom's eyes widen. "Not a big deal?" she says. "Luca, you've been *investigating* your own sister's *murder*. Do you know how reckless that is? Do you know how much danger you're putting yourself in?" She drops the paper and reaches out, to take Luca's hand. "Look at me."

Luca doesn't, won't, until her mom squeezes her fingers hard enough to bruise and Luca snatches her hand back, glaring. "That *hurts*."

And her mom shakes her head. "I'm sorry," she says, "but I need you to look at me when I say this, okay? I need to know you hear me." Her voice is raw, stretched thin. "I already lost one daughter. I can't lose you, too."

Luca shouldn't say anything, she knows, but there is something about the exhausted ache in her mother's voice and the gleam of tears in her eyes that cracks her resolve. "I know," she says, moving quick to sit beside her mother now. "That's what I was trying to make sure didn't happen. Because the curse, it's not just the stories people tell, it's really real, and I thought that if I could figure it out, then I would know how to stop it coming for me, too. And now Detective Charles is all like 'you knew them both' like it's my fault somehow, like Polly was my fault, and I thought I was looking for a way out of all this but it seems like there is no way out and I don't think anyone is ever going to pay for what they did—"

Luca stops herself.

Her mom is staring, her face fixed in surprise, and Luca knows she has royally fucked up.

"Mom, I'm not . . ." *Crazy*, is how that is supposed to end, but her parents don't like when she uses that word, and besides, it isn't true.

But her mom is nodding. "I know," she says, "I know. This is just—this is a hard time for all of us. Okay? It's hard and it's all right that you're feeling this way." She touches her thumb to Luca's cheek. "I'm going to make an appointment with Dr. Ramirez. How does that sound?"

Luca closes her eyes. How does it sound?

Like her parents always sound when they have to deal with her mental illness, like they don't understand her, can't comprehend what it's like inside her brain and think therapy is some kind of instant fix for when things go wrong. *That's not how it works,* she always wants to tell them. Therapy can help her, antidepressants can help her, but none of it changes who she is, fundamentally. There is no making it go away, only learning to live with it, how to cope.

But they want me to be fixed, Luca thinks. *They think I am broken.*

I am not broken.

Her mom is watching her intently, waiting for an answer, and because Luca can't gather the energy to push back, she nods. "Fine," she says. "It sounds just fine to me."

38

The night before the wedding.

Late, dark.

In Luca's bedroom, in her bed, Naomi lies on her side facing Luca. Her eyes are closed but she's not sleeping yet, Luca can tell. "Naomi," she says in a whisper.

"Yeah?" Naomi answers without opening her eyes.

"If you didn't know me," Luca says, "if you'd never met me and you heard about what had happened—would you think I was involved?"

Naomi's eyes open and she stares at Luca, so serious. "No."

"No?"

"Not at all."

"But why not?" Luca turns on her side too, her tank top sliding off her shoulder. "If you heard a girl had been murdered and she was last seen arguing with her sister, wouldn't even a small part of you wonder 'what if'?"

"People fight," Naomi says simply. "People do all sorts of things. I always think, when people are talking about things like this, they're always looking for the thing that someone did that makes no sense, but they don't recognize that we all do out-of-the-ordinary things every day."

"Do we?"

"The other day," Naomi says. "Why did you go to the beach?"

"Because."

"Because what? You wanted to sit by the fire? You wanted to talk to someone?" Naomi exhales. "No. You just wanted to. Not everything has some great big reason behind it. What if you and Whitney had gotten into a fight? Could've been about anything. Could've been that she wore your shoes without asking and you were pissed and then five minutes later it's over. You're sisters."

No great big reason.

"One more question," Luca says, touching her bottom lip. "Do you think I'm a crazy bitch?"

Naomi smiles at her. "Yes," she says. "Absolutely. It's why I like you so."

"Because I'm crazy?" Luca says. "Or because I'm a bitch?"

"Little of both."

Luca turns on her back. "On the beach, they were talking about Whitney," she says to the ceiling. "Like she was nothing. Talking about how she looked when she died, what happened to her, like she was some doll or a toy they could pick up and put down whenever they felt like it. Because they'd put her down soon and move on to something shinier." She scratches at her neck, warm. "I don't want to say you had it better but, like—at least the way your Anya died was cleaner."

Naomi props herself up on one elbow, her face like, *Okay, Luca, now I really do think you're crazy.* "Cleaner?"

Luca clicks her tongue. "That was the wrong word," she says. "I mean . . . definitive, you know? A car accident. What is there to say other than it happened? It's the kind of thing people think is sad, sure, but they understand it. No one understands the things that happen here. They don't even try."

Naomi's quiet for a moment, watching, and then she says, "Aren't you tired?"

For a moment Luca thinks she has upset Naomi and she really didn't mean to, it's just that she can't stop thinking about the girl Naomi was friends with, how she was here one moment and gone the next and Naomi is still getting over it, yes, but at least she *knows*, the who and what and why of it all.

But then Naomi places a finger at the point just above Luca's breasts and runs it up her throat and under her chin. "Come on," she says, not sounding mad at all. "Try to sleep."

So Luca rolls over, her back to Naomi, the way she always sleeps when they're next to each other. Her hands pressed together and tucked under the pillow, one of Naomi's hands resting on her hip. A comfort Luca doesn't know how to go without now.

Before long she hears Naomi's breath deepening, stretching out.

Luca breathes along with her, hoping it'll work tonight, that she'll fall asleep and stay that way and there won't be any dreams of bad things—or worse, of the good; Whitney, alive. Polly, flipping her the bird and laughing.

She waits and she breathes and she thinks about the hundred ways she might die at any moment, how the curse may get her, and only then can she sleep.

39

Madison's wedding falls on the first day of July, the first Saturday of a new month.

They sleep late—or at least, Naomi does, and Luca pretends to be sleeping as she lies there beside Naomi. Bone-tired and not really sure who or where or what she is anymore, like she's somehow slipped between the bonds of time and space. Only way to deal with what has happened, keeps on happening, to her.

When Naomi does wake up, they get ready for the evening's festivities. Makeup and shoe selections and straightening irons smoking hot, Naomi running waves through her hair, Luca pinning hers out of her face with golden slides. Normal, normal, just be normal.

Naomi zips Luca's dress and skims her fingers across the back of Luca's exposed neck. "All done."

Luca squirms away with a breath of completely involuntary laughter. "Stop," she says, and then, "Thanks."

Naomi pulls Luca in front of the mirror and wraps her arms around her waist from behind. "Look," she says. "We look good."

They do, and it is a marvel to Luca, still, that this girl does want her, that she found somebody who so perfectly fills the space left behind by loss. So she tries a small smile at their reflection, her eyes finding Naomi's in the mirror. "You're beautiful."

Naomi's the one to squirm now. "You are."

Luca smiles. "Do you think I should wear the gold shoes or the black?"

"Pink," Naomi says. "With the ankle ties. I like those." She kisses Luca's shoulder, softly, and Luca closes her eyes.

Can't deny the effect Naomi's mouth on her skin has on her.

Naomi's kisses swing from one extreme to the other, Luca has quickly learned: sweet and delicate and the kind of gentle that makes Luca feel like a porcelain doll in her hands. Or desperate and ferocious and starving, hands gripping so tight that the other day Luca found half-moon imprints on her right thigh, a companion to her self-inflicted permanent bruise.

They're gone now, but she can still run her hand over the spot and remember the feel of them.

It's like Naomi knows exactly what she needs.

"Come on," Luca says, opening her eyes and extricating herself from Naomi's embrace. "Madison will kill us if we're late."

It's a beautiful day. But in Parris, it always is.

They enter the estate and there are flowers everywhere— *everywhere*. Welcoming them to the house, and lining the path laid out down to the seating, and strewn across the aisle, and on the back of every gilded chair. Roses and peonies and ranunculus, sprays of white flowers Luca doesn't know the name of, lilacs tied with thin gold ribbons.

While the cellist plays, somebody comes around and hands them these tiny glass bowls, filled with petals, to throw once the ceremony is over.

They are bloodred and beautiful.

When Madison comes down the aisle in the gauzy floral creation that she'd spun around in for Luca up in her bedroom, Luca can't quite catch her breath.

Naomi leans to whisper in her ear. "She looks beautiful."

Luca nods, unable to tear her gaze away from Madison. "Beyond belief," she says, trying to smile. Trying, trying, trying.

The ceremony itself is sweet and solemn. Madison makes her vows with this boy—man, maybe—who she has told Luca she loves so many times, and when she says it up in front of everybody it sounds so true, her voice like happiness, and Luca doesn't want to be the cliché girl crying at the wedding, but it is love.

Madison and her new husband walk up the aisle hand in hand, and everybody throws their petals. Luca throws her petals and Madison's smile blooms wide and it is all almost enough to forget that Whitney should be there, behind Madison.

She has no bridesmaids; was never having any. Only Whitney, her maid of honor. It was all she needed, Madison said.

Luca is glad, now, that her parents decided not to attend,

even though they were of course invited. How shattered would they have been, how hard would they have cried, being present for this moment in Madison's life that they won't ever get to witness for their own daughter?

There is just an empty space where Whitney should be, in a dress that matches Madison's, wearing a smile that mirrors her, believing in love on this beautiful day.

But she is not there and Luca throws the last of her petals and gives up on trying not to cry.

When they are seated for dinner is when she feels it.

That hauntingly familiar chill that knifes up her spine and settles around her neck, as if the curse has wrapped itself around her throat like a necklace.

Luca touches a hand to her neck like that will force it away, turning as she rubs her fingers across her skin. That's when she notices that people are looking at her.

Not boldly, not for long, but she sees them. Catching her in secretive glances.

Her hand stills as she keeps turning, scanning the tent set up not far from where the ceremony took place. People are definitely looking. *Looking at the girl they think killed her sister,* she thinks, and in that moment she is not sure whether the chill on her skin is the curse or the feeling of all these eyes on her, the weight of their judgment.

Luca whips back around to look ahead. She's at a table with Carter and Beth, putting on their perfect couple act. A space for herself, and a seat next to it for Naomi, and for a moment Luca wonders if Naomi is sitting where Whitney was supposed to be.

The other few places at their table are empty.

"What do you think?" She says it into Naomi's ear, leaning close. "Madison left them like that on purpose, or nobody else wants to sit with the murder suspect?"

"Stop," Naomi says. "It's not—"

"Everybody's thinking it," Luca whispers. "I'm not stupid, Naomi. You're not either."

Naomi lets out a long breath. "Well, fuck 'em," she says. "They can all choke."

That, Luca manages to smile at.

They sit through dinner, course after course of tiny, delicious things, slices of steak and chunks of lobster in creamy sauce and bite-sized pastries oozing with cheese. Tomatoes in blistered skins and sharp sorbets and rich chocolate gelato.

After dinner there are speeches, and Luca tunes most of them out but then Madison stands, microphone in hand, and starts speaking. "I know it's not customary for the bride to make a speech," she says, "but I think that's antiquated bullshit and it's my wedding day, so I'll do what I want."

This raises a laugh from everybody around Luca, and she watches as Madison smiles. "I want to thank everybody for being here with us today," she continues. "Some of you have come a long way to be with us, some of you have known us both as long as we've been alive, some of you are newer friends—but no less close." She pauses and looks down, and Luca watches Peter, her husband now, touch a single finger to her wrist. And Madison looks up. "I wanted to take a moment to . . . I don't know, exactly. Honor? Let's go with that. To honor my best friend, who isn't here today." A pause again, to clear her throat. "I wish she was, and I wish she'd been there with me to walk down the aisle, but—"

Luca feels the tension in the room swell, suddenly, a tight pressure. And a pressure in her wrists, which she only registers when she looks down at her hands to see she's clutching on to her napkin like she's strangling it.

The weight of a hundred-plus gazes on her is heavy enough to drown under. But what can she do, in this moment? She wants to weep for her sister, but they'll say *fake*, they'll say *acting*, they'll say, *Could she make it any more obvious?* Even anyone in here who doesn't buy into the rumors, they want to see her cry, get their fix of her pain.

And if I don't, she thinks—more evidence that she is cold, hard-hearted, not in pain at all.

"Anyway," Madison says, and she's holding a champagne flute up now. "Let's raise a toast to Whitney, and to all of you."

The ceremonial clink of a hundred glasses bursts the tension, everybody all at once laughing and cheering, as if thankful to have gotten that required moment of remembrance over with, as if they couldn't care what Luca did or didn't do at all.

Luca raises her glass halfway but no more, the hardness in her chest cracking.

Across the table Carter clears his throat and pushes his chair back. "Excuse me," he says. "Bathroom."

Luca watches Beth watching him go. So many performances today. So much fun at the circus.

She turns away, to Naomi, and kisses her on the cheek because she doesn't know what else to do. "Sweet," Luca says flatly. "Don't you think?"

Naomi doesn't say anything. Only tips her glass back, draining it in one fast swallow. "Long night," she says. "Better be prepared."

40

Later.

She doesn't know where she's going, but then she sees the girl in the floor-length gown, emerald green with thin straps, and a slash of red lipstick that makes her look as dangerous as she really is.

Jada.

So she follows.

It's the first she's seen of Jada all day, to her surprise. Not that she's really been looking for her, but she had half expected Jada to find her, to gloat, to revel in her pride at having gotten exactly what she wanted. But no. And it's a surprise, but maybe, Luca thinks, maybe she is playing it safe tonight. She wanted to be here so bad and now she is, and maybe finally there is something more important to Jada than wreaking havoc.

Jada's at the end of the bar now, the bartender sliding a drink across to her, and Luca watches as she plucks an ice cube from the glass and bites it clean in half.

Then she slips away, and Luca follows again.

Jada leaves the tent and walks along a short path that leads to a cluster of trees that have been transformed into a magical grotto—lights strung up everywhere and huge jewel-toned ottomans scattered around for guests to recline on. To one side a table of sweets is set up, tiny tarts and bites of chocolate-covered things, and Luca pauses at the entrance as Jada peruses the selection, her eyes lit up.

Luca isn't sure what she's doing, following Jada like this. She just—wants to see her there. See that it is worth it, to Jada, what she's done to be here. Leveraging Whitney's death for her own gain. See how happy it's made her.

Jada picks a dessert up and pops it whole into her mouth, chewing with her eyes closed.

And then— "You're a terrible spy," she says suddenly, and spins around to face Luca. Eyes open. "Seriously? Come on."

Luca tries to act like she hadn't been meaning to hide, and steps forward into the grotto. "Having fun?"

"Oh, bunches." Jada leans back against the table, kicking out one stiletto-clad foot. "Just like old times, huh? You and me. If only Polly were here, right? If only she wasn't dead."

Luca hears what Jada isn't saying. *If only you hadn't let her die.*

A flicker of anger rises in Luca but she tries to keep it tamped down. Not let Jada stoke it too much, because that's exactly what she wants, and Luca is tired of giving in to her demands. "Are you ever going to stop blaming me?"

Jada tips her chin up. "Are you ever going to stop blaming a made-up curse?"

Luca opens her mouth before she is even sure of what

she's going to say, but then there is a noise from outside, loud enough to stop them both, and—

"Isaac! Isaac, man, you can't go in there."

"What? You gonna stop me?"

Luca looks toward the sound coming from outside the grotto, and then back to Jada, whatever she had been about to say next gone. "Your brother's here?"

Jada groans. "For Christ's sake," she says. "I'm going to kill him myself."

"Quiet." Luca holds her hand up, listening.

"—can't be here, Isaac, it's her *wedding*. Are you serious right now?"

"She doesn't love him."

"What, but she loves you? Jesus, you went out for a while when we were kids, Isaac, and look at you. You're wasted. What are you gonna do, go in there and attempt some grand romantic gesture while you can't even stand up straight?"

"God, this is pathetic," Jada says, and Luca moves away from her, peering through the trees, trying to pick out faces in the low light. If Isaac is one of those voices, then the other sounds like—

"Fuck you," Isaac says, voice carrying loudly through the trees. "You know what, Carter, I'd be careful if I were you."

Yes, then: Carter.

"Okay," Carter says, sounding tired to Luca's ears. "I'll make sure to do that."

"I'm serious," Isaac says. "I know all about you." A pause, only for a beat. "You and Whitney."

Luca stills. For a moment there she had been wondering why Carter was even bothering with Isaac—let him do what he wants. It's Isaac Charles; no real threat.

But now she sees this going another way—the stupid fragile-ego-man way, the pissing contest turning to something more serious.

Jada turns to Luca and opens her mouth; Luca puts a finger to her own lips.

Don't.

In the trees she can see them now, facing off, Isaac's lean giving away his altered state.

Carter moves around him, and it's quiet, only the distant sounds of the party seeping through, until Carter says, "You don't know what you're talking about."

"I don't?" Isaac's laugh is loud. "Convenient, isn't it. Her dying. Takes care of that whole baby problem for you, doesn't it?"

The words sink into Luca's stomach.

Baby. Problem.

Carter's voice is sharp. *"What?"*

And Jada looks to Luca again. "Yeah," she says softly, quiet so they aren't discovered, but her eyes are sharp. "What the hell is he talking about?"

"It'll all be out there soon enough," Isaac says. "Medical examiner's findings and all that. How she was pregnant when she died. And I wonder who they'll think of first . . . the asshole she was hooking up with? Maybe."

Medical examiner's findings.

Luca's breath catches, stuck on something in her throat

that might be sickness or might just be hurt. Medical examiner means autopsy. Isaac talking about the findings means the autopsy report is done. Isaac saying *that whole baby problem*—

"You're so full of shit," Carter says, yells almost. "Honestly, *fuck* you. You don't know a thing about Whitney or me or what happened to her."

"My dad's the head of the police department," Isaac says, and the gloat is audible in his voice. "You have no idea what I know."

There's a noise then, a thud, and a loud grunt, and then Carter's voice again. "Stay down," he says. "Where you belong."

Luca keeps still, her gaze flicking from Jada to the place in the trees where the two boys are—were? Carter has disappeared, and Isaac—

There's another groan, and he is still on the ground, Luca understands.

So she looks at Jada and says, voice low, "Tell me your brother is lying his ass off." Takes a step toward the other girl, her hand half-raised, finger pointing. "Tell me he can't know what her autopsy report said because there hasn't *been* an autopsy report yet, not that I know about, so he has to be lying."

"Luca—"

"Tell me."

"Fine," Jada says, narrowing her eyes. "There's no autopsy report."

Except Luca can't believe her, can she, not when she's forced Jada to say it. So if what Isaac said isn't wrong, if he has seen the report, then it's real, and who knows how long Detective Charles has had it for, how long he's been keeping it from Luca and her parents—

And if Charles has it, and it's real and a medical examiner has opened Whitney up and looked at her bones and whatever flesh was left inside her and written it all down—

And if she had been pregnant and Carter had known, then the easiest way to make that problem go away was—

"Your fucking family," Luca says, and in the dark, where Jada can't see, she rakes her nails down the inside of her left forearm. Not what she really wants but she just needs something, something, to hurt more than she does inside.

41

Luca leaves Jada there in the trees and walks, legs numb, back inside the tent.

She passes beneath the floral arches, through the light, between the tables scattered with half-empty crystal glasses, abandoned. Everything remains so beautiful even as things shatter.

Takes care of that whole baby problem.

She feels stupid for being even the sharpest slice of surprised. But that changes everything, doesn't it? Because Carter said he loved Whitney, and Luca believed him, but now, now—

Luca knows how it is, boys like Carter. Especially boys who work for their daddies, who are being groomed for takeover, who have trust funds and clauses in those trust funds and soon start to see the world through a lens of who keeps them from what they feel they are rightfully owed and who doesn't. Boys who don't need pregnant girls running around threatening their shiny-bright futures.

She is inside now, and Naomi's right there, straight ahead.

She's dancing, with Madison. Hands twisting in the air above their heads and their dresses swirling together, Naomi spinning graceful tight pirouettes, and it makes her ache to see the both of them. Wishes she could be there with them, slow-motion swaying under the soft lights, but it would feel like a betrayal. How could she dance when Whitney needs her?

Everything, everything she does now feels small and insignificant because Whitney isn't there, and Whitney will *never again* and Whitney *can't* and Whitney *won't*.

Luca's palms itch. What does she do now?

She watches Madison spin Naomi, both laughing like they've been friends for a lifetime, and suddenly she wants Naomi. Just to hold her, just to feel the press of someone else's warm skin and beating heart, to feel the reassurance of living. And to hear Naomi whisper into her ear that they can do this, that Whitney won't fade into nothing.

Luca steps onto the dance floor, and that is when she sees him.

Carter.

Across the dance floor, leaning with a drink in his hand. His tie undone and shirtsleeves pushed up and god, he's always such rumpled rich-white-boy perfection that if she didn't know him, Luca would hate him in this second.

If I didn't know him, she thinks.

Do I really know him?

Carter's watching Naomi and Madison, everyone's watching Naomi and Madison, even Madison's brand-new husband, standing off to the side with this pathetic lovesick smile.

Then Carter's eyes are on Luca, and she forces herself not to give anything away as he gives her this two-finger salute that she knows is supposed to mean only *I'm here* but feels closer to *I see you, Luca.*

Which is illogical, because he doesn't know that she overheard him and Isaac. He doesn't know what she's thinking now.

(That he killed Whitney.)

(That Carter killed Whitney.)

Luca forces herself to smile back at him, *killermurdererkiller*, and then the band ends the song and before she can move Naomi's there in front of her, fingers wrapping around Luca's wrist. "You," she says. "Dance with me."

"No," Luca says, and Naomi's smile drops a fraction. "I need to tell you something. Come with me so I can tell you something, okay?"

She slides her wrist through Naomi's grip, until their hands are pressed together, Naomi's warm where hers is cold. The pulse in Naomi's thumb tick-ticks against Luca's skin. *A-live, a-live,* it seems to tell her, and Luca exhales.

Yes, she thinks. *But for how long?*

42

Luca drives with the top down, hands tightly gripping the wheel as the island blurs past.

Naomi's hand rests on Luca's knee, but Naomi doesn't say anything, not even about the sky, which fills with fireworks behind them.

When Luca pulls into their street it is like they are back, weeks ago, so much different but the scene outside Luca's house the same.

The police cruiser angled on the driveway, and lights on inside the house.

Luca gets out of the car and walks in the house without really registering it, just barely recognizing that Naomi is following right behind her.

There, in the kitchen. Just Detective Charles this time, and her parents sitting there, her mom with her head in her hands and her dad already crying, and all three look up when they hear Luca's heels on the tile.

She is half-afraid and entirely electric because she is still his suspect, isn't she, and just because she heard what she did doesn't mean that he is going to do the right thing and follow the correct path, so maybe he is here for her, again, but she has to know—

"The autopsy," is all she says, tilting her chin up. "The autopsy?"

And if Detective Charles is surprised that she says it, somehow already seems to know, then he doesn't show it. Instead he looks at her for a long minute, like he's weighing what to say.

In the end he says nothing. Only nods.

And Luca knows.

Not me.

Carter.

43

—*blunt force trauma.*

cracked skull.

almost instantaneous death but—*also showed*—*and the medical examiner believes*—

—*yes, that is what it means. Pregnant. I know it's*—

Doing everything we can.

44

If she can't have her sister, she can have the next best thing.

When she gets to Madison's house, it's in disarray: the remnants of the wedding being swept out of sight, caterers clearing up, maids cleaning.

Madison meets her at the door, red-eyed, but whether that is from the drinking or grieving, Luca can't tell. "What a way to start married life," she says when she sees Luca. "My husband's on a plane halfway across the world and I'm here finding out my best friend was most likely murdered by the boy she loved. Because she was *pregnant?* Luca—"

She pulls Luca toward her, and Luca falls into her hug. "Tell me they're going to get it right this time," Luca says, in a crackly whisper that is all she can manage. "Tell me they're going to do something about Carter."

Madison squeezes her harder, pressing the air right out of Luca's lungs. "God, I hope so," she says. "And then I wonder if it even matters because it won't bring her back, and then I get mad for even thinking that—"

"No, no." Luca disentangles herself. "No, I know exactly

what you mean. Like, sometimes—" She catches herself. *Sometimes I wonder why I am trying so hard to escape the curse, sometimes I wonder what the point of being alive even is if I have to do it without Whitney now too,* but those are the kinds of things she can't say out loud. Not unless she wants people making panicked phone calls and watching her take her meds, like anytime she talks about suicide means she's inches away from actually doing something. People who don't constantly think about killing themselves don't understand the difference between the active and the passive. The plan, and the just ever-present knowledge that it's an option. Even Madison wouldn't understand that when Luca thinks, *What is the point of being alive without my sister?* she doesn't mean she's going to kill herself. She takes her meds, she goes to therapy when she needs it. She manages. She is safe.

From herself, at least. From the curse?

Never.

Madison's looking at her intently. "What?" she says. "What is it?"

Luca scrubs a hand across her face. "I don't know," she says, but she is thinking about *safety*, and the curse, and how much danger she is putting both Madison and Naomi in by being around them. By allowing herself to love them. If the curse is taking everything and everyone that matters from her, then how long is it until it destroys them, too?

And she is thinking about what her mother said before, about justice. *None of it's going to bring her back.* "I just feel like . . . nothing here is ever going to really change."

"It will," Madison says. She takes Luca's face in her hands and watches her for a long minute, her eyes bright, shimmering through the red. It is grounding, to Luca, the steady touch and the long stare. Like Madison is a counterweight to her pain, balancing her. "It will, Luca. Or at least, that's what I want to believe."

Luca nods, Madison's fingers warm on her cheeks. It will. It will.

45

Luca stands on her balcony, watching as her mother swims slow, serene laps of the pool.

Her mom never goes into the pool. Doesn't like the way the chlorine sticks to her skin, or what it does to her highlights. But it's been three days since the wedding, three days since Charles came and told them about the autopsy, and it has thrown them all, Luca thinks. Like discovering Whitney is dead all over again, the slicing and measuring of her body a secondary sentence.

Pregnant, Luca thinks for the thousandth time. Yet another thing Luca didn't know about her sister. *Would Whitney have told me, eventually?* She doesn't even know what Whitney would have done, what she was maybe already planning on doing. Luca would have assumed Whit would choose an abortion, but that was before, when she thought she knew everything there was to know about her older sister. She never spoke about wanting kids, but maybe she did. Maybe Whit would never have told Luca and gotten it taken care of. Maybe she would have asked Luca to go with her, and afterward they would have shared tacos and a hysterical laugh that Whitney came that close to upending her whole life.

It doesn't matter now. Carter made the choice for all of them.

Luca makes her way downstairs and outside, skin instantly clammy from the midday sun. Today is the Fourth of July. She has invites to a handful of parties sitting in her inbox, and she imagines people hesitating before adding her name to their lists, wondering whether it's worse to invite the dead girl's sister or to *not* invite her.

Today is the Fourth of July, Luca thinks. *Today marks the day that Laney Hart died.*

When she reaches the edge of the pool, she sits and slides her feet into the water, and her mom swims over.

"Hi, baby," she says, and Luca remembers not *that night* but the day preceding it, how Whitney came in from wherever she'd been and kicked off her heels. How Luca was the one in the pool and Whitney was sitting right where she is now.

"Hi," Luca says to her mom. "What are you doing?"

Emilia smiles. "I was looking at the water," she says, "and it seemed silly, all of a sudden. That I never swim in here, because I don't like the way it smells. What kind of reason is that, really? I like to swim. So I thought I should do it, while I can."

There's the unsaid that lingers around everything lately, the whole *because life could end for any one of us at any moment* thing.

But Luca doesn't say anything about that, only nods and looks beyond her mother, to the sea.

"We're getting closer," her mom says, the words floating up to Luca's ears. "It'll be over soon, Luca."

She looks at her mom, hair wet, no makeup, the mirrored creases between her eyebrows. She believes it, Luca can tell. That this might really be the end of things.

And Luca wishes she could feel the same, but she won't, not until Carter is in custody, has confessed to the truth of everything.

"You know what that means?" Emilia squints up at her. "You don't need to keep looking for anyone or anything. You can stop."

"I have," Luca says. "I'm done with that. I don't know what I was thinking."

"I know," her mom says, and she pushes off the wall, gliding through the water turned diamond by the sun. "Look at that," she says, turning onto her back. "It's almost over."

46

The next day she and Naomi are lying on her bed, her head by Naomi's feet, the hushed sound of the ocean coming through the open balcony doors. "I love that sound," Luca says, and she closes her eyes. "Sometimes I feel like I shouldn't. Like I shouldn't love the water at all anymore, because of how Polly died. But I still do. Do you think that's weird?"

"You are a water sign." Naomi's voice drifts down to her. "It makes sense to me."

"You stopped driving," Luca says without opening her eyes. "Maybe I should be more like you."

"I didn't—" Naomi pauses. "You should do whatever you want. You should swim in every ocean in the world, if that's what you want."

This is painful, Luca thinks. Look at them. Listen to them. Talking about the ocean because there's nothing else to talk about, not while they're in this limbo. Purgatory waiting period.

She opens her eyes. She's hungry now.

Luca draws a fingertip across Naomi's ankle, watching for a reaction, the way Naomi's foot flexes. "Tickles," Naomi says.

"Yeah?" Luca turns her head and kisses the same spot. "What about that?"

It's that graying early-dusk light in Luca's bedroom, when the sun is still there but the brightness is fading, and the idea of artificial light is too much of an intrusion to bear. It's the kind of light she likes to look at Naomi in. Her soft, dark eyes, heavy lids, half a smile. She is made for dusk and purple sunsets and starlight.

"Sometimes I wonder how I ever thought I wasn't gay," Naomi says, and then she's rolling over, pushing up on her knees and crawling up to Luca, on the same level now. "Hi."

Luca stretches up, puts her arms around Naomi's neck, and pulls her down. She presses her face into Naomi's skin, always ocean salted. Not afraid anymore. "Hi."

"I miss you."

"I'm right here."

"Not always," Naomi says, her words warm beside Luca's ear. "Not all the time."

"I'm here now," Luca says, and sinks into the feel of Naomi. Her girl.

Sometimes she is turned on, thinking sex, thinking how she wants to touch Naomi, feel her, make her come. Sometimes she wants this the most. The slow, quiet embrace. The weight of Naomi around her.

I love you, she thinks. A revelation. *I love you.*

The buzzing of one of their phones cuts through their quiet, and they roll apart, each searching. Luca finds hers first, and it's hers that is ringing.

Naomi puts her chin on Luca's shoulder. "Who is it?"

"Beth," Luca says, and then answers with a clipped, "What do you want?"

"Luca," Beth says, her voice faraway, and Luca can't tell whether it's the connection or her own ears or the fact that somehow, suddenly, she absolutely knows what Beth is about to say. "It's Carter."

Luca curls her other hand into a fist, nails digging into skin. "What about him?" *Say it. Say what I want to hear, Beth.*

"They just arrested him," Beth says. "They just arrested Carter for Whitney's murder."

47

It takes them only ten minutes to cross the island, Luca driving too fast like she always does lately, speeding toward the station.

"*Luca,*" Naomi says, and first Luca thinks it is because of the speed, she forgets how Naomi hates it, but then she realizes it's the red light Naomi is pointing to. She slams on the brakes, snapping both of them forward a little.

"Sorry," she says, as the light goes green, as she pulls away and takes the next turn.

Naomi says nothing, only puts her hands on the dash as Luca swings sharply into the parking lot.

And there ahead of them is a car, with its lights off, an officer climbing out of the driver's side.

If it were a movie, Luca thinks, the moment would be in slow motion. It would probably be raining, not another now-purple sunset, and the cruiser's lights would be on, flashing blue and red against that rain. The camera would pan their faces as they watched Carter being taken from the back seat, his hands cuffed behind his back, and a suitably dramatic song would soundtrack it all—a piano cover of some eighties song turned mournful for the moment.

But of course none of that happens.

All that happens is that she throws the car into park and they get out, in time to watch the officer take Carter from the police car and up the steps, toward the station doors.

And then, as if he knows the cinematic version that Luca wants, Carter turns right before the doors. Finds the two girls on the other side of the parking lot.

She hears his words in her mind: *I loved her. I still love her.*

Luca holds her breath as he stares at them, his eyes shockingly blue in a blood-drained face.

I see her. I think I see her, every day.

The officer pulls him in and Carter keeps watching them, even as he disappears inside the building.

I don't know if that's better or worse than never seeing her at all.

48

It's another sunset when Luca takes the road she so rarely does. The one that winds and climbs its way above the water they were never supposed to swim in. Above the slice of soft sand that cradles the sharp rocks, far down beneath the bridge that is the only real way out of this place.

Two days.

That's how long Carter has been in custody, not free to go home yet even though his daddy's lawyers are working on it, she knows, and that means he'll be out soon.

Luca would give anything to know what was said in the station after he went inside, to know the panic he was feeling—

Was it panic?

Or was he calm, maybe? Does he know exactly what he's doing, does he have full faith that he's going to get through this unscathed?

Luca turns a sharp right without really looking, cutting across two lanes of traffic and leaving angry horns behind her. It's too much for her, this island, tonight. Feels too much almost always, lately.

She's been sitting in her house all day wondering about Carter and missing her sister. Wishing she could be someplace else, somewhere this isn't happening, and then before she could think too much she had her keys in her hand. Out to the car, twisting the key so hard in the ignition it could snap clean in half, but it didn't and then she was driving and then she was heading for the bridge.

Now it rears up out of the darkening sky, the steel that holds it steady in the high winds far above, and Luca tightens her grip on the steering wheel. It's empty, like it usually is at this hour. Sometimes people race across it, winter Friday nights with nothing better to do, nothing they could ever want to do more than make a mockery of the escape route, because who would ever want to escape?

I do. I do.

The bridge is right there and Luca pushes her car faster, faster, almost—

She hits the brakes.

Seat belt tight across her chest, a flat punch, and she exhales a rush of air but the car stops.

At the edge of the world, it feels like.

Luca sits there for a minute before pulling over to the side and turning the engine off. There's only the rush of water below and the pounding of blood in her ears. Nothing else. No one coming for her, no one knowing even that she's here, what she knows, what she can feel burying her.

She gets out of the car.

Walks up to the bridge but stops short of setting foot on it.

Down below is the place where Polly's demise began. Across, the other side is not so far, really, but it's a distance enough. Another world over there.

She looks at her feet, black flats she doesn't remember putting on. Doesn't remember most of what she wears lately, just picks something from the floor of her bedroom and goes.

Walk.

One step. All you need is one step, and you'd be off the island. Isn't that what you want?

So walk, *Luca.*

Luca turns around, turns her back on the world outside Parris. Instead she looks down at the water beneath her, the water that filled Polly's lungs until she was no more, and wonders what it would be like to drown too.

Her therapist has told her, before, that these ideas of hers, they're only thoughts. Whenever she thinks about picking up a kitchen knife to stab herself through the arm, envisions herself pinned to the counter, the knife sliced cleanly through flesh and bone—it is only a thought. Not something she has to act on, not even something she has to give weight to.

Luca thinks, sometimes, that they're her comfort. At first they were terrifying, yes: nobody *wants* to constantly be thinking of a hundred different ways to end their life. But as you get used to it, as you learn how to differentiate between active and passive, as you learn that this is just the way your brain functions and not always an indicator that you don't want to be on this earth anymore—

The familiarity, the pattern, it becomes close. For Luca,

anyway. They became something she could rely on, something she didn't worry about.

Times like now. When Carter, a boy she has known as long as she can remember, is suspected of killing her sister.

The wind off the ocean whips her hair into her face, and Luca catches it, drags it out of her eyes and mouth. Makes her think of the good part of that summer, the weeks before Polly died, riding their candy-colored bikes, and Luca's hair always getting in the way and Polly always laughing at her with that rainwater sound.

She wants to smile at the memory, but beneath her the white-tipped waves serpentine, ivory foam like veins of marble, and all she can think is that Polly doesn't get to laugh anymore. Whitney doesn't get to dance barefoot, curls stuck to her lip gloss, dress slipping off a shoulder.

Maybe today is the day she does it. Takes a step off the edge, the step she's always thinking about.

Luca turns her face away from the water, up to the sky, and watches the last pieces of sun break through her eyelids.

No, she thinks. *Not before I get my answers.*

49

She's sitting outside the station now and she's checking her phone and she's looking at her texts to Naomi, left on *delivered*.

thinking about doing something real stupid

u wanna stop me???

Obviously not.

Luca flips the mirror down and attempts deep, steadying breaths as she applies a slick of red lipstick, pulls at a spiral strand of curls, narrows her eyes with liner smudged beneath. A look of armor.

Then she gets out of the car.

The minute she walks into the station, though, Officer Harold is there, barring her way. Gently, though, as if his frame in front of the corridor leading to Charles's office is only a coincidence. "Ms. Thomas—"

Luca cuts him off. "Ms. *Laine* Thomas," she says, as always. No one in this place can get it right. "Is he here?"

"Detective Charles is not available," Harold says. "But why don't you take a seat—"

Luca looks beyond him and can see, clearly, the shape of

Charles behind his office door. "Tell him I'm here," she says, curt, forceful. "I need to speak to him."

And she sees behind Harold as the door swings open and Charles comes down the hall, a weariness to his walk. "It's okay, Greg," he says, clapping his colleague on the shoulder. "I'll handle this."

Officer Harold glances at Luca and then nods, once. "Sure thing."

He disappears into the hall, and Charles sighs as he looks at Luca. "What can I do for you this time?"

"I need to talk to Cart—"

"Absolutely not." Charles doesn't even let her finish, and he's looking at her now like she's lost it. "He's a suspect in custody. You are the victim's family member. I can't let you do that."

Luca scans the room, the bulletin boards with sparse notices, the empty desks, the receptionist out front acting like she's not listening intently. "I'm not going to *do* anything," she says. "I'm not going to do something to screw up the process or whatever it is you think I'm going to do. I just—"

Charles narrows his eyes. "You just what, Luca? Don't you think you've inserted yourself into this investigation enough?"

"Me?" She stares. "*You* were the one who accused me, made me a suspect."

He softens a little, like he's actually sorry. "It was all in the course of the investigation—"

She holds a hand up. "Please," she says, and hates the way it sounds, hates that she's pleading with this man who not so long ago thought she was responsible for her sister's death. "I need to hear him say it. I need him to tell me what he did."

Charles puts a hand on her shoulder and bends so he and Luca are eye to eye. "You need to go home," he says. "Go home, Luca."

She walks out—not like she has another choice—but she doesn't get into her car, will not obey Charles.

Instead she walks along the side of the building and takes out a cigarette, lighting it with trembling hands.

I just wanted to hear him say it, she thinks. Just wanted to look him in the eye and get the truth, a thing that she is finding fucking rare on this island lately.

Luca exhales, flicks the ash from her cig. Would it have been so hard for Charles to let her in, talk to the boy who killed her sister?

Boy. He's a man, really. Shouldn't infantilize him. He was man enough to cheat with Whitney, to get her pregnant, to make the choice about how he was going to fix that. Deal with his mess.

Her hands won't stop shaking and she lets the cigarette fall to the ground, grinds it out with her heel. It's quiet outside the station. The parking lot is half-empty, the only sound wind in the trees that line the perimeter.

What now?

Luca pulls her car keys from her back pocket and is about to move when a cop whose name she doesn't know comes out the front doors. She is followed by a girl.

Dark hair, long legs, burnished-sand skin.

Luca stills. *Naomi?*

It is so jarring, unexpected, to see Naomi here that Luca doesn't do anything but watch as she hurries down the front steps, leaving the officer behind. She crosses the parking lot without a look behind her, heading for a car in the corner with its lights on bright, and then she gets in fast, and Luca watches as the car—Naomi's mom's, she sees now—rolls out of the station and away.

She's gone so fast that Luca could almost believe she was never really there, that she hallucinated the entire thing.

But then there is another cop coming up the steps, Browning, she thinks, and he nods at the one who brought Naomi out. "What was that about?"

The first officer steps forward, moonlight glancing off her blond hair pulled back into a severe bun. "Charles wanted her in," she says. "Wanted to shore up the sister's alibi."

Luca steps back, pressing herself to the wall so she is hidden in the shadow of the entryway. The sister. *Me.*

"Thought that was all settled," Browning is saying.

"Yeah, but you know he wants to nail this," the woman says. "Wants to make sure the Muszynski kid and his lawyers can't pull up another viable suspect."

"She stick to it?"

The woman nods and the two of them begin walking into the building. "She was a mess in the room, though. Turns out she was involved in something a couple years ago, in her hometown. Almost killed a girl in a car wreck."

Axis tilt.

Luca should be used to it by now, but it still takes the ground from beneath her, a feeling in the pit of her stomach like gravity has gone.

Almost killed a girl in a car wreck.

But that's Naomi they're talking about, and she never did anything, and Anya isn't *almost* dead, she's *d-e-a-d* dead.

The officers are still talking as they disappear into the station, but Luca can't listen anymore, because all she can think is—

Almost?

50

When she gets home she can see lights blazing at Naomi's house, but she doesn't go over there. It would be too easy, she knows, to let Naomi give her exactly what she wants, to hear her raspy voice explain it all away. *No, Luca, of course I didn't lie. No, Luca, why would you even listen to anything they say? No, Luca. No.*

Instead she goes inside and up to her room, knowing what she's going to do. Almost resigned to it, already tired thinking of what she's about to unreel.

But she does it anyway.

She gets her laptop and opens a new browser window. Taps her thumb on the space bar.

Anya, Naomi has always said. Just *Anya,* no last name. The accident that killed her happened on a Saturday, and it was a violent and instantaneous death, and that's all Luca has to go on.

So first she brings up Naomi's social media and scrolls back as far as she can, looking for this girl. She hasn't done this before, because— Well. The nice reason is to say it felt like a violation.

The real reason is that she didn't want to see Anya at all, to see this girl that Naomi had loved. What if she were prettier? What if she were better?

Even though she was dead. That's the kind of bitch Luca is, deep down, jealous of a dead girl.

But there's no sign of anybody else in any of Naomi's photos. Mostly landscapes and blurry night-sky images, the things Luca's seen her posting of Parris mirrored in these older pictures. Nobody tagged in anything, and any old comments lead to locked accounts.

Luca sits back. So.

In the search bar she types the name of Naomi's hometown followed by *Anya*, followed by *crash*.

Simple, easy, but it works, because when she presses the return button, the page fills with results.

Crash Closes Highway

York Heights Teen Involved in Highway Accident

Teen Crash Driver Twice Legal Limit

York Heights Gymnast, Crash Victim, Finds New Hope

Luca stills. It's dated more recently than the others, only three months ago.

That's what she's looking for, isn't it?

She clicks.

The text loads faster than the pictures, and for that she's glad, because she still doesn't want to see this girl. Not until she knows she's wrong, that this article isn't actually saying what she thinks.

But—*"What?"*

She breathes the word as she touches fingers to her lips, reading slowly.

> *Anya Pearson, 17, was coming home from a party with her gymnastics teammates last year when the car she was in crashed into the median. The driver of the vehicle, who we cannot name for legal reasons, escaped without injury, despite her blood alcohol level being twice the legal limit. Ms. Pearson, a former state champion, was not so lucky: her injuries were so extensive that she was placed in a medically induced coma for three weeks while surgeons tried to save her, putting her acceptance to Louisiana State University into jeopardy. But a year later, she's almost fully recovered and about to embark on her most challenging journey yet: staging her gymnastics comeback. Ms. Pearson says—*

Not dead.

51

She does not sleep.

At sunrise she goes down to the ocean, sits and watches the small morning waves wash onto the shore, pull back out, repeat. Rhythmic and hypnotic, but not enough to wipe what she has learned from her mind.

Anya Pearson is not dead.

Naomi has lied.

The thought makes her sick. Physically, viscerally—she threw up several times throughout the night, the sourness coating her tongue after. Naomi lied. Naomi *lied*.

Naomi—

"Hey."

Luca startles and looks up at the shadow blocking out the rising sun. Naomi is here, finally.

"Where were you?" Luca asks.

Naomi sits beside Luca, pushing her hair behind her ears. She's wearing cutoffs and a fraying sweatshirt, defense against the slight chill that comes before the sun reaches full power. She looks like nothing can touch her, the epitome of summer girls, rich girls, armored against the worst thing.

But perhaps she *is the worst thing,* Luca thinks.

"Busy," is all Naomi says in answer to Luca's question.

"Busy," Luca repeats. "Busy, busy, always busy. Wanna know where I've been?"

"Somewhere stupid?"

Luca tips her head to the side. "So you do actually *read* my messages. You just choose not to reply. Nice to know."

Naomi has the grace to look at least some small part ashamed. "I didn't—"

"I've been thinking," Luca interrupts. She stares out at the water, calm on the surface, its riptides and stealth deadly currents hidden beneath. Just like herself: calm on the surface, raging below. "I've been thinking about you."

"Me?"

"And Anya." Luca shifts, turns a fraction so she can see Naomi's expression. "I mean, it's hard. Right? All this with Whit, with Carter. I know it's different. The way she died, it was different. But . . . I don't know. I feel like maybe you don't feel like you can talk about it, like I'll think you're being self-centered or something, but I won't. So you can tell me, you know. Tell me all about it."

Going too heavy, perhaps, but even though she already knows, Luca still wants to give Naomi a chance. Maybe not an out, because how is there a way out of this, but—

God, she just wants it not to be happening. She wants to go back to the time when Naomi was the girl she loved and she still had something *good* in her life.

"It's . . ." Naomi raises her shoulders. "It's not about me right now. I don't need to talk about her."

"Come on," Luca says. "It's okay. I don't mind."

"Well, I do," Naomi says. "I don't want to talk about her."

Luca digs her toes into the sand. Right. Right, she never does. Which made some kind of sense before because Luca knows what it is to be exhausted by the memories. To want to keep it all to yourself, sometimes. Selfish.

But that's not what this is, is it?

"Did you ever look Polly up?"

Naomi's head snaps up. "What?"

"I don't know if you ever did," Luca says. "I didn't look Anya up. I thought it would be wrong, somehow. She was yours, after all. Not mine. And you told me everything about her, everything about what happened, and I had you here. I had you to talk to about it all so I didn't need to look anything up, I didn't need to be that person I hate, looking for all the bloody details. Did you?"

"No," Naomi says, the word drawn out. Confused. "No, I never looked her up."

Luca nods, at first just the one motion but then like she can't stop, head rocking and rocking, parallel to the waves. "You could have," she says. "But you would only find out everything I already told you." She pauses. "Because I told the truth. And you—"

She fixes her stare on Naomi. "You lied."

There is an interminable moment when there is no sound but the sea, no movement but the rise and fall of chests.

A slow pause in time where, Luca feels, things could possibly go back. Things could at least stand still. She could still live in a version of her world where she gets to hold Naomi's hand, where this girl is her girl, where somebody knows who and what she is.

And then Naomi says, "You don't understand."

Every calm surface inch of Luca is burned off in the anger spiraling up. "I don't *understand*? What is there to *understand*, Naomi? She's not *dead*. I looked her up, and Anya Pearson, your best friend, the girl who you told me died in that car accident, is *not dead*! So tell me what about that I don't *understand*."

"I lost her," Naomi says, hands twisting together. Nerves or a show? "Okay? That's still the same, that was always the same. I never lied about that and how it felt. She almost died in the accident and I haven't seen her since then, I couldn't see her—"

"Because you were driving the car." Luca shifts away from Naomi, the weak sun hitting so that she can barely see Naomi's face. "Because you almost ruined her life, because it was *your fault*."

Naomi shakes her head, and for a split second Luca thinks she's saying, *No, you got it wrong*, and she would gladly accept that, except then Naomi says, "It was a *mistake*. It could have easily been the other way around—"

"But it wasn't!" Luca can't stand it a second more, scrambles to her feet, kicking up sand. "It *wasn't* the other way around. And she *almost* died. And you *don't* know what it's like to lose somebody, then."

"I do—"

"You *don't*! She's not dead, is she! She's alive. You could go there right now and see her again." Luca wipes at her cheeks, salty. "See her face. Touch her. Feel how alive she is. But my girls, they're gone. Whitney and Polly, they're forever gone. There's nothing left of them for me but you, you could have her. And instead of being grateful for that, instead of being honest with me, you lied."

"You think I wanted to lie?" Naomi's up on her knees, those dark eyes of hers searching, hungry. "I didn't come here like, oh yeah, I'm going to tell everyone I have a dead friend, like— who would do that? I wasn't going to tell anyone about Anya at all. But then I met you and it just came out, her name just came out, and I knew I couldn't tell you the truth. The whole reason I wasn't going to tell anyone was because I know what happens when I do, things like this happen, people decide they know everything about me and they decide I'm a bad person, and this was supposed to be a fresh start for me. A place to get away."

Luca laughs, bitterly. "You picked the perfect place."

"Maybe this place is a mess, but I got here and there you were," Naomi says. "And I didn't know about Polly when I said Anya was dead. I didn't do it on purpose. But once you told me about Polly, it was too late. And then I thought— it wasn't entirely untrue. You lost a friend. So did I. It just wasn't exactly the same, and I knew if I told you everything it would ruin us before we ever started—"

"There was no 'us,'" Luca says. "You were you and I was me, we were nothing and no one to each other—"

"Not to me." Naomi's shaking her head earnestly. "You were never *nothing* to me. As soon as I saw you, I was—it's still the same, Luca. It's still us. You, me. I get you, you get me, all that."

But Luca's backing off. "It's not the same still," she says, through the knot that has formed in her chest and climbed into her throat. "There's everything I told you because I trusted you, and now that's gone. And all those moments like—you said you don't drive because of what happened to her, but it's really because *you* happened to her. You told me you couldn't remember her *voice* anymore. And I *felt* that, I *got* it, but it's another *lie* because you know what, you *could* hear it again."

"Wrong," Naomi says, standing now too. "I can't hear her. I can't see her. She'll never see me."

"And why?" Luca takes a step forward, looking up at Naomi. God, she is so beautiful. That is all she can see, looking up at her. She is so beautiful still, and she looks wretched right now, and there is still so much of Luca that wants nothing more than to wrap her arms around Naomi, hold her close, feel their hearts beat out of time.

But she can't, because it's all falling apart now. Their relationship. Their friendship. All built on a false foundation, cracking into a hundred pieces now that Luca's unearthed it.

Anya isn't dead, but Whitney still is, Polly still is. So what now? What's left?

"She won't see you because *you* did that to her," Luca says. "It's your fault. It's all your own fault except you refuse to own up to it—"

"That's all I'm trying to do!" Naomi explodes. "*God*, Luca, you think I wanna be in therapy all those hours, listening to her tell me all the things I did wrong? But I go even when I don't want to because she's trying to teach me how to accept what I did, how not to *blame* myself forever while not forgetting what I did. Because I know, I know what I did to Anya. Of course. You think you forget something like that? You think I quit gymnastics because I *wanted* to? I got kicked out of my gym and ostracized from everywhere else because Anya Pearson, state champ, had her career ruined by me. You think you forget that it was *your fault* when all you can ever think about is the wreck you walked away from?"

Luca shakes her head, curls flying around her face. "It doesn't matter," she says. "Because you decided for me how I was going to feel about it. How I was going to feel about *you*. Before you knew me at all. You wanted to lie more than trust me, and then once you did know about Polly, you didn't come clean. You decided to keep on going, to use it, to use *her*, instead of being honest."

"You never would have wanted me," Naomi says, and she's crying now, same as Luca, trying her hardest to get the words out. "If I had told you what really happened, you never would have looked at me again, and I needed a friend. I needed you."

It digs deep into Luca, latches beneath her skin, that word. *Needed.* No one has ever needed her. And no one has ever wanted her the way Naomi did. Does.

And as much as she blames Naomi for all of this, there is a tiny seed of guilt blooming inside herself. Because wasn't that how she felt too? That she needed Naomi. Or needed *someone*, and then Naomi came along and Luca decided yes, she was the one, she would fix it all. Put all her hopes and raw emotions into this stranger, because how much does she really know about Naomi, anyway? Never asked her too much about her life before Parris, if she missed it, what she was like as a kid. What she wants to do next, who she wants to be when she is twenty, twenty-five, thirty.

No. Luca just saw a girl who would fill the void and that was enough for her.

She finds herself reaching toward Naomi, fingers stretching across the gap between them. An inch farther, and she could touch her. Have Naomi back.

Naomi pushes dark hair out of her face, shaking. "Luca," she says, "please—"

Luca pulls her hand back.

It's too late.

"I thought I knew you," Luca says. "I thought you were everything I ever wanted, but you're a liar." Like everybody, Luca is finding out: Whitney and Carter and Beth and now Naomi, all liars, all hiding things to keep themselves protected, and fuck anybody it hurts, right?

The gap between them widens, Luca can feel it. The tension building, taut and unbearable. "*You* are a fucking curse, Naomi."

She turns her back on the chasm before she can fall right in.

52

She's been driving around for hours. Aimless, worthless.

Can't talk to anyone, because who does she have left now? Only Madison, and she can't quite bear to tell Madison what an idiot she's been. How she let this liar into their lives, let her become part of their grief when she is only another vulture.

You do things so sexy and you don't know it.

Let Naomi claw her way in because she said pretty little things like that, did pretty little things like letting Luca cry and smiling at her and being the perfect kind of bitch for Luca to fall for.

She ends up in the hills but stays away from the memorial. *Maybe they'll put Whitney's name up there,* she thinks. Now that they know who killed her. She can have her plaque, and Carter can rot, and life can go on. Like it did after Polly, like it seems to do after every horror on this island.

Somehow she falls asleep right there, drifts off into a nightmare of crashing cars and laughing monsters.

When she wakes it's with a jolt, and she rubs at her eyes, disoriented when she sees the clock on the dash and how much time has passed. "I have to go," she whispers under her breath, talking to no one. "I have to—"

When her phone rings, Luca stares at it where it lies on the passenger seat. Maybe it's Naomi.

So she won't answer. That's all she has to do, not answer. Not even look, not let herself look. What could Naomi even say to make this better, right? There's nothing. Luca gave every raw, flayed inch of herself to Naomi, and in the end it was nothing but a lie.

Luca closes her eyes and presses her hands over her ears. The worst part is how not surprised she feels. On one level, close to the surface? Yes. She thought she knew the story, and now it's all different. Of course it hurts, of course it's a pain like being caught in a current, scraping your flesh against hidden rocks beneath the water. But when Luca searches for a deeper shock, some kind of confusion, there's . . . nothing.

Her phone's still ringing, or ringing again, maybe, and she doesn't want to give Naomi the satisfaction of answering, but she can't bear to hear its insistent buzzing any longer.

So Luca snatches it up to turn it off, get some peace, but then it's not Naomi calling at all.

It's Jada's name on the screen, and she can't imagine why Jada of all people would be calling, but she answers. "What?" she snaps. "What is it?"

She expects a standard retort from Jada. This is how they work now, isn't it? One of them says something too sharp, the other bats it back. But Jada's voice almost hums when she speaks. "Meet me at the market," she says. "Same as before. Parking lot. I have something you want to see."

53

When Luca pulls into the parking lot, Jada's already there, leaning against her car, flipping something between her fingers.

Luca parks but doesn't take her hands off the steering wheel. Exhales as she stares out the windshield. She's not sure why she came, except that hum of Jada's voice called to her.

Sounded like the Jada from before. When they were the kind of friends who laughed high and loud at whatever they felt like, when it was still the three of them.

After a moment she gets out, begins walking over to Jada. Her pixie cut is growing out a little, the ends curling against her neck, and she nods when she sees Luca. "Get in," she calls, gesturing to her beat-up car.

"Where are we going?" Luca calls back.

When Luca is closer, Jada shakes her head. "Nowhere," she says. "I need you to see something, and I need no one else to see it."

"Fine." Luca slides into the passenger seat, sinking into the softness.

"Just you?"

"What?"

Jada's watching her. "No Naomi," she says. "What, you have a fight or something?"

"None of your fucking business," Luca says, even though it's stupid and will only make Jada dig further.

Except Jada only rolls her eyes. "Whatever." She reaches into the back and returns with a laptop, balancing it on the center console. "So. I was . . . I don't know. I know they have Carter. I know it's all kind of done now, but—"

"But what? You wanted to screw with me some more?"

"Will you *listen*? Jesus." Jada leans back. "I was looking for . . . I don't know. Something. Everything. I don't like that somehow my dad managed to get something past me. The autopsy report, you know? Like—how did Isaac know about it before I did? Was I not paying enough attention? How did I miss that?"

"Okay, you were a bad spy," Luca says. "So what?"

"So I was looking on his computer," Jada says. "And I found the autopsy report."

Luca sinks, her shoulders, her spirit. "That's it?" she says. "Jada. I already know what it says. Everyone knows what it says."

"Yeah, I didn't think it mattered either," Jada says. "Until I saw the second one."

There is a moment of silence as what Jada has just said ticks its way through Luca's brain.

The *second* one. The second one?

"What?" Luca's breath catches on the word, barely making it out. "Jada. What?"

Jada plugs a flash drive into the laptop and taps on the trackpad before turning it so Luca can see the screen. "Let's play a game," she says.

"No games—"

"It's an easy one," Jada says. "Spot the difference."

Luca swallows. It's hard to tell whether Jada's for real, like always. She's good at that. Making herself hard to read.

But there's a hardness in her eyes right now, the kind of serious that says maybe it is real, maybe this matters.

So Luca looks.

Jada has focused in on one particular section, and Luca finds herself grateful for that. She doesn't have to read anything more about Whitney's shattered skull, her blood. Just a short section—on the left:

Female genital system: The structures are within normal limits. Examination of the pelvic area indicates the victim had not given birth but was pregnant at the time of death. There is no evidence of recent sexual activity. Vaginal fluid samples are removed for analysis.

And on the right:

Female genital system: The structures are within normal limits. Examination of the pelvic area indicates the victim had not given birth and was not pregnant at the time of death. There is no evidence of—

She stares over the laptop at Jada. "They're the same," she says. "They're the same except for one of them says Whitney was pregnant, and the other says she wasn't."

A grim smile spreads over Jada's face, slow. "Right," she says. "So—"

"She wasn't pregnant," Luca says, and then again, to herself. "She wasn't pregnant?"

The new information pushes up against the old in her head and she thinks, *Whitney wasn't pregnant when she died* and it makes a quick, relieving kind of sense. Because if there was no pregnancy, then there was no secret—about this, anyway. Whitney wasn't keeping it from her and it's like a piece of her is returned to Luca, suddenly. Maybe she wasn't as far from her sister as she's been beginning to think.

But if she wasn't pregnant—

"Here's the thing," Jada says, cutting into Luca's thoughts. "The one that says she was pregnant is the official report, the one everyone's heard about. The other one? It's dated before the official one. And it was in a pretty deep-down place on my dad's computer. You know, almost like he was trying to hide it."

"So, what?" Luca says. "Either somebody made a mistake, or—" She swallows hard, again. "Somebody really wanted to make it seem like she *was* pregnant."

Neat.

Slick.

"Because what a great way to prove your suspect had a motive, right?" Jada says. "Especially if your victim was having a secret relationship with someone you'd love to say killed her."

Luca's already shaking her head, hair sweeping over her shoulders. "No," she says. "You're saying someone's setting Carter up. That they just want to make it look like he did it."

No. No, Carter *did* do it, he did kill Whitney, because who else could have killed her but the boy who'd gotten her pregnant and stood to lose his girlfriend, his reputation, his entire inheritance?

Except.

It all falls apart, if there's no pregnancy.

If that part is a lie.

Luca pushes back against the seat, hand pressing against the window. This space is too small, the air is too small—

"This is what I wanted," she says, shaking her head again, feeling her teeth catch the inside of her cheek as she speaks quickly, too quickly. "Carter, I mean. Once I heard what your brother said, I wanted him arrested, I wanted him to pay, I believed it was him. I *believed* he did it, but that's what I was supposed to think, wasn't it?"

"The way I see it, this could mean two things," Jada says, and she glances out the window, like someone could be hovering around her car, just waiting to catch them. "One: he did it, but they didn't have the evidence."

"So they faked it."

"Right," Jada says. "Maybe they figure they get him in with this and in time he breaks, confesses. Or two—"

"He didn't do it." Luca exhales. He didn't do it. Is that possible? Is that real?

"He didn't do it, but they know who did," Jada says. "And they're willing to frame Carter to protect this person."

"'They' are willing." Luca eyes Jada. "You know who 'they' is, right?"

"I'm not an idiot," Jada says flatly. "My father. Right? He's clearly a part of this. These are official reports, which I found on my dad's computer. It's not like someone made a fake autopsy report and tried to pass it off as real. This is—they're both real. It's just that one tells the truth, and the other is a lie. So someone with the necessary access and authority changed their findings, and put it in black and white."

Luca swallows hard. Her whole life the curse has felt like a ghost breath on her skin, an apparition of a touch, tight squeeze around her ribs. But this is no ghost. This is solid, real evidence of someone—multiple someones?—twisting the narrative of her sister's life for their own benefit.

"He sat there, in my house, and told us what the autopsy said," Luca says now. "He said it out loud, lied out loud."

"He's good at that," Jada says.

Luca looks at the flash drive, stuck in the laptop. There's the part of her that feels relieved, yes, but there's another part that only sees that drive as yet another piece of her sister ready to be passed around. Hasn't Whitney been through enough, haven't they all gotten their fill of her? *Is there no dignity in death?* she thinks. *How much more of her can be peddled and pawned by the people on this island?*

Luca snatches the drive from Jada's laptop, and Jada glares. "Hey!"

"I have to go," Luca says, and she climbs out of the car, walks fast back to her own, with Jada scrambling to keep up. *What do I do now?*

Her fingers curl around the metal. She is once again unmoored. She was so eager to believe it was Carter, but this throws that all into doubt and maybe it was him, but maybe it wasn't, and her mind just keeps saying the same thing over and over and over again.

What do I do?

"Luca, wait—"

"Go home, Jada." Luca pulls out her keys.

Jada calls out, "You can't just—"

Luca wrenches her driver's-side door open, turns back just for a second to look at Jada. "Thank you for showing me this," she says. "Now go home."

54

Luca drives with the flash drive on the passenger seat and her knuckles white on the wheel.

She can't take this to her mom, not with how she reacted to Luca's investigating before. Her dad—he'll take her mom's side, start fishing out the therapist numbers immediately.

And Naomi—

Luca sucks in a breath between her teeth. No. There's only one place she can go, really, one person she has left. Maybe Madison will know, maybe she'll tell Luca what she should believe. At the very least, maybe she'll look Luca in the eye and tell her it's all going to be okay, even if they both know it's a lie.

Madison is the only one Luca has left.

The gates to the Rivers estate are open, and Luca drives straight up to the main house. She parks haphazardly, the way Whitney always did when they came over, like she was in too much of a hurry to get to Madison to bother straightening out.

She steps out of the car, phone already in hand, and is

about to text Madison, say *i'm outside your house, where are u? bedroom?*

And then there is a shattering crash, a splintered noise coming from inside the house.

Luca's hand slackens, her phone almost falling to the ground. She is about to call out when she catches herself.

No. That sounded like breaking. Sounded like violence.

"Shit." It is quiet, slipping out between closed teeth, and Luca stays still right where she is.

There is somebody inside Madison's house.

Of course there is, her mind whispers. *The curse has come for her, too. The last person you have left. Didn't you always know this was how it would end?*

Luca inhales slowly, like it will slow her hammering heart. She looks at her phone in her hand. Call 911?

For what? So they can help Madison like they helped Whitney, helped Polly?

She lets the breath out in a rush. They're not the only ones who didn't help before, are they? Luca wasn't there to save Polly, or her sister. But this time she is here, and Madison is in there, needing her.

That is the only thing she needs to propel her forward, to the front door that opens with only a push.

Luca steps inside.

55

When they were younger, riding those pastel bikes around the island, they didn't wear helmets, no safety. Why worry about that? Just ride, face to the sun, breeze sketching over your skin. Until the day Luca fell off and shredded both her knees raw, dripping blood onto the sand-dusted road.

It's what she's thinking of as she walks through the Rivers house, so quiet. Her blood, drops spattering on the ground, the sting of grit embedded in her flesh, how Whitney came to get her and said, *I told you* as they cleaned the wounds out together.

She is imagining those blood spatters, like tiny planetary explosions. Imagining finding new ones now, on her way through the house. In the kitchen, maybe. Madison, stretched out over the countertop, the blood pooling on marble before waterfalling to the floor. Or in the living room, sprawled on the floor, gasping for air.

Maybe outside, in the pool, facedown. That drowning Luca's always dreamed of.

Something splinters beneath her shoe.

Luca stills at the sound and looks down. A fragment of

china. Curved, thin; the handle of something, maybe.

She crouches and slides it out from beneath her shoe, silently. But on the air, a faint sound.

Luca closes her eyes and tilts her head in the direction of it. Sounds like voices. Sounds like voices coming from outside, she thinks.

Through the kitchen, still holding her breath a little and relaxing only when she passes through the empty space. Everything in its place and shining. It's dusk now, the sky through the double-height windows pink, and Luca turns, walks through the living room and its artwork staring down at her, toward the wide-open doors leading out to the pool.

The voices start again, and Luca lifts her chin. *Listen.*

". . . going to leave?"

"Yes! Like I always planned to."

"But not *now*," the first voice says, and it's deep, a little pleading. "Not after everything."

"That only makes it more important for me to go." Madison; Luca knows her voice as well as anything. "I'm not changing my plans. Neither should you. Just act normal, okay? Keep acting like everything's fine."

"But it's not."

And Madison sweeps into view now, barefoot in yoga pants and a knotted tank.

Luca shrinks back against the wall inside. From here she can see Madison still, but not the other person. Who? She knows everyone Madison knows, in Parris at least. It's not her dad. Not Carter, clearly. Peter? *But Madison said he was out of the country,* she remembers. After the wedding, flying out to London, where Madison is supposed to meet him soon.

So it can't be him.

Can it?

"Please," Madison says, and beside her the lights beneath the pool water shimmer. "Come on. I'm here, aren't I? I'm with you right now, aren't I? What did you think, I was going to call off my engagement, my marriage? Think about how that would have looked."

The words whir through Luca's mind. *Cheating? She's seeing somebody else?*

"But you don't have to leave."

"There's only so much I can *do* for you. This is fucked-up enough without complicating things even more."

"So what am I supposed to do?" He—whoever he is, whoever Madison is talking to—raises his voice. "Forget everything about that night? I'm risking everything, I'm lying to everyone about *everything*—"

"You've been doing it fine so far," Madison snaps. "What happened that night—you chose to do what you did."

Time slows, and Luca feels the walls of her throat close in.

That night.

There is only one night.

They are out under the navy night sky, stars speckling, and there's whiskey in a plastic cup and music loud and Whitney's there. "Are you having a good time?" she says. "Come, dance with me and Beth. Luca's a good dancer. Show her what a good dancer you are, baby sister."

Her entire body is sparking volts and Luca shakes her head to clear the memory but she can't, because Madison is talking about that night, the night Whitney died, the night her best friend died, and she is saying things that don't make sense to Luca, and whoever she is talking to, they have done something too, and Madison knows, and *what happened that night—you chose to do what you did—*

Luca's heart thrums as she begins to piece it all together.

Madison, knowing more than she has pretended to.

"You chose it, and you've been fine with it all, up until now," Madison is saying, "so what's different? What's changed? You were okay with all of this before and now suddenly you want to tell?"

Somebody else, part of that night.

And this person—the reason Carter is in jail right now, the one Detective Charles is covering for—

Madison's voice wavering. "You can't play this game with me. I'm done with that, Isaac—"

Luca's head snaps up, so hard she hits the wall and has to bite her tongue to keep her *fuck* from echoing through the night, as he steps into the light.

As Isaac Charles steps up in front of Madison and who else, who else would Detective Charles protect if not his own kid, his own son.

Jesus I am so stupid it is so clear—

"You," she says softly, to Isaac, even though he can't hear her, hasn't ever heard her. "You killed my sister."

56

Isaac paces, drawing his hands through his hair, an air of desperation in his movements.

"Before was different," he says now, voice ringing out around the pool. "Now we're putting someone in jail for something he didn't do. Jesus, Madison, I know this whole thing is fucked-up anyway, but this? What are you doing?"

"I'm *protecting* you," Madison says, and then she steps up close to Isaac, stilling him with a hand on his chest. "You think I don't care about you? Just because I'm married now doesn't mean I don't *care*. And we're going to be okay, as long as we keep doing what we've been doing. They have Carter. Your dad made it perfect. No one will ever know." Her voice takes on a pleading tone. "Don't ruin this for me."

Your dad made it perfect.

Luca presses herself farther into the shadows and watches as Isaac sinks into a chair, head dropping into his hands. Madison goes to the bar and makes herself a drink, like nothing is wrong at all—slicing a lemon with a small knife, pouring vodka into a glass, sucking something from her thumb.

Isaac. And Madison. Together?

Together in this, now, at least.

Luca's breaths are strangled. *Isaac, he killed—he killed Whitney, but—why would he, she never did anything to him, he never—and Madison, Madison, Madison knew, she's known all along, and she's—*

Luca squeezes her hands tight, nails pressing hard into her skin, the way she likes, the way she needs when she feels like this.

She thought Madison was the one person she had left, the girl she could still trust, but no. She is like all the rest of them, all hiding some ulterior motive, all willing to sacrifice whatever they must to get what they want.

And it is her own stupid fucking fault. Never learns, refuses to learn from all the lessons this island has given her this summer. Right? All this time she has trusted Madison, and that was her biggest mistake. She should have known, once she discovered how well her own sister could lie to her. Should have seen, when she found out Madison lied for Whitney, too.

She can still hear them arguing outside and she tries to focus, tries to steady her breathing.

At least that made sense, though. Madison, helping Whit keep a secret.

This, though? Isaac Charles?

Lying for him, covering up for him, for what he did to her best friend?

Luca pushes away from the wall, looking out of the shadows and into what little of the evening light remains. No.

No more guessing, no more trying to figure out motivations she can't possibly fathom. They are going to tell her what she wants to know.

It's darker, but not so much that Luca can't see the expression on Madison's face as she moves outside, out of the shadows. The fastest flash of confusion, quickly masked with a smile. "Luca?"

Isaac's head snaps up at the sound of her name, and when he sees her, he doesn't smile, doesn't look surprised. "Luca."

He looks—

Afraid.

Of me, Luca thinks, as she takes slow steps toward them. *Because I know.*

I know what he did.

57

Madison's holding her glass out. "You want something to drink?" she's saying, easy. Like it isn't at all strange for her to be here with *him*, for Luca to have just shown up, melting out of the dark. "Let me make you—"

"Do you love him?" Luca asks, the words falling out in a hot rush. "Do you love him, more than you ever loved her?"

"What?" Madison shakes her head, a little bemused laugh to accompany it. "What are you talking about?"

"Don't," Luca says, and it freezes everything. Madison, Isaac, her, the three of them stuck in a still frame. "I heard you. I heard it all."

There's a long stretch of silence then, a held breath.

Then Madison slowly sets her glass down on the bar, carefully, eyes on Luca. "Okay," she says. "I don't know what you think you heard—"

"Stop! Stop *lying*. You." Luca stabs a finger into the air, gaze fixed on Isaac. "It was you. *You* killed her, you *took her* from me."

"No." Isaac takes a step back and finally opens his mouth. *"No*, I *didn't*, you—"

"You're a fucking liar, fucking *coward*. And *you*." She whips her head around, staring Madison down. "You chose him over Whit? Why? What makes him better than her? How could you love him more than her?"

Madison's perfectly controlled expression cracks then, for the briefest of moments, but Luca sees it.

The flash of mourning that came when Luca said Whitney's name, and how Madison pulled it all back, minute muscles in her face working to cover it back up. "You're wrong," she says. "I loved Whitney more than anyone."

"Not more than me," Luca says, and she looks back at Isaac. "Your dad, he did a good job," she says. "Acting like there was a real investigation going on. Getting the autopsy report changed. Giving Carter such a good motive, *wow*—" She claps, the noise a crack in the quiet. "And I ate it all up, didn't I?"

Isaac takes a step toward Luca, his face ashen. "You have this all wrong," he says. "I *did not* kill her."

"Isaac, stop—" Madison throws a hand out. "Luca, please—"

"I sat there and I told you, over and over, how I just wanted to know what happened to my sister." Luca shakes her head, can't stop it. "And you let me. When you knew. You've known all along—"

"Don't make it sound like I'm some—some evil *monster*," Madison says, and there's a catch in her voice. "You don't even know what happened, you don't know what they said they would do if I told—"

Something inside Luca shatters. "So it's true, then," she says, because up until this very second, she realizes now, she has been waiting for Madison to say the one thing that will make this all make sense. Turn her back into the girl she thinks of as her second sister, but now—this begging, this sad little voice—

"Tell me," Luca says to Isaac. "Tell me what you did to her."

Isaac looks to Madison, his eyes glazed with a wild sheen, and back at Luca. "It was stupid, okay," he says, his tone pleading. "It was a huge mistake. I didn't know what to do—when she called, I just did the first thing I could think of, and when I got here there was nothing else—"

"When you got here?" Luca stares at him. "When she called?"

58

Madison shakes her head, her shoulders dropping like she's giving up, giving in. "After the party," she says, her voice barely a whisper, "Isaac came over. It was stupid, I know, it's not like I planned to cheat on Peter but—anyway, he came over, but I didn't know that Whitney was on her way too—she was pissed, I guess, and we were both just so messed up that it all got out of hand so fast and it's not like he meant to do it, he didn't mean to hurt her—"

Isaac's head snaps in Madison's direction. "I *didn't* hurt her." His face shines in the night light, sweat on his forehead, trickling beneath the neckline of his white tee. "You wanna know what happened, Luca?"

"She fell, really," Madison's saying, like she can't even hear Isaac, and she's looking up at the night sky like she can see it, still, like she's living it again. "He pushed her, yes, but—"

"She was dead when I got here," Isaac says, loud, blunt. "That's why you called me here, to help you." He turns toward Luca, a tautness to his limbs that she can feel from here, and it makes her skitter backward. "She called. I came. She lets me in, and there's Whitney, lying on the floor already dead, and she says that Whitney slipped, fell and hit her head, and she didn't know who else to call."

"What are you doing?" Madison shifts away too, quick steps back from Isaac's palpable anger. "It's over, Isaac. You and your dad can't keep me quiet anymore. She knows it was you. Soon everyone will know it was you. Stop making it worse, stop *lying*."

Isaac stabs a finger in Madison's direction. "No," he says, his mouth a snarl. "I'm telling the truth, which I should have done weeks ago. Because that did happen, Luca." He looks to her. "I came over and there was your sister and I didn't know what to fucking do. When Madison said she needed help I thought . . . I don't know what I thought but it wasn't *that*. So I called my dad because I knew he would know, and I'm sorry, Luca—I'm sorry she's gone and for what I did, but I swear to you, I did not kill her."

"You didn't kill her." When Luca speaks, her voice is a sharpened knife, a razor cutting quick and decisive through the night, the way she used to cut through the layers of her own skin and flesh until the blood welled, perfect. "Right. And you didn't move her body either, right? You didn't toss her like she was *nothing*, Isaac? You didn't know about the autopsy report your dad doctored, how it was Carter who was going to pay for everything?"

She shifts toward Isaac now, looking straight into his eyes. Challenging him. *Come on, keep lying. I want to see how far you'll go so you don't have to say what you did.*

"Yes," he says, and the single word echoes.

Yes is not what Luca expected. "What?"

"Isaac," Madison says, her voice vibrating.

Isaac's shoulders slump with what seems like relief, letting out what he has been keeping in for too long. "I helped move her. First I covered her up. I couldn't—I couldn't look at her like that. I moved her out of the foyer. I put her in my car and then I didn't know what to do next, so I called my dad. Me and him, together, we took her to somewhere we knew she would be found quickly and then we came back here and we cleaned everything up. My dad—he said we would never mention any of it again. That we would never tell anybody what we did. He was going to make it all go away. But I swear to you, Luca, that was all I did."

That was all. Like it was nothing, like everything Luca is now seeing in her mind—the blood from the crack in Whitney's skull and how he must have wiped it all away, Isaac and his father sharing the weight of her body between them, pulling her out of Isaac's car and then tossing her to the ground like spoiled meat into the trash—was *nothing.*

"Why?" Luca asks. "What did she ever do to you that you had to do that to her?"

"I *didn't,*" Isaac says, stress cracking his voice. "Madison, will you tell her the fucking truth?"

Yes, tell me, Luca thinks, and she looks to Madison, expecting fury.

But Madison is crying.

The body-racking, air-stealing kind of crying, with both hands clasped to her chest.

It's the kind of crying, Luca knows instantly, born of guilt.

59

"No." Luca closes her eyes like that'll make it all go away, like when she opens them again Madison will be put back together, ready to convince Luca that this was all Isaac's fault.

She opens her eyes.

Tears are still running down Madison's face. "I can't," she says, a strangled gasp. "I don't—Luca, I'm sorry, I'm so sorry, he's not lying—"

"Stop it."

"I thought if I just—and you'd think—but I can't, it was an accident, she fell, it was an accident—"

"No." Luca presses her hands over her ears. It was bad enough when she thought Madison had known what Isaac did and kept it to herself this entire time, but now she's backtracking, unsaying all the things she just said and that means Isaac wasn't lying and Madison—

Madison wipes the back of her hand across her face and takes a shuddering deep breath. "Please don't hate me," she says. "I just, I didn't know what to do because it happened so fast, we were just fucking around like we always did, you know, we were having *fun*, and then she said she was thirsty so she was going to the kitchen. . . ." She rushes toward Luca then, grabbing hold of her by the elbows. "One second she was there and the next she was at the bottom of the stairs and I didn't even understand what had happened at first, I couldn't process it, but then I saw how she wasn't moving. She wasn't *breathing* and there was so much *blood*, and I was out of my mind when I called Isaac but it was all I could think of, and I have hated myself every second of every day since then, Luca, I swear—"

"Stop it!" Luca pushes Madison away, shoving her hard in the chest with all the force she can gather.

"Please, Luca, I'm so sorry, I was so scared. . . ."

Madison's pleading fades into a static buzz as Luca looks at her hands.

Her hands that pushed Madison, the pressure against Madison's chest.

And she is remembering Whitney, laid out on the table, the purple-gray bruises that had bloomed on her chest.

Luca stares at her hands, shaking, and looks up at Madison, her mouth still moving.

The question slithers across her brain, a harsh whisper-thought. *If Whitney slipped—*

then where did the bruises come from?

Time slows, a single moment stretched out elastic and endless.

Across from her Madison's mouth stops moving, her crying face twisted in a way that should make her ugly but somehow doesn't. Never does, Madison. Always looks beautiful, glowing, golden.

And Whitney is dead, decaying, rotting.

She looks and finds Isaac sunk into a crouch, wiping his hands over an ashen face.

Luca turns her hands over, gazing at her palms.

Then she curls her fingers in, feels her nails biting into her flesh, and everything snaps back into place, and there is a bright clarity that almost hurts.

"What about the bruises?"

Madison swipes the back of her hand across her nose, and it's good, a quick cover, but not so good that Luca doesn't see the way Madison's entire body stiffens. "What?"

"She had bruises. On her chest. Like maybe a person would have if someone had hit them. Or pushed them." Luca lets her hands fall, and asks the question softly. "If she slipped, then where did the bruises come from?"

Behind her Luca senses movement, Isaac rising up to his full height. "Madison," he says, "what does she mean?"

Madison blinks, slowly and deliberately. "I have no idea—"

But Luca has grasped the silken thread of this untruth and she can't help but pull on it, feel how it all begins to unspool. "You said she slipped," Luca says. "You say that's the truth, but right before that you were standing there telling me Isaac killed her, Isaac was responsible for everything."

"I got *scared*—"

"You said you were messed up." Luca's words come out loud, an echo drifting across the pool and its warm-water haze. "Earlier. You were *both* so messed up, you and Whit."

"Right," Madison says, and she's not crying anymore. "Exactly. And it was—"

"An accident? Yeah. You've said." Luca wets her lips. "You also told me Whit wasn't using. Not since college. Remember? I asked you if she had a problem and you told me no, not now. Nothing now." *And so what if she had? People make choices and sometimes those choices are a mistake, but they shouldn't follow you around forever*, Madison said, during her engagement party.

And Madison said other things, too.

Your dad made it perfect.

No one will ever need to know.

Don't ruin this for me.

For me, *for* me, Luca thinks.

"So what, she *was* using? She was high that night, is that what you're saying? You were lying when you said all that other shit to me? Or are you lying now?" Luca takes a step closer with each word, Madison taking a corresponding step back like this is a dance between them, a practiced routine, until she is backed up against the bar and can't go any farther.

"You don't know what you're talking about," Madison says. "She—"

"Was Isaac there when she died or not? Was it just the two of you? Just you there, when she slipped?"

"Luca—"

"But what about the bruises? What about the bruises, Madison? How did she get those *bruises* like somebody *pushed* her—"

"I had no *choice*, she was going to ruin *everything*!"

60

Luca takes two unsteady steps back, the impact of Madison's words knocking her off-balance.

She was going to ruin everything.

"Jesus," Isaac's saying, "Jesus fucking *Christ*, Madison, you pushed her?"

"You did, didn't you." Statement, not a question, and Luca searches Madison's brimming blue eyes for something, any sign of the truth, or regret, remorse, a part of her that is still human. Luca is looking for any sign that Madison is the same girl she's known since before she can remember. The girl whose bed she slept in, whose ear she whispered kid secrets in, who has always been there, right behind Whitney, the shadow of her sister.

Madison stares back, her gaze steady. And then, finally, eventually, she speaks. "It's not like I planned it," she says. "It's not like I *meant* to—"

Luca lets out a low moan as her chest heaves and she is crying, sobbing as she speaks. "Oh my god, oh my god," she is saying, because it's clearer than anything to her now. "Madison—"

"She just showed up," Madison says, a sudden rush of words as her hands twist through the air. "She showed up here and god she could be such a judgmental *bitch* and she got so mad at me over nothing, she was all 'what did you take, what did you take, I thought we had a deal' and she started saying she was done, she was going to tell everybody about the pills, and she *knew* what that would do to me, but ever since that fucking DUI—she's held it against me all this time, when it's not like I forced her to take the blame, she was *fine* with it, but all of a sudden it was different, she starts saying she's sick of me, she's going to tell everyone, she hopes my dad *does* cut me off, she hopes Peter leaves me, and she was my *best friend*, how could she say all those things to me? I kept thinking, how can she be so cruel, and then before I knew what happened . . ." Madison sighs, an empty exhalation. "She was at the bottom of the stairs."

Isaac's eyes are wide, no color left in his face.

"You could have called somebody." Luca hears herself as if from a hundred miles away, somewhere outside her body where she doesn't have to process what Madison has just confessed, that Whitney is dead because Madison didn't want her daddy to take away her credit cards, didn't want to lose her soon-to-be husband, didn't want to *ruin* her reputation.

What a waste.

Luca tastes her salt tears on her lips as she speaks. "For help," she says. "Why didn't you call for help?"

"I *did*." Madison closes the distance between them, diamond-bright tears gliding down her cheeks, effortless as always, and her hands grab at Luca's elbows, shoulders, the sides of her face. "I called Isaac because I knew I could fix it, I knew I could make it okay and I did, didn't I? Even you thought Isaac did it, for a moment at least. Imagine what everybody else is going to think when they hear what he did. Because he did those things, Luca, him and Charles, they took her body, they cleaned up, Charles screwed with the investigation—see how guilty they look?"

"That's why you called me," Isaac says, the slow realization audible in his words. "You lied to me, Madison. You told me she fell. You told me you were afraid of getting in trouble and I was the only one who could help you."

"That wasn't a lie," Madison says, her eyes still on Luca, hands still gripping tight. Luca doesn't miss the way her voice changes, how the pleading edge has vanished, replaced by sharp irritation. "It just didn't mean exactly what you *thought* it did."

"You said you needed me," Isaac says. "You said you wanted *me*, not anybody else. I did all that for you because I thought you were really in trouble, but you—"

"You did that because you thought I would owe you." Madison releases Luca and whips around, staring Isaac down. "You thought if you could be the hero I needed that I would have to be with you, right, I'd have to pay you back. *That's* why you did what you did, Isaac."

"No," he says, shaking his head. "No. Whitney was dead, in your house, and you *asked* me to do it—"

"I asked you to come over," Madison says slowly. "I said I

needed help. I said it was an accident. You know what I never said? 'Call your dad. Drag her body out of here. Make it look like she was never even here.' I didn't ask you to do all that, Isaac. You got there all on your own."

Isaac's mouth hangs open for a minute, his eyes flicking side to side as he takes in what Madison is saying. Then he throws his hands up and gives a mirthless laugh. "You fucking bitch," he says, moving away, back from the two of them twisted together at the bar. "You fucking *bitch*, Madison. No. I'm done. I'm done with all of this, I'm done with *you*."

Luca's watching Madison, so calm now, poised, and thinks, *Who are you?* "You can't blame him for this," she says, and inside her ribs her heart thrums.

Isaac's stabbing a finger at the air, picking up the pace now as he keeps backing away, beginning to turn. "This is the problem with all of you, you people with money," he's saying, voice raised loud enough to carry, "you think you can control everything, you think the rest of us are just here to serve you and when you're done with us, you're done. You think nothing can touch you—"

"It was you who pushed her," Luca says to Madison. "*You* are the reason she's dead."

Madison's gaze snaps back to Luca. "Don't," she says, that one word soaked in sorrow, fresh tears spilling down her face. "I loved her, Luca, I swear, you know how much I loved her, you know I would never *mean* to hurt her."

"But you *did*!"

"That's not what the story has to be," Madison says.

"When everybody hears what I have to say, they'll believe it."

How, Luca is about to say, but the word catches in her throat, the rest of the question—*how will anyone believe you when Isaac tells his version?*—swallowed back down, because she knows.

In the second before Madison whispers, "I can still fix it," before Madison presses her lips to Luca's forehead fast, desperate, Luca knows.

And yet it still surprises her when Madison pushes her away, when she snatches a knife from the bar, the tip of it catching on Luca's forearm, a surface slice that stings. *"Shit—"* Luca looks up. "Madison!"

She trips back as Madison rushes past her with the sharp, slick knife tucked into her hand, stalking her way toward Isaac, and it's fast.

The way she walks, the way she raises her arm, the way Luca hears herself from some distance calling out Isaac's name—

But the way Isaac turns is slow, and then his face as he sees Madison's hand raised, his arms going up too late. "Mad—"

She cuts him off, sliding the knife up and into the side of his neck, like it's nothing. Nothing at all.

Luca forgets about the single slice on her arm and her stomach lurches, the threat of throwing up. It takes her a moment to think again, to get past the flash of the knife and the small sound it made, but when she does, she stumbles forward. "Madison," she says, and hears herself repeat it, over and over. "Madison, what did you do?"

Isaac, voiceless, grapples for the knife in his throat, and

Luca isn't sure if he's trying to pull it out or keep it in, which one would be better, but then he drops to his knees and Madison, quick as a snake, reaches in and yanks the blade out.

He staggers forward, two unsteady steps, and drops to his knees. Blood seeping through his fingers, spilling down his chest.

And Madison turns to Luca, dropping the knife to the ground. "See?" she calls to Luca, and there's a fear across her features, but Luca isn't sure whether it's real or just another construction. "He was here, he was angry. Just like the night of the party, when he came here, when I called him here to tell him to leave me alone. You remember, right? When we were younger, after we dated, how he was obsessed with me. He scared me, then, tonight. I didn't know what else to do, after what he did to Whitney—" She lifts her hands, wet with Isaac's blood. "I couldn't let him hurt you, too, could I? I couldn't let him hurt somebody else."

Luca can't take her eyes off Madison's hands. They shine in the moonlight, the glaze of blood.

This place is cursed.

It crashes over her like a wave, the weight of the ocean on a wild day, the powerless feeling that comes with getting caught in a rip.

Not a new thought, no. But everything is crystallizing, coming into clear, sharp focus.

Madison, bloody over a body in front of Luca, and her sister's shattered skull, and the pills they never talked about, the ones that Beth traffics in now, and the girl Naomi left

with a ruined life, and Polly Polly Polly who never did anything to deserve such a violent end—

The curse is real. But it is not the kind she believed in before.
There are no beasts, except for the ones she lives among. There
is no unseen vengeful force, besides that hiding inside every
person she knows. There is nothing causing these bad things
to happen except people on this island, what they'll do to get
what they want, who they'll willingly, happily destroy in the
process.

Something inside her swells and snaps, all the air swept
right out of her. This whole time she was terrified that the
curse was coming for her, and it was, it did, but look. *Look,*
she tells herself, willing herself to meet Madison's eyes. *She's
right there, it's all been right there all along, hasn't it?*

Because it's Parris, isn't it, and all of them who call the
island home. This perfect place, beautiful Parris, where the air
is always sweet and the sun is always shining and the ocean
is always warm and you can forget the rest of the world even
exists because you don't need the rest of the world, not when
you're here.

And at what cost? she thinks. *A few dead bodies? A few horrific incidents every decade or so?*

But they don't matter, not really. Not if you mytholo-
gize them, spin them into stories to scare after the sun goes
down. No, then this place remains perfect, and you don't
have to look too closely at yourself, acknowledge the bargain
you have entered into. Where the bad things that happen
are nothing but something to bear. A fair exchange, for the

sunlight and the warmth and the pleasure of this place. Where you look away and forget because it didn't happen to you, you are still safe, you do not have to look into the rotten center of things.

But now Luca is face-to-face with what lies beneath the veneer of perfection, Madison there with her careful frightened expression and Isaac, Isaac making this horrific wet, sucking noise, until he isn't making it anymore.

Until he is still.

Dead.

Madison sighs, and it is like the ending of a musical phrase, a release from the moment.

"Madison," Luca says, tasting the salt on her lips and how bitter the name is in her mouth, hearing how far away she sounds to her own ears. "Why did you do that? You didn't have to do that."

"Yes, I did." Madison moves close to Luca, puts her hands on either side of Luca's face just like before except there is blood now, still warm and painting Luca's face with every shift of Madison's touch. "I couldn't let him hurt another girl," she says, and she is so earnest, like she truly believes the words she's saying, like she needs Luca to understand.

Luca can't move, can't pull herself away even as the feel of Isaac's blood on her skin tells her she will never truly feel clean again. "But *you* did it," she says, willing the words out. "*You* killed—"

And Madison presses a hand over Luca's mouth. "*He* did it," she says, almost feral, but then she seems to remember what role she needs to play and her voice softens again, the delicate tremble returning. "But it's okay, Luca. I fixed it, see?"

Luca stays still, unsure what is worse: the blood across her mouth or the look in Madison's eyes.

No curse besides this, her mind whispers. *What they'll do. Who they'll destroy.*

"It's all going to be okay." Madison smiles. "You're safe now."

61

"Can you tell me where you're hurt?"

Luca looks at the EMT asking her the question, this calm-voiced white lady with beautiful amber hair and concerned eyebrows snapping latex gloves on. "I'm not," Luca says, monotone. "It's not my blood."

There's a sheet covering Isaac's body.

Not my blood, only his, from his neck have you ever seen someone's neck sliced open it really pours out—

"This looks like yours," the EMT says, her fingers gently probing the slice on Luca's arm. "I think that's gonna need some stitches. Can you follow my finger?"

Luca does as she is told and the EMT nods. "Good," she says. "Stay right here for me, okay?"

Don't leave me, Luca wants to say, even though she knows Madison was taken inside the house right when the cops arrived, is in there still with Harold and the female officer Luca heard talking about Naomi. Theoretically, nothing can happen to Luca, but still she thinks, *Don't leave me, please.*

Except by the time she has thought it the EMT is already

back, carrying supplies, and she lays a white gauze dressing over the wound. "Give me your hand," she says, and again Luca does what she's told, letting the woman hold her hand against the dressing. "Keep pressure on that," she says. "We'll get you to the hospital soon enough."

"I'm fine, I don't need—"

The EMT gives her a look. "You're not fine," she says, and she crouches, so she is eye level with Luca. "You have a wound that needs taking care of, and you're most likely in shock. You experienced something traumatic tonight."

"Right," Luca says, and the word comes out on a breath of laughter, a sound that makes the EMT's expression turn uncertain.

Because she's right, this woman, except she doesn't even know how she's right, and there's no pointing trying to explain it to her because she wouldn't believe it, anyway. This much Luca knows, understood in the time it took from Madison's 911 call to the cavalry arriving.

No one will believe her, if she tells the truth. How it wasn't Isaac who killed Whitney, but Madison. How it wasn't self-defense or a drive to protect Luca that put the knife in his neck tonight, but Madison still trying to protect herself. *Why would they believe me? The only other person who was there that night is dead now. I don't know what Charles believes happened, but I know he was willing to frame Carter to make sure Isaac was protected. And Madison—*

Madison called the cops herself. Admitted what she had done, in words soaked with panicked guilt, another perfect performance. And what guilty person would call the cops themselves, right? What person with something to hide would willingly confess to killing?

Luca presses the dressing to her arm, hard enough to feel the sting, the throbbing hurt of her splayed-open flesh.

The strange thing about growing up on this island, having it be a part of you and you part of it, is that you forget these events don't happen everywhere, not in the way they happen here. You forget that not everywhere has the stories Parris does—Polly, lungs filled with salt water.

Isla Hollinghurst, burned to ash.

Evelyn Mortimer, the pageant queen left for dead in an alley, and Laney Hart poisoned on the yacht, and *Whitney*, now, too. All of them, these violent bursts that rip through Parris, leaving razor-edged holes behind.

And these holes, Luca knows now, are sewn up quickly, roughly, stitching the tales into the very fabric of the island but looping off the damage. Neat, tiny stitches that leave only the barest scar, invisible in most light.

Luca closes her eyes. She has always been able to see them, these marks that remain, but tonight it is like there is a new light scattered across them, making the scars gleam differently. And now she knows for certain, finally, in her cracked-china heart, that Polly's death was no accident.

The specifics—they're still unknown, will always be that way. Who killed her, what exactly happened beneath the bridge that day? Luca will never know for sure. But she knows that Polly didn't go into the ocean all by herself, that somebody else put her there. And she knows that whoever killed Polly did it because they wanted to.

They saw her, and they took what they wanted, and they left her there halfway to dead while they slipped right back into their day, back into their perfect life.

She opens her eyes and finds the brightest string of stars in the sky.

No, she'll never know every single piece of that crime. But she knows she was right. The curse did come for Polly.

And it came for Madison, too, in its way, she tells herself, exhaling slowly. *Or she became it, or—I don't know. But I know I was searching this whole time for some mistake Whitney made, something she did that brought the curse on her, when the only* mistake *she made was the same one I did, over and over.*

I trusted Madison.

The EMT is speaking to her again. "Can you stand up for me, honey?"

On the ground, one corner of the sheet covering Isaac's body has flipped up, exposing half his pale, slack face. Far down on the drive the lights on the police cruiser are still on, strobing into the darkness.

And then, on the other side of the pool, Officer Harold steps out of the house. He is followed by the other officer, and she is guiding Madison along, one arm around her waist, supporting her as they take her not to their cruiser but to the second EMT.

See? See how it starts? See how easily the narrative begins to take shape?

Luca focuses on the woman in front of her. "Do you believe in curses?"

"What?"

Then Luca points at the house. "My sister," she says, "my sister died in there. Right there."

The EMT shifts uncomfortably, and when she speaks again, the soothing demeanor is gone. "Let's get you to the hospital," she says, all business. "Come on."

Luca lets the woman pull her to standing, lets herself be led past Isaac's body and around to the front of the house. It's lit up inside now, and it looks so regal still, as if nothing terrible could ever take place inside those gilded walls. It's a lie, of course, but then so is the island. Every part of it, every person. That's the real rot, isn't it? They are all complicit in what goes on here. It touches everything, is deep down in the blood of Parris, infecting everything and everyone.

So I will never escape the curse, Luca thinks, and she tips her head back, face up to the starless sky.

As long as I am part of this place, I am doomed.

62

At the hospital Luca is stitched back together by a young doctor.

Someone who introduces themselves as a forensics technician takes scrapings from beneath her fingernails and a sample of her saliva, and folds her clothes into a plastic bag.

She is allowed to shower then, making sure to keep her fresh stitches dry, the blood coming off her with the sting of medical soap and the rough push and pull of her own hands.

When she comes out of the shower, she sees that someone has left hospital-issue clothes on the bed for her. Luca pulls on the sweatpants, far too tight, and doesn't bother with the sweatshirt that she knows won't fit over her chest, slipping the paper hospital gown back on instead.

She gives her statement to Officer Harold and the female officer, both wearing the same careful sympathetic expression that Luca doesn't believe. And even if she did, she wouldn't tell them the truth: they belong to here, where no one can be trusted.

And Luca has seen what Madison can do. She put her

hands on Whitney to make sure she kept quiet. She put a knife in Isaac's throat to keep him from talking.

Luca does not want to test her, to see what she might do to the next person who threatens her.

So she tells the officers what they want to hear. *Yes, Isaac was acting irrationally. Yes, I was scared. Yes, I think I could have been hurt.*

Tell them what they want and let them make whatever story out of it that they need to. What does it matter?

She isn't going to be around for the fallout.

The officers are still talking, questioning, when Luca hears her mother's voice, the call coming down the hallway, the echo of her name as the door swings open wide.

"*Luca.*" Her name from her mom's mouth is a gasp, and her dad is behind, holding a hand to his mouth, brown skin ashen.

Luca feels every piece of dust that makes her up reaching toward her mother. "Mom—"

Officer Harold lifts his pen. "We're not quite done—"

"Yes, you are," her father says, in the kind of cold voice he uses only when he must. "You have kept us out there for hours. Now you can leave, and come back later, or better yet, leave our daughter alone entirely. She's been through enough tonight."

The officers exchange a look but then they leave, disappearing out the door like they were never even there.

"Luca," her mom says again. "When we heard—I thought—"

Thought it happened again, Luca thinks. *First Whitney, then me.*

"Madison," Luca says, and her mouth is dry, words hard to get out. "She—"

"I know," Emilia says, and she sits on the edge of the hospital bed, reaches over and smooths a hand across Luca's forehead. "I know."

Of course they *don't* know. No one knows, besides her, and Madison, and Isaac, dead now.

But they'll believe the story, like everybody else, and they'll get some kind of closure. They'll get to believe that they know who killed their daughter, that the monster is gone now, vanquished by the avenging princess.

That will be enough, Luca thinks. *Enough for them.*

Her dad is shaking his head, and Luca can see where he's been crying, the glassy sheen in his eyes. "All along," he says, quiet crack in his voice. "We trusted Charles, and it was his own—"

"Nick." Her mom says it softly, a warning. *Not now.* And then her mom lifts Luca's arm, gazing at the row of stitches in wonder. "I'm so sorry. What you've been through, what happened tonight—nobody should have to see something like that. When I think of how afraid you must have been . . ."

For a moment Luca feels her resolve wavering, uncertainty creeping back in.

But then she remembers: *as long as I am part of this place, I am doomed.*

If she stays, she is doomed. If she lets the way her parents are looking at her now keep her here, then she'll be locked into this for the rest of her life, she'll stay complicit.

"I love you." Emilia brings Luca's hand to her mouth and kisses her palm. "We love you, you know that, don't you? We love you so very much."

Luca feels the exhaustion bone deep, a stain that won't come out of her, but she nods and attempts a smile. "I know," she says. "I love you, too."

63

It is easy to slip out.

Hospitals never really get quiet, not even in Parris, where the hospital is small and made to look more like an expensive hotel than a medical building. No dove-gray paint or Egyptian cotton towels can mask the nurses calling down the corridors, those constant life-monitoring machine sounds, the wailing of a baby from behind a closed door.

Her mom is at the nurses' station, filling out paperwork, and her dad is on his way to the cafeteria in search of coffee.

So it is easy for her to get off the bed and slide her feet into the slippers someone put there, to pick up the ziplock bag that contains her belongings.

It is easy to walk out of the room and down the corridor, take the elevator down, and pass unnoticed through the emergency room, where she follows the arrows on the floor until she is through the sliding doors and outside.

Free.

Luca exhales.

It's still dark; far away, right at the very edge of the sky, there's the barest touch of azure threatening to bleed into the remnants of night. Luca wonders if the sky here is that different from anywhere else, or if she'll look up one day, far away from here, and see the same sunrise, sunset.

She closes her eyes for a second.

When she opens them, Jada is standing across from her.

They are far enough apart that it feels to Luca as if they are in two different worlds, a brass handrail surrounded by small green flowers slicing the space between them.

Jada looks—actually, she looks no different from normal. No different from when Luca saw her last, less than a day ago now. The only hint of anything being wrong, of the fact that her brother was just killed, are the red rings around her eyes that she has tried to cover with makeup.

She has always been like this, Luca knows. Can't show what she's really feeling, because that's weakness, right? And she can't afford to be weak, not when she already has so much else stacked against her here.

You always knew, didn't you? Luca watches Jada, just like Jada watches her. She has always known, hasn't she, all along—what the real curse of Parris is. She never believed in Luca's version because she knew the truth.

And yet.

She's still here, helping Luca, bargaining her way into Madison's wedding.

Even as she knew this place was rotten, she wanted to be a part of it more than anything, Luca thinks. And now she is. Right? Now her brother is dead, will be painted as a murderer, her father guilty of covering it all up.

What could bind you more with Parris than becoming a story to tell in the dark all by yourself?

For a moment Luca thinks about telling Jada. *Your brother didn't kill Whitney. Madison did. Madison didn't kill him to protect me. She did it to protect herself.*

When she opens her mouth to speak, though, all that comes out is, "I don't have my car."

Jada tips her chin up, that defiant, tough-girl veneer she's spent so long hiding behind. "You're leaving. Right?"

There is a weight to the word, *leaving*. Like it doesn't mean *going home*, or *getting away from the hospital*, but like she knows exactly where Luca's going after this. Like she understands.

Luca swallows down the rush of remorse that hits. Of course she understands. They used to be everything to each other, used to be able to know what the other was thinking with the quickest look. Luca thought that was gone, fractured away with everything else. But she has been wrong about so much.

"Yeah," she says finally, softly. "I'm leaving."

Jada nods once, looking at the keys in her hand. Then she throws them, tosses them into the air, and they carve a high arc, flashing silver as they sail toward Luca.

She snaps her hand out and just about manages to catch them, small wind chime sound as she wraps her fingers around them. "Jada—"

"Take mine," Jada says, and then she is gone, a streak of

black vanishing up the steps and into the hospital before Luca can even answer her.

Luca weighs the keys in her hand.

"Okay," she says to the place where Jada used to be. "I will."

64

The house looks muted, in the sunrise light.

Luca leaves Jada's car on the drive and lets herself in. She leaves the hospital slippers in the entryway, sheds the clothes with their bleach smell as she walks upstairs.

In her room, half-naked, she catches sight of herself in the mirror and sucks in a breath. The stitches on her arm are ugly, blunt crosses on her skin, and her face is shadowed, full of ghosts.

"But you are not a ghost," Luca says to her mirror self.

Not yet.

And then she starts, quick, before she can think too much about it.

Gets dressed in her own clothes, first, some kind of equilibrium returning as she pulls one of her many dresses over her head, slides her feet into one of her dozens of pairs of sandals. Then Luca pulls her carry-on luggage out of her closet, lays it on the floor, and begins to fill it fast. Underwear and jeans and a couple more dresses, swimsuits, shoes.

Her favorite lipstick, her meds.

Laptop.

One book, cracked spine.

From her bathroom she collects shampoo, toothpaste, razor—*razor blade*, she thinks, and then *no, stop, not now*—toothbrush, ribbon hair ties.

All goes into her bag, and then she leaves her room. Down to her mother's office first, for paperwork. Passport, birth certificate, things she'll need. A stack of cash from the safe that her dad thinks she doesn't know the combination to, enough to survive on while she figures out what it is she's doing, where she's going. At least she doesn't have long to wait until her birthday: it has crept up on her without notice, the fact that in less than two weeks she'll be eighteen. Then she can keep on going, doing whatever she decides, and no one can stop her.

She leaves the office and goes back down the hall.

Whitney's door has been closed for so long, it seems, almost like if they open it, whatever's left of her in there will dissolve into the air. But now Luca steps inside, and she wants to look around at everything, lie down in Whitney's sheets and see if they still smell like her, but she doesn't have time.

Instead she stands in front of the dresser where Whitney always left her jewelry scattered, where it remains carelessly cast aside just the way she left it.

Luca scans the jewels quickly, pinks and blues and the brightness of diamonds gleaming back at her. It doesn't matter which one, not really. Only that she has something. A touchstone for her sister, to take with her, because she's leaving.

It's the only way, she knows. All this time she has been

searching for it, how to escape the curse, but now she sees the only real way *out* is *off*. Off this island, away from everybody here and all the things they've done. The things she has done too.

She picks up a ring, opal on a gold band, a halo of pale pink stones around it. Slips it onto her pinkie, the only finger it'll fit, and then takes it off and holds it tight in her curled fist.

Luca closes her eyes. "I love you, Whit," she says to the air, and then she leaves, closing the door behind her, sealing the tomb back up.

She goes back to her bedroom and hides the ring deep down inside her bag, and she is pulling the zipper along the soft leather when she hears something from downstairs. No, not something; someone.

"Luca? Luca, are you in there?"

She sways to the sound of Naomi's scratchy call and lets the bag drop.

It was stupid, naive, to think she could get away without doing this. Seeing her.

So Luca goes downstairs, through the quiet house, to where she knows Naomi will be.

And there she is, at the back door, the glass slid open to frame her. There are dark circles under her eyes, and she has the look of someone who just chain-smoked an entire pack, but her shoulders drop and her mouth makes an uncertain smile as she sees Luca approach.

Luca stops, an arm's length away. Naomi looks awful but still, she is so beautiful. "What are you doing here?"

But her words are lost in Naomi reaching across the gap toward her, pulling her close. "Holy fuck," Naomi says, breath hot against Luca's skin. "Jesus, I was so fucking scared. I'm so glad you're okay, holy shit."

Her fingers dig into Luca's skin and she's holding her so tight it almost hurts, but only almost.

Luca gives in to it, letting Naomi hold her for longer than she knows she should. Memorizing the parts of Naomi that she doesn't want to forget.

The smell of her skin, the amber perfume and cigarettes and sunscreen; the way their bodies press together, soft on softer; the way Naomi's touch feels like a tether to a more grounded realm, a careful place to land.

It feels so good to be held by her.

And maybe if she let it go on long enough, it would undo the damage Naomi wrought on them. *Maybe if I stay like this long enough, I can forget what she did.* Except she knows that's not true, that there is no way out of this but the one she's already chosen, and she doesn't have time for this. Any moment now her parents will be discovering the hospital bed empty and her gone, and she can't be anywhere near here when they do.

With a gentle twist, she separates from Naomi. "What are you doing here?" she says again.

"I heard," Naomi says. "Everybody heard, and I thought— I called you, about a thousand times."

Luca looks at her empty hand and then up, at the ceiling. "Oh," she says, picturing her phone, no charge, and left on her bed because maybe she's being overly cautious but she doesn't want anyone to be able to track her. No credit cards, no phone. No trace.

She looks back at Naomi. *I heard. Everybody heard.*

What they heard is not the truth, though, and Luca knows that if she told Naomi what really happened, she would believe it. She would be on Luca's side, she would understand.

But she can't. Those kinds of secrets, truths, are only for somebody she trusts. And Naomi is not that person anymore.

"So you heard," Luca says, a chill to her voice. "That doesn't explain why you're here."

"I—why wouldn't I be?" Naomi says, and takes a step forward, half in and half out of the house still. "After last night—"

Luca moves the other way, forcing Naomi back, so they are out of the house, standing on the still-cool patio with the ocean glittering beyond.

"Last night had nothing to do with you, or us," Luca says. "It didn't change anything. Or did you forget? Did you forget that we're done?"

Naomi flinches. "Luca," she says. "You could have *died* last night. You get that, right? What did you think, I would just not come find you? Like I don't care at all? Because we had one fight—"

"Don't." Luca holds her hands up, pressed against an invisible wall between them. "Don't try to rewrite it like it was some stupid petty argument over nothing—"

"I'm not," Naomi says. "I'm sorry, I shouldn't have said that, I'm just—I know it was more than that." She's nodding solemnly, her hands pressed together. "I'm sorry about every-thing. About lying to you. And I know, I know, it doesn't change things and you've heard this same thing too many times from too many people now, but that doesn't mean I won't say it still, because I have to. Because it's true. I am so sorry."

Luca takes a step back, watching the way Naomi is watch-ing her. "That doesn't undo it, does it? Nothing can undo you lying to me like that, for so long."

"I didn't *lie*—"

"You did. You *lied*, Naomi, on purpose. To trick me. To manipulate me, to make me want you. So you wouldn't have to own up to what you did to that girl."

Naomi inhales sharply and then she is suddenly crying, no sound but salt tears slicking down her face. "I didn't want to trick you. I only wanted someone who could look at me without seeing a monster."

"You don't know what I would have seen," Luca says. "You don't know what I would have thought. You never gave me the chance. And then you never tried to make it right, come clean. You let me believe Anya was lying in a grave somewhere and we were the same, in that way."

Naomi is quiet for a long moment, and behind her the sun is breaking through, the world around them coming awake and alive. "I didn't know what else to do," she says eventually, so quietly. "I didn't know."

"Right." Luca laughs, a single, caustic breath of it. "And now you want me to say I forgive you, to say it's all okay. Which is so fucked-up, because you know the reason I loved you was that you never made me feel less than for not being okay. For feeling bad or being angry, having a brain filled with weird thoughts. It was nothing to you, it was fine, it was . . . what?" she says, because Naomi's staring at her now. "What?"

"You loved me?" Naomi says, and Luca realizes her slip. How she never said it before, only kept it inside and now here it is, finally spoken but at the worst possible time. "You loved me," Naomi says again, not a question this time.

Luca answers anyway. "Yes."

Naomi wipes her cheeks with the back of her hand, a graceful, fluid movement. She is like Madison, so pretty even when she's weeping. "But you don't love me now?"

Luca's breath is a noisy rush in the quiet. "I do," she says, exactly how true that is a surprise even to herself. "I love you, still."

And Naomi looks hopeful, like she has found her loophole, like Luca will have to forgive her now, because that's what you do. You forgive the people you love, right? You do anything for the girl you love, right?

"I love you," Luca says again, but she is not finished. "But it doesn't fix anything. It doesn't mean we should be together. I used to think you were different, but in the end, you are exactly like everybody else. That's why this has to be it for us."

"No," Naomi says, and she presses a hand against her throat, holding on. "It doesn't have to be it, we don't have to be over, we can—I will make things right. Luca, please. I've never known anyone like you. There is nobody else who comes close to you."

It should be sweet to hear that, it should be the kind of moment Luca will remember forever, but instead it's such a sharp pain that she has to catch her breath. Naomi is so earnest, so painfully sincere, as if she believes there is a way out of this for them. And sure, Luca can imagine saying, *Okay, let's do this, run away with me* but it is nothing more than a fantasy. Luca has spent so long living in a world half-built from fantasy, and all along the truth of the curse was right in front of her, wasn't it, except she wouldn't let herself see it. So now here is this girl, here is Naomi, and Luca must force herself to see what is in front of her. They are not meant to be. They had a time, but that time is over, and Luca wishes it wasn't but that is a wish she can add to the list of things that will never come to be.

"Luca," Naomi says, that beautiful rasp in her voice. "I love you, too."

Luca touches her fingertips to the delicate skin beneath her eyes, finding wetness there. "I know," she says. "But it isn't enough. We were good, you know. You made me feel . . . I never felt alive these last few years until you looked at me the way you do. It was like I woke up for the first time. You know? You changed me and I wouldn't undo that, I wouldn't undo us, but I can't put us back together." She shifts closer. "I love you, but that isn't everything."

She waits for a moment, for Naomi to say something, but she doesn't. Only stands there, hand on her throat, breaths coming in shaky gasps.

In the distance the sea is beginning to stir, the sun creeping higher. *There's no time,* Luca thinks.

She brings herself as close to Naomi as she can, puts her hands on either side of Naomi's face, and kisses her. Just once, just soft.

"I think you should go," she breathes, when they come apart.

Naomi nods and slips out of Luca's hands. Turns her back and retraces her steps the way she came, toward the sand and the ocean so blue.

Luca wants to watch her go, but time, again. She has so little left.

So she turns and walks back inside the house, leaving Naomi behind.

65

Luca puts her bag on the passenger seat of Jada's car and gets in.

She takes a breath before turning the key in the ignition. Once she's on the other side, somewhere she can catch a train or a bus or whatever will take her far enough away, she'll mail the keys back to Jada, with a note telling her exactly where she can find the car. *And maybe thank you too, she thinks, for giving me a way out.*

For a second she just sits, bathing in the sound of the engine, the feel of it vibrating up her spine.

Then she takes a last look at her home, and she watches as it grows smaller in the rearview mirror, vanishes out of view as she steers the car out onto the road and leaves.

It's still early enough that the island is quiet as she drives across it. Not that it's ever busy, really, but the roads are almost completely empty, every light green as she heads toward the bridge.

She is calmer than the last time she came this way, but she is also a different girl from the one who couldn't bring herself to cross before. There will be no last-minute slam on the brakes, no seat-belt burn across her chest, because this time, she knows, she isn't stopping.

She reaches across and dips a hand into her bag, her fingers closing around what she wants. She takes her hand out and unfurls it, and the flash drive sits in the center of her palm.

It's all the evidence she has. The only thing that says, *There's more to this story than you know*, and she has no idea where she's going, or how long she'll be able to stay gone, but maybe she will find someone on the other side who will want to know the truth.

She tips her hand and lets the flash drive fall back among her clothes. *Maybe, someday, somewhere.*

When the bridge rises up in front of her, morning light making the metal gleam, Luca exhales. She has no music on, and the windows are down; she wants to hear the water, hear it as it rushes beneath her. A different sound from the wave crash she's so used to.

Up ahead—closer—closer still—

And then she is there, on the bridge.

Luca tightens her grip on the steering wheel as she drives straight, steady. Here she is, somewhere between Parris and the rest of the world, and the ocean below calls to her but not like it so often does, not a plea for Luca to come join it. Rather a whispered urge, to go on, go faster, *go.*

She laughs, a nervous, breathy sound all her own. It's really not that far, she realizes, the distance from here to there. It's not as vast as she's felt, her whole life. Already the island is beginning to fade behind her, smaller and smaller with each passing second. And ahead, coming into focus, the world beyond.

Goodbye, Parris, she thinks. *And fuck you. On behalf of everybody you stole from, the lives you ruined, the people you destroyed. The ones who weren't as lucky as me.*

The wind through the open windows stings her eyes, whips her curls across her face. *Fuck you from Isla and Evelyn and Laney. Fuck you from Whitney. From Polly.*

She wishes more than anything in the world that she wasn't doing this alone, leaving Parris without them. But she can hear Polly's laugh in the ocean below, feel Whitney in the wind tugging at her hair and it's as if they are running alongside her, keeping her company, keeping up until they can't anymore. Until Luca is more than halfway across and up ahead she can see the end of everything. The bridge that curves into the mainland, a long ribbon road that is unspooling before her.

Luca presses on the gas; the speed tick-tick-ticks up.

Almost there.

She does not know where she is going, but all that matters is that it won't be Parris. She used to think the island was special, curse and all, like she would stay here forever even when she hated what it had done to her. But now she knows it is better to be lost out there than rotting in Parris.

The stitches in her arm pull, like a reminder of that rot, and Luca glances down at them. There will be a scar when they're gone, a permanent reminder of this place. That night.

She remembers the feel of Madison's hands on her face, her touch slippery with Isaac's blood. *You're safe now,* she said, like she believed it.

"No," Luca says aloud, barely more than a breath. "But I will be."

She takes one hand off the wheel and holds it out the window, feeling the wind twist and spin over and around her fingers. The other side is right there now, close enough to taste.

Luca pulls in a breath. Holds it. Lets go.

The sun is so bright and the air so sweet, and she is almost there,

almost

almost

almost—

Acknowledgments

Thank you to my incredible agent, Suzie Townsend, who took me and this book on when it was nothing more than a few chapters.

Thank you to Kate Sullivan, for asking the question that made me rewrite the entire book and finally find the story it was supposed to be.

Thank you to my amazing editor, Kate Prosswimmer, who understood everything I was trying to do with this book and helped it become a thousand times better than I thought it could ever be.

To Carla Hutchinson, for giving this book my first UK home and loving these cursed girls.

To Dani Segelbaum and everybody at New Leaf.

To everyone at Margaret K. McElderry Books and Hot Key Books.

To Janet McNally, the best podcaster of all time. To Diana Hurlburt, for reading early drafts and always sending the best floral updates. To angel Nicole Chiarella. To Ashley Woodfolk, for being an early (and beloved) cheerleader. To MK Pagano,

Paige Cober, Hannah Whitten, and Carlyn Greenwald, for always supporting. To anyone I talked to about "this, like, sad island book" over the years.

To my family as always.

Finally, thank you to Maggie Horne and Rory Power, two of the best and weirdest friends a girl could ask for.

REBECCA BARROW

Rebecca Barrow is the critically acclaimed author of *Interview with the Vixen*, *This Is What It Feels Like*, and *You Don't Know Me But I Know You*. *Bad Things Happen Here* is her UK debut. She is a lover of sunshine, Old Hollywood icons, and all things high femme. She lives and writes in England. Visit her at rebecca-barrow.com.

Thank you for choosing a Hot Key book.

If you want to know more about our authors and what we publish, you can find us online.

You can start at our website

www.hotkeybooks.com

And you can also find us on:

We hope to see you soon!